TWO BOTTLES OF RELISH

In this attractive collection of tales Lord Dunsany mixes reality with fantasy to entertain us with a series of modern detective stories. Some are macabre such as the one called 'The Two Bottles of Relish'. Others have a lighter and more amusing touch but all are invested with the author's own compelling brand of writing. The variety and originality of plot in all these twenty-six tales stimulates the imagination and carries the reader along in a state of continuous excitement and anticipation.

In this volume we meet the acknowledged master of the short story at his best—a delight to the reader and a model for others to follow.

TWO BOTTLES of RELISH

THE LITTLE TALES OF SMETHERS AND OTHER STORIES

LORD DUNSANY

COLLINS
CRIME
CLUB

COLLINS CRIME CLUB
An imprint of HarperCollins*Publishers*
1 London Bridge Street
London SE1 9GF
www.harpercollins.co.uk

HarperCollins*Publishers*
Macken House, 39/40 Mayor Upper Street,
Dublin D01 C9W8, Ireland

This paperback edition 2023

1

First published in Great Britain as
The Little Tales of Smethers by Jarrolds 1952

Introduction by Ellery Queen from *Queen's Quorum: A History of the Detective-Crime
Short Story as Revealed by the 125 Most Important Books Published in this Field
since 1845* published by Biblo and Tannen, New York, 1948

A catalogue record for this book is available from the British Library

ISBN 978-0-00-815938-2

Typeset by Palimpsest Book Production Ltd, Falkirk, Stirlingshire
Printed and bound in the UK using 100% renewable electricity at CPI Group (UK)

CONTENTS

INTRODUCTION

ONE of the most unforgettable short stories of detection-and-horror ever written—Lord Dunsany's 'The Two Bottles of Relish', about detective Linley—first appeared in book form in an anthology titled *Powers of Darkness* (London: Philip Allan, 1934). The story, an unqualified *tour de force*, has an interesting and revealing history. Lord Dunsany was amused to notice that people were reading gruesome stories of murder in preference to his own more delicate tales. He wondered if he could write a story 'gruesome enough for them'. So, with 'tec tongue in cheek but writing with grim seriousness, Lord Dunsany fashioned 'The Two Bottles of Relish'.

The story proved 'gruesome enough'—indeed, it far exceeded Lord Dunsany's original intent. Editors were fascinated by the tale, but they frankly confessed that it made them ill. As a matter of fact, no male editor in England or America would publish the story. Finally, a woman dared—Lady Rhondda, who printed it in *Time and Tide*, November 12-19, 1932. Lord Dunsany has always thought that Lady Rhondda, a militant feminist, published the story as an example of sheer realism, saying to herself, 'That is just how men do treat women.' Gradually the widespread nausea (to use Lord Dunsany's own phrase) seems to have worn off . . .

Lord Dunsany informs us that there are seven other tales about detective Linley, and that he hopes to include all eight in his 1951 volume of short stories. Needless to say, this book, when published, will be selected for *Queen's Quorum*, for if Lord Dunsany had written only the very first tale of detective Linley, without the seven 'sequels', this single achievement would have earned Mr Linley's creator a permanent seat at King Edgar's Round Table.

ELLERY QUEEN
1948

THE TWO BOTTLES OF RELISH

SMETHERS is my name. I'm what you might call a small man, and in a small way of business. I travel for Numnumo, a relish for meats and savouries; the world-famous relish I ought to say. It's really quite good, no deleterious acids in it, and does not affect the heart; so it is quite easy to push. I wouldn't have got the job if it weren't. But I hope some day to get something that's harder to push, as of course the harder they are to push, the better the pay. At present I can just make my way, with nothing at all over; but then I live in a very expensive flat. It happened like this, and that brings me to my story. And it isn't the story you'd expect from a small man like me, yet there's nobody else to tell it. Those that know anything of it besides me, are all for hushing it up. Well, I was looking for a room to live in in London when first I got my job; it had to be in London, to be central; and I went to a block of buildings, very gloomy they looked, and saw the man that ran them and asked him for what I wanted; flats they called them; just a bedroom and a sort of a cupboard. Well, he was showing a man round at the time who was a gent, in fact more than that, so he didn't take much notice of me, the man that ran all those flats didn't, I mean. So I just ran behind for a bit, seeing all sorts of rooms, and waiting till I could be shown my class of thing. We came to a very nice flat, a sitting-room, bedroom and bathroom, and a sort of little place that they called a hall. And that's how I came to know Linley. He was the bloke that was being shown round.

'Bit expensive,' he said.

And the man that ran the flats turned away to the window

1

and picked his teeth. It's funny how much you can show by a simple thing like that. What he meant to say was that he'd hundreds of flats like that, and thousands of people looking for them, and he didn't care who had them or whether they all went on looking. There was no mistaking him, somehow. And yet he never said a word, only looked away out of the window and picked his teeth. And I ventured to speak to Mr Linley then; and I said, 'How about it, sir, if I paid half, and shared it? I wouldn't be in the way, and I'm out all day, and whatever you said would go, and really I wouldn't be no more in your way than a cat.'

You may be surprised at my doing it; and you'll be much more surprised at him accepting it; at least, you would if you knew me, just a small man in a small way of business; and yet I could see at once that he was taking to me more than he was taking to the man at the window.

'But there's only one bedroom,' he said.

'I could make up my bed easy in that little room there,' I said.

'The hall,' said the man looking round from the window, without taking his tooth-pick out.

'And I'd have the bed out of the way and hid in the cupboard by any hour you like,' I said.

He looked thoughtful, and the other man looked out over London; and in the end, do you know, he accepted.

'Friend of yours?' said the flat man.

'Yes,' answered Mr Linley.

It was really very nice of him.

I'll tell you why I did it. Able to afford it? Of course not. But I heard him tell the flat man that he had just come down from Oxford and wanted to live for a few months in London. It turned out he wanted just to be comfortable and do nothing for a bit while he looked things over and chose a job, or probably just as long as he could afford it. Well, I said to myself, what's the Oxford manner worth in business, especially a business like mine? Why, simply everything you've got. If I picked up only a quarter of it from this Mr Linley I'd be able to double my sales, and that would soon mean I'd be given something a lot harder to push, with perhaps treble the pay. Worth it every time. And you can make a quarter of an education go twice as far again, if you're careful with it. I mean you don't have to quote the whole of the Inferno to show that you've read Milton; half a line may do it.

Well, about that story I have to tell. And you mightn't think that a little man like me could make you shudder. I soon forgot about the Oxford manner when we settled down in our flat. I forgot it in the sheer wonder of the man himself. He had a mind like an acrobat's body, like a bird's body. It didn't want education. You didn't notice whether he was educated or not. Ideas were always leaping up in him, things you'd never have thought of. And not only that, but if any ideas were about, he'd sort of catch them. Time and again I've found him knowing just what I was going to say. Not thought-reading, but what they call intuition. I used to try to learn a bit about chess, just to take my thoughts off Numnumo in the evening, when I'd done with it. But problems I never could do. Yet he'd come along and glance at my problem and say, 'You probably move that piece first,' and I'd say, 'But where?' and he'd say, 'Oh, one of those three squares.' And I'd say, 'But it will be taken on all of them.' And the piece a queen all the time, mind you. And he'd say, 'Yes, it's doing no good there: you're probably meant to lose it.'

And, do you know, he'd be right.

You see, he'd been following out what the other man had been thinking. That's what he'd been doing.

Well, one day there was that ghastly murder at Unge. I don't know if you remember it. But Steeger had gone down to live with a girl in a bungalow on the North Downs, and that was the first we had heard of him.

The girl had £200, and he got every penny of it and she utterly disappeared. And Scotland Yard couldn't find her.

Well I'd happened to read that Steeger had bought two
bottles of Numnumo; for the Otherthorpe police had found
out everything about him, except what he did with the girl; and
that of course attracted my attention, or I should have never
thought again about the case or said a word of it to Linley.
Numnumo was always on my mind, as I always spent every day
pushing it, and that kept me from forgetting the other thing.
And so one day I said to Linley, 'I wonder with all that knack
you have for seeing through a chess problem, and thinking of
one thing and another, that you don't have a go at that
Otherthorpe mystery. It's a problem as much as chess,' I said.

'There's not the mystery in ten murders that there is in one
game of chess,' he answered.

'It's beaten Scotland Yard,' I said.

'Has it?' he asked.

'Knocked them endwise,' I said.

'It shouldn't have done that,' he said. And almost immediately
after he said, 'What are the facts?'

We were both sitting at supper and I told him the facts, as I
had them straight from the papers. She was a pretty blonde, she
was small, she was called Nancy Elth, she had £200, they lived
at the bungalow for five days. After that he stayed there for
another fortnight, but nobody ever saw her alive again. Steeger
said she had gone to South America, but later said he had never
said South America, but South Africa. None of her money
remained in the Bank, where she had kept it, and Steeger was
shewn to have come by at least £150 just at that time. Then
Steeger turned out to be a vegetarian, getting all his food from
the greengrocer; and that made the constable in the village of
Unge suspicious of him, for a vegetarian was something new to
the constable. He watched Steeger after that, and it's well he
did, for there was nothing that Scotland Yard asked him that he
couldn't tell them about him, except of course the one thing.
And he told the police at Otherthorpe five or six miles away
and they came and took a hand at it too. They were able to say

for one thing that he never went outside the bungalow and its tidy garden ever since she disappeared. You see, the more they watched him the more suspicious they got, as you naturally do if you're watching a man; so that very soon they were watching every move he made, but if it hadn't been for his being a vegetarian they'd never have started to suspect him, and there wouldn't have been enough evidence even for Linley. Not that they found out anything much against him, except that £150 dropping in from nowhere; and it was Scotland Yard that found that, not the police of Otherthorpe. No, what the constable of Unge found out was about the larch-trees, and that beat Scotland Yard utterly, and beat Linley up to the very last, and of course it beat me. There were ten larch-trees in the bit of a garden, and he'd made some sort of an arrangement with the landlord, Steeger had, before he took the bungalow, by which he could do what he liked with the larch-trees. And then, from about the time that little Nancy Elth must have died, he cut every one of them down. Three times a day he went at it for nearly a week, and when they were all down he cut them all up into logs no more than two foot long and laid them all in neat heaps. You never saw such work. And what for? To give an excuse for the axe was one theory. But the excuse was bigger than the axe: it took him a fortnight, hard work every day. And he could have killed a little thing like Nancy Elth without an axe, and cut her up too. Another theory was that he wanted firewood, to make away with the body. But he never used it. He left it all standing there in those neat stacks. It fairly beat everybody.

Well, those are the facts I told Linley. Oh, yes, and he bought a big butcher's knife. Funny thing, they all do. And yet it isn't so funny after all; if you've got to cut a woman up, you've got to cut her up; and you can't do that without a knife. Then, there were some negative facts. He hadn't burned her. Only had a fire in the small stove now and then, and only used it for cooking. They got on to that pretty smartly, the Unge constable did, and the men that were lending him a hand from Otherthorpe.

There were some little woody places lying round, shaws they call them in that part of the country, the country people do, and they could climb a tree handy and unobserved and get a sniff at the smoke in almost any direction it might be blowing. They did that now and then and there was no smell of flesh burning, just ordinary cooking. Pretty smart of the Otherthorpe police that was, though of course it didn't help to hang Steeger. Then later on the Scotland Yard men went down and got another fact, negative but narrowing things down all the while. And that was that the chalk under the bungalow and under the little garden had none of it been disturbed. And he'd never been outside it since Nancy disappeared. Oh, yes, and he had a big file besides the knife. But there was no sign of any ground bones found on the file, or any blood on the knife. He'd washed them of course. I told all that to Linley.

Now I ought to warn you before I go any further; I am a small man myself and you probably don't expect anything horrible from me. But I ought to warn you this man was a murderer, or at any rate somebody was; the woman had been made away with, a nice pretty little girl too, and the man that had done that wasn't necessarily going to stop at things you might think he'd stop at. With the mind to do a thing like that, and with the long thin shadow of the rope to drive him further, you can't say what he'd stop at. Murder tales seem nice things sometimes for a lady to sit and read all by herself by the fire. But murder isn't a nice thing, and when a murderer's desperate and trying to hide his tracks he isn't even as nice as he was before. I'll ask you to bear that in mind. Well, I've warned you.

So I says to Linley, 'And what do you make of it?'

'Drains?' said Linley.

'No,' I says, 'you're wrong there. Scotland Yard has been into that. And the Otherthorpe people before them. They've had a look in the drains, such as they are, a little thing running into a cesspool beyond the garden; and nothing has gone down it, nothing that oughtn't to have, I mean.'

He made one or two other suggestions, but Scotland Yard had been before him in every case. That's really the crab of my story, if you'll excuse the expression. You want a man who sets out to be a detective to take his magnifying glass and go down to the spot; to go to the spot before everything; and then to measure the footmarks and pick up the clues and find the knife that the police have overlooked. But Linley never even went near the place and he hadn't got a magnifying glass, not as I ever saw, and Scotland Yard were before him every time.

In fact they had more clues than anybody could make head or tail of. Every kind of clue to show that he'd murdered the poor little girl; every kind of clue to show that he hadn't disposed of the body; and yet the body wasn't there. It wasn't in South America either, and not much more likely in South Africa. And all the time, mind you, that enormous bunch of chopped larch wood, a clue that was staring everyone in the face and leading nowhere. No, we didn't seem to want any more clues, and Linley never went near the place. The trouble was to deal with the clues we'd got. I was completely mystified; so was Scotland Yard; and Linley seemed to be getting no forwarder; and all the while the mystery was hanging on me. I mean, if it were not for the trifle I'd chanced to remember, and if it were not for one chance word I said to Linley, that mystery would have gone the way of all the other mysteries that men have made nothing of, a darkness, a little patch of night in history.

Well, the fact was Linley didn't take much interest in it at first, but I was so absolutely sure that he could do it, that I kept him to the idea. 'You can do chess problems,' I said.

'That's ten times harder,' he said sticking to his point.

'Then why don't you do this?' I said.

'Then go and take a look at the board for me,' said Linley.

That was his way of talking. We'd been a fortnight together, and I knew it by now. He meant go down to the bungalow at Unge. I know you'll say why didn't he go himself, but the plain truth of it is that if he'd been tearing about the countryside he'd never have been thinking, whereas sitting there in his chair by the fire in our flat there was no limit to the ground he could cover, if you follow my meaning. So down I went by train next day, and got out at Unge station. And there were the North Downs rising up before me, somehow like music.

'It's up there, isn't it?' I said to the porter.

'That's right,' he said. 'Up there by the lane; and mind to turn to your right when you get to the old yew-tree, a very big tree, you can't mistake it, and then . . .' and he told me the way so that I couldn't go wrong. I found them all like that, very nice and helpful. You see it was Unge's day at last; everyone had heard of Unge now; you could have got a letter there any time just then without putting the county or post-town; and this was what Unge had to show. I dare say if you tried to find Unge now . . .; well, anyway, they were making hay while the sun shone.

Well, there the hill was, going up into sunlight, going up like a song. You don't want to hear about the Spring, and all the may rioting, and the colour that came down over everything later on in the day, and all those birds; but I thought, 'What a nice place to bring a girl to.' And then when I thought that he'd killed her there, well, I'm only a small man, as I said, but when I thought of her on that hill with all the birds singing, I said to myself, 'Wouldn't it be odd if it turned out to be me after all that got that man killed, if he did murder her.' So I soon found my way up to the bungalow and began prying about, looking over the hedge into the garden. And I didn't find much, and I found nothing at all that the police hadn't found already, but there were those heaps of larch-logs staring me in the face and looking very queer.

I did a lot of thinking, leaning against the hedge, breathing the smell of the may, and looking over the top of it at the larch-logs, and the neat little bungalow the other side of the garden. Lots of theories I thought of; till I came to the best thought of all; and that was that if I left the thinking to Linley, with his Oxford-and-Cambridge education, and only brought him the facts, as he had told me, I should be doing more good in my way than if I tried to do any big thinking. I forgot to tell you that I had gone to Scotland Yard in the morning. Well, there wasn't really much to tell. What they asked me was, what I wanted. And, not having an answer exactly ready, I didn't find out very much from them. But it was quite different at Unge; everyone was most obliging; it was their day there, as I said. The constable let me go indoors, so long as I didn't touch anything, and he gave me a look at the garden from the inside. And I saw the stumps of the ten larch-trees, and I noticed one thing that Linley said was very observant of me, not that it turned out to be any use, but any way I was doing my best; I noticed that the stumps had been all chopped anyhow. And from that I thought that the man that did it didn't know much about chopping. The constable said that was a deduction. So then I said that the axe was blunt when he used it; and that certainly made the constable think, though he didn't actually say I was right this time. Did I tell you that Steeger never went outdoors, except to the little garden to chop wood, ever since Nancy disappeared? I think I did. Well, it was perfectly true. They'd watched him night and day, one or another of them, and the Unge constable told me that himself. That limited things a good deal. The only thing I didn't like about it was that I felt Linley ought to have found all that out instead of ordinary policemen, and I felt that he could have too. There'd have been romance in a story like that. And they'd never have done it if the news hadn't gone round that the man was a vegetarian and only dealt at the greengrocers. Likely as not even that was only started out of pique by the butcher. It's queer what little things may trip a man up. Best to keep straight is my motto. But perhaps I'm straying a bit away from my story. I should like to do that for ever; forget that it ever was; but I can't.

Well, I picked up all sorts of information; clues I suppose I should call it in a story like this; though they none of them seemed to lead anywhere. For instance, I found out everything he ever bought at the village, I could even tell you the kind of salt he bought, quite plain with no phosphates in it, that they sometimes put in to make it tidy. And then he got ice from the fishmongers, and plenty of vegetables, as I said, from the green-grocer, Mergin and Sons. And I had a bit of a talk over it all with the constable. Slugger he said his name was. I wondered why he hadn't come in and searched the place as soon as the girl was missing. 'Well, you can't do that,' he said. 'And besides, we didn't suspect at once, not about the girl that is. We only suspected there was something wrong about him on account of him being a vegetarian. He stayed a good fortnight after the last that was seen of her. And then we slipped in like a knife. But, you see, no one had been enquiring about her, there was no warrant out.'

'And what did you find,' I asked Slugger, 'when you went in?'

'Just a big file,' he said, 'and the knife and the axe that he must have got to chop her up with.'

'But he got the axe to chop trees with,' I said.

'Well, yes,' he said, but rather grudgingly.

'And what did he chop them for?' I asked.

'Well of course, my superiors has theories about that,' he said, 'that they mightn't tell to everybody.'

You see, it was those logs that were beating them.

'But did he cut her up at all?' I asked.

'Well, he said that she was going to South America,' he answered. Which was really very fair-minded of him.

I don't remember now much else that he told me. Steeger left the plates and dishes all washed up and very neat, he said.

Well, I brought all this back to Linley, going up by the train that started just about sunset. I'd like to tell you about the late Spring evening, so calm over that grim bungalow, closing in with a glory all round it, as though it were blessing it; but you'll want to hear of the murder. Well, I told Linley everything, though much of it didn't seem to me to be worth the telling. The trouble was that the moment I began to leave anything out, he'd know it, and make me drag it in. 'You can't tell what may be vital,' he'd say. 'A tin-tack swept away by a housemaid might hang a man.'

All very well, but be consistent even if you are educated at Eton and Harrow, and whenever I mentioned Numnumo, which after all was the beginning of the whole story, because he wouldn't have heard of it if it hadn't been for me, and my noticing that Steeger had bought two bottles of it, why then he said that things like that were trivial and we should keep to the main issues. I naturally talked a bit about Numnumo, because only that day I had pushed close on fifty bottles of it in Unge. A murder certainly stimulates people's minds, and Steeger's two bottles gave me an opportunity that only a fool could have failed to make something of. But of course all that was nothing at all to Linley.

You can't see a man's thoughts and you can't look into his mind, so that all the most exciting things in the world can never be told of. But what I think happened all that evening with Linley, while I talked to him before supper, and all through supper, and sitting smoking afterwards in front of our fire, was that his thoughts were stuck at a barrier there was no getting over. And the barrier wasn't the difficulty of finding ways and means by which Steeger might have made away with the body, but the impossibility of finding why he chopped those masses of wood every day for a fortnight, and paid as I'd just found out, £25 to his landlord to be allowed to do it. That's what was beating Linley. As for the ways by which Steeger might have hidden the body, it seemed to me that every way was blocked by the police. If you said he buried it they said the chalk was undisturbed, if you said he carried it away they said he never left the place, if you said he burned it they said no smell of burning was ever noticed when the smoke blew low, and when it didn't they climbed trees after it. I'd taken to Linley wonderfully, and I didn't have to be educated to see there was something big in a mind like his, and I thought that he could have done it. When I saw the police getting in before him like that, and no way that I could see of getting past them, I felt real sorry.

Did anyone come to the house? he asked me once or twice. Did anyone take anything away from it? But we couldn't account for it that way. Then perhaps I made some suggestion that was no good, or perhaps I started talking of Numnumo again, and he interrupted me rather sharply.

'But what would you do, Smethers?' he said. 'What would you do yourself?'

'If I'd murdered poor Nancy Elth?' I asked.

'Yes,' he said.

'I can't ever imagine doing of such a thing,' I told him.

He sighed at that, as though it were something against me.

'I suppose I should never be a detective,' I said. And he just shook his head.

Then he looked broodingly into the fire for what seemed an hour. And then he shook his head again. We both went to bed after that.

I shall remember the next day all my life. I was out till evening, as usual, pushing Numnumo. And we sat down to supper about nine. You couldn't get things cooked at those flats, so of course we had it cold. And Linley began with a salad. I can see it now, every bit of it. Well, I was still a bit full of what I'd done in Unge, pushing Numnumo. Only a fool, I know, would have been unable to push it there; but still, I *had* pushed it; and about fifty bottles, forty-eight to be exact, are something in a small village, whatever the circumstances. So I was talking about it a bit; and then all of a sudden I realized that Numnumo was nothing to Linley, and I pulled myself up with a jerk. It was really very kind of him; do you know what he did? He must have known at once why I stopped talking, and he just stretched out a hand and said: 'Would you give me a little of your Numnumo for my salad?'

I was so touched I nearly gave it him. But of course you don't take Numnumo with salad. Only for meats and savouries. That's on the bottle.

So I just said to him, 'Only for meats and savouries.' Though I don't know what savouries are. Never had any.

I never saw a man's face go like that before.

He seemed still for a whole minute. And nothing speaking about him but that expression. Like a man that's seen a ghost, one is tempted to write. But it wasn't really at all. I'll tell you what he looked like. Like a man that's seen something that no one has ever looked at before, something he thought couldn't be.

And then he said in a voice that was all quite changed, more low and gentle and quiet it seemed, 'No good for vegetables, eh?'

'Not a bit,' I said.

And at that he gave a kind of sob in his throat. I hadn't thought he could feel things like that. Of course I didn't know what it was all about; but, whatever it was, I thought all that sort of thing would have been knocked out of him at Eton and Harrow, an educated man like that. There were no tears in his eyes but he was feeling something horribly.

And then he began to speak with big spaces between his words, saying, 'A man might make a mistake perhaps, and use Numnumo with vegetables.'

'Not twice,' I said. What else could I say?

And he repeated that after me as though I had told of the end of the world, and adding an awful emphasis to my words, till they seemed all clammy with some frightful significance, and shaking his head as he said it.

Then he was quite silent.

'What is it?' I asked.

'Smethers,' he said.

'Yes,' I said.

'Smethers,' said he.

And I said, 'Well?'

'Look here, Smethers,' he said, 'you must 'phone down to the grocer at Unge and find out from him this.'

'Yes?' I said.

'Whether Steeger bought those two bottles, as I expect he did, on the same day, and not a few days apart. He couldn't have done that.'

I waited to see if any more was coming, and then I ran out and did what I was told. It took me some time, being after nine o'clock, and only then with the help of the police. About six days apart they said; and so I came back and told Linley. He looked up at me so hopefully when I came in, but I saw that it was the wrong answer by his eyes.

You can't take things to heart like that without being ill, and when he didn't speak I said: 'What you want is a good brandy, and go to bed early.'

And he said: 'No. I must see someone from Scotland Yard. 'Phone round to them. Say here at once.'

'But,' I said, 'I can't get an inspector from Scotland Yard to call on us at this hour.'

His eyes were all lit up. He was all there all right.

'Then tell them,' he said, 'they'll never find Nancy Elth. Tell one of them to come here and I'll tell him why.' And he added, I think only for me, 'They must watch Steeger, till one day they get him over something else.'

And, do you know, he came. Inspector Ulton; he came himself.

While we were waiting I tried to talk to Linley. Partly curiosity, I admit. But I didn't want to leave him to those thoughts of his, brooding away by the fire. I tried to ask him what it was all about. But he wouldn't tell me. 'Murder is horrible' is all he would say. 'And as a man covers his tracks up it only gets worse.'

He wouldn't tell me. 'There are tales,' he said, 'that one never wants to hear.'

That's true enough. I wish I'd never heard this one. I never did actually. But I guessed it from Linley's last words to Inspector Ulton, the only ones that I overheard. And perhaps this is the point at which to stop reading my story, so that you don't guess it too; even if you think you want murder stories. For don't you rather want a murder story with a bit of a romantic twist, and not a story about real foul murder? Well, just as you like.

In came Inspector Ulton, and Linley shook hands in silence, and pointed the way to his bedroom; and they went in there and talked in low voices, and I never heard a word.

A fairly hearty-looking man was the inspector when they went into that room.

They walked through our sitting-room in silence when they came out, and together they went into the hall, and there I heard the only words they said to each other. It was the inspector that first broke that silence.

'But why,' he said, 'did he cut down the trees?'

'Solely,' said Linley, 'in order to get an appetite.'

THE SHOOTING OF
CONSTABLE SLUGGER

I ONCE told a story about a murderer called Steeger. It got into *Time and Tide*, and rather shocked some people: quite right too. Smethers is my name. And my friend Mr Linley found out how Steeger did it. But they couldn't hang him: that was another matter. So of course the police watched him, and waited. And one day Inspector Ulton called at our flat and shook hands with Mr Linley, and said: 'Steeger's done it again.'

Linley nodded his head and said, 'What is it now?'

And Inspector Ulton said: 'He has killed Constable Slugger.'

'What?' said Linley. 'The man that helped you so much over the other murder?'

'Yes,' said Ulton. 'He had retired. But Steeger never forgave him. And now he's killed him.'

'What a pity,' said Linley.

'It's a damned shame,' I said.

And then the inspector saw me. I'm a small man, myself, and he hadn't noticed me.

'I speak quite suppositiously,' he said. 'You understand that it's purely a suppositious case.'

'Oh, quite,' I answered.

'Because it wouldn't do to go saying outside this room,' he went on, 'that anyone said as Steeger had murdered anyone. Wouldn't do at all. Render yourself liable. Besides, I never told you anything of the sort.'

'Quite,' I repeated.

'He quite understands,' said Linley. 'How did Steeger kill poor Slugger?'

The inspector paused a moment and looked at me, then at Linley, and then he went on. 'That's what we can't make out,' he said. 'He lived in the house opposite Slugger's, in the village of Otherthorpe, only four or five miles away from the scene of his other crime. And we'd have said he shot Slugger across the street as he sat at an open window. And he had a big shot-gun that could have done it, an eight-bore, and there was a ghastly great wound in Slugger's neck, going downwards into the lung.'

'Did they find the gun?' asked Linley.

'Oh, yes,' said the inspector. 'Of course it was all clean and packed away in its case by the time the village constable got in, and he had heard a shot; it was that that made him go, and he went at once; he went to Slugger's house first. Yes, he found the gun all right; but our difficulty is that whether the doctor got the bullet out and was careless enough to lose it, though he says he didn't, or whatever happened, there's no sign of any bullet; no exit wound and no bullet in the body, just the one enormous wound, the sort of thing you might make with a crowbar, and no weapon of that sort discovered, so we can't prove anything and we've come to you again. We must get Steeger this time.'

'What did he want an eight-bore for?' Linley asked.

'Well, to shoot Slugger really,' said the inspector. 'But unfortunately he's got a perfectly good excuse for it; he does actually shoot ducks with it on Olnie Flats, and sells them. We can't go into Court and say what he really bought it for, after that.'

'No,' said Linley. 'Did the constable find Steeger when he called?'

'Yes,' said the inspector, 'at the back of the house: he was digging in the garden.'

'Digging?' said Linley. 'When did this happen?'

'Last Wednesday,' said the inspector.

'But it was freezing hard last Wednesday, wasn't it?' replied Linley.

'Well, pretending to dig,' said the inspector. 'But we can't hang him on that. No one would dig while it was freezing that hard; but we can't prove it; and we couldn't hang him on it if we could.'

'No, it just shows you and me that he's up to his old tricks again.'

'That's all,' said the inspector.

It was snowing even as they spoke, and had been freezing all the week. I sat quite still and just listened, and I think they forgot me.

'He had a good heap of earth to show for his digging,' Inspector Ulton said, 'but that didn't say that he'd only just done it. Lots of people heard a shot, though nobody saw it. We've had the whole body photographed by X-rays and there's no sign of a bullet.'

'Could he have hit Slugger with a pick-axe through the window?'

'No, first floor,' said the inspector. 'The room upstairs. And Steeger shot him from his upstairs room too, only there's no bullet. The wound goes a little downwards, and Steeger's upper storey was the higher one of the two. If you could only find that bullet for us.'

'A deep wound, I suppose.'

'Oh, very,' said Ulton.

'He must have extracted it.'

'Oh, no one crossed the street after the shot. Mears; that's the constable there; lives in the very street, twenty-eight doors away and he was out of his house in ten seconds; the whole street was empty.'

'He didn't have the bullet tied to a thin wire,' said Linley; 'you'd have thought of a thing like that.'

'Yes, we thought of that,' said the inspector. 'But a big bullet like that would have left blood-marks somewhere, either on Slugger's sill, or the street, or the wall of Steeger's house; and there weren't any.'

'What cheek,' said Linley, 'going and living right opposite Slugger's house.'

'Yes,' said the inspector. 'And Slugger knew what Steeger was waiting for too. But he wasn't going to give up his house on that account. Steeger thinks he can do what he likes, having escaped the first time.'

'Slugger had his window open, you say?'

'Oh, yes.'

'You can prove that?' said Linley. 'Because you'd have to prove it, considering the weather.'

'Oh, yes,' said Ulton, 'Mears will swear to that. Slugger had his window open in all weathers. He was sitting beside it reading. The paper was in his hand.'

'It certainly looks as if Steeger shot him through the window,' said Linley.

'It stands to reason he did,' said Ulton. 'But, without the bullet to show, you know what a jury would do. They'd go and let him off.'

'Yes,' said Linley. 'How wide was the street?'

'Ten yards from wall to wall,' said the inspector. 'Barely that. Nine yards two feet.'

'Well, I'll think it over,' said Linley, 'and let you know tomorrow how I think Steeger did it.'

'I'd be very glad if you would,' said the inspector, and he turned to go away. And at that he noticed me again, and told me that any suggestion from me that Steeger had ever killed anyone would be highly criminal, as though he hadn't been slandering Steeger (if that's the word for it) himself for the last fifteen minutes. I said I wouldn't say a word against Steeger, and the inspector left.

'What do you make of it?' asked Linley.

'Me?' I said. 'If he shot Slugger and the bullet didn't go through, it must be still in the body.'

'But they've found that it isn't,' said Linley.

'Let me go down there and have a look,' I said.

'No, Smethers,' he said. 'You won't find anything Scotland Yard has missed.'

'Well, what are you going to do?' I said.

'Think,' said Linley.

'What about?' I asked.

'Evaporating bullets,' said Linley.

'Are there such things?' I asked him.

'No,' said Linley.

'Then what's the use of thinking about them,' I said.

'Because it's happened,' said Linley. 'When a thing's happened you've got to admit it, and try and see how.'

'What about a big arrow,' I said. 'And pull it back by a string.'

'Worse than the bullet tied to a wire,' he answered. 'Still more blood-marks.'

'What about a spear ten yards long,' I said.

'Ingenious,' was Linley's only comment.

I got a bit huffed when he wouldn't say more than that, and began to argue with him. But Linley was right. They didn't find any spear, for one thing, when they searched Steeger's house; and, for another, there wouldn't have been space for it in the upstairs room.

And then the telephone-bell rang. It was Inspector Ulton. Linley went to the 'phone. 'They've found a wad in the street,' he said.

'A wad?' said I.

'A wad of the eight-bore,' he answered. 'Between the two houses.'

'Then he shot him,' I said.

'We know that,' said Linley.

'Well, what's the difficulty,' said I, 'if you know it already?'

'To prove it,' said Linley.

He sat thinking in front of the fire for a long time, and I could do nothing more to help him. And after a while he said, 'Ring up Scotland Yard, Smethers, and ask if there was any sign of burning about the wound.'

I did it and they said No. The doctor had thought for a moment that he felt some small foreign particle, which made them think that he might have lost the bullet, but he said that he was mistaken, and that there was nothing there, and no sign of burning.

I told Linley, and all he said was, 'Then it was nothing that burned away.'

And he was quite silent again.

So was I, for I could think of nothing. I knew it was Steeger, just as he did; but that was no good.

'We must hang Steeger,' he said after a while. And I knew that he was thinking of Nancy Elth, the girl Steeger murdered the last time. He sat silent for so long then that I thought it had beaten him. Time passed and I was even afraid that he had given it up, which I knew he ought not to do, because I was sure he could solve it.

'How did Steeger do it?' I asked after a while.

'He shot Slugger,' said Linley.

'How?' I asked.

'I don't know,' he said. 'And I never shall.'

'Oh, yes, you will,' I said, 'if you give your mind to it.'

'Oh, well,' said he, 'give me a chess-problem to look at.'

'No,' I said. 'If you get looking at them you'll never leave them alone. Let's solve this problem first.'

For I saw he was just on the verge of giving it up.

'Oh, well,' he said, 'then give me some fresh air. I must have a change of some sort.'

So I opened the window and he leaned right out, breathing the frozen air of the late evening. And there the whole mystery was, the moment he put his head out of the window. What funny things are our minds. Here was one of the brightest minds I had ever known, hard at work on a problem, and yet he had to see what he was looking for by shoving his face into it, and that purely by chance. Yes, there were icicles of all sizes hanging about the window, and he almost bumped his face into them. He drew in his head and said, 'They won't get Steeger yet. They'll never prove this to a jury. The bullet was made of ice.'

AN ENEMY OF SCOTLAND YARD

INSPECTOR Ulton came to see Mr Linley today. I am glad to say that he has got used to me; the inspector, I mean. He just said, 'You're Mr Smethers, aren't you?' And I said I was. And he said, 'Well, you'll understand that all this is strictly private.' And I said I would. And then he started talking to Mr Linley.

I'd met Inspector Ulton before over the murder at Unge, and the shooting of Constable Slugger. Mr Linley had helped him a lot.

'I've come to you again, Mr Linley,' were his first words.

'Is it Steeger again?' asked Linley.

'We don't know who it is,' said the inspector. 'We usually know at the Yard who has done a murder. It's not very difficult. Motive usually points straight at somebody; and we can easily find if he was in the neighbourhood at the time. Proving it is the only difficulty. This time we can't even find out who it is. We thought you might help us, Mr Linley.'

'What is it?' said Linley.

'It's a bad case,' said the inspector; 'as bad a case as we've had for a long time.'

'I'm sorry to hear that,' I said.

He didn't pay any attention to me, but I somehow saw from his look that I'd said a silly thing. Bad cases were their job. If they stopped, where would Scotland Yard be? I was sorry as soon as I'd said it.

'We got a letter at Scotland Yard last week,' he said, 'threatening that if Mr Cambell went again to his club, or Inspector Island went to watch a billiard-match at Piero's, or Sergeant Holbuck played football either at the Scramblers Football

Ground or the old Sallovians, each one of them that did so would be killed. Holbuck is one of our best football-players, and those are the only two grounds he ever plays on. Watching billiards at Piero's was what Inspector Island always did when he could.'

'But wait a moment, Inspector,' said Linley. 'That's a preposterous threat. The man could never carry it out.'

'Mr Cambell and Inspector Island are dead already,' said Ulton.

'Dead?' said Linley. And I never saw him so flabbergasted.

'Mr Cambell went to his club, the Meateaters, in Holne Street, the day that we got the letter, and was poisoned. And Inspector Island went to Piero's next day to watch a game of billiards, and a piece of the wall above the door fell as he went in, and killed him.'

'A piece of the wall fell?' exclaimed Linley incredulously.

'Yes,' said the inspector. 'It was in the papers, though very little about it, as they've not held the inquest yet. But we are working on the other case first, as we have a clue there.'

'What is the clue?' said Linley.

'We've the finger-print of a waiter at the club, who disappeared on the night of the murder, before Mr Cambell was taken ill. Of course he must have given the poison, but we don't know much about him or who he really is, and we don't think he was the man who planned it all.'

'Can I see the finger-print?' asked Linley.

And Inspector Ulton brought an envelope out of his pocket and took from it a sheet of paper, and on the paper was the finger-print, very completely in ink. It was one of two sheets of papers for members' bills, and in the middle of it, very black, was the finger-print. Linley looked at it for a long time.

'And Piero's?' he said at last.

'That baffles us,' said the inspector. 'We have found out that the masonry that killed Island was dislodged by a small explosion that took place very effectively at a joint between two big stones. And the explosive was set off by a delicate mechanism that must have been inserted in the wall from the inside. We can find very little of the machine, not only because the explosion took place inside it, but because it was all mixed up with some stuff called thermite, which burns very fiercely, and which destroyed everything except a few small bars. Anyhow there *was* a machine that fired the explosive that brought down those pieces of masonry, but what we can't find is any wires controlling it. The fire was soon put out, and the damage only local, and we have searched all round the door; both sides, above and below; but there's no sign of a wire.'

'Could one have been pulled away?' asked Linley.

'Not across the open without being seen by someone,' said Ulton, 'and there were plenty there. And not underground. We've searched; and we've made sure there's no wire, or a channel that it could have run in. It must have been a time-fuse.'

'Was Inspector Island as regular as all that?' said Linley.

'Well, he had regular habits,' said Ulton, 'and he got off duty at a certain hour and the game began at a certain time.'

'To the very second?' asked Linley.

'Well, not to the very second,' he said.

'And it would have to be about half a second,' went on Linley. 'No, the time-fuse won't do.'

'I don't suppose it will,' said Ulton.

And they were both silent awhile.

'Well,' said Linley after a bit, 'I can tell you one thing. Whoever that waiter was . . .'

'He called himself Slimmer,' said Ulton.

'Whoever he was,' said Linley, 'there's something a bit deep about him. Deeper than you've had time to go yet, I mean. That finger-print shows you that. When did he make it?'

'It was found after he'd gone,' said Ulton. 'What's odd about it? We find thousands of finger-prints.'

'Simply,' said Linley, 'that a man who is committing a murder doesn't make a finger-print in ink right in the middle of a sheet of paper, quite so neat and tidy as that, and then leave it where the police can find it handily.'

'What then?' said Ulton.

'Why, it's not his finger-print. It's some kind of fake. So that you are dealing with very queer people; people clever enough to forge finger-prints, which I have never heard of being done. Have you?'

But Inspector Ulton would not say what they knew at the Yard and what they didn't know.

'I might have,' he said.

'It might be done on rubber by a good forger, I should think,' went on Linley. 'But the people that did that might be capable of carrying out their threats, which at first I hardly thought possible. Now about the explosion at Piero's. That must have been controlled by someone who could actually see Island coming. He might have had warning that he was coming when he was fifty yards away, or any other distance, but that would never have been exact enough to kill him. He must have seen him go into Piero's.'

'And, if he did, how could he make the thing explode?' said Ulton.

'That's what we've got to think about,' said Linley. 'What houses are there from which he could see the inspector going up to the door?'

'There's several,' said the inspector.

'And what about the third man?' said Linley. 'Holbuck, didn't you say?'

'Yes, Sergeant Holbuck,' said the inspector. 'He's going to play football tomorrow. He won't stop for the threat. None of them would. But we're going to see that he's safe. It's on the Old Sallovians' ground. Everyone playing on his side will be members of the Force, and we know every man on the other side. They are all right; and the whole front line of the crowd looking on will be our men, and we'll have a few extra dotted about behind, all the way round the ground, not to mention the ones that will watch every man coming in at the gate. And then we'll see him safe back when the game is over: we are not telling anybody how we are going to do that, but we shall not let Holbuck take any chances.'

'Tomorrow,' said Linley. 'May I come?'

'Yes,' said Inspector Ulton. 'This ticket will let you in, but you won't be allowed to stand in the front row.'

Mr Linley saw me looking at him. 'Could I have a ticket for my friend?' he asked. 'You'd like to come and see what happens, Smethers, wouldn't you?'

Like to see what happened? Of course I would. And Inspector Ulton looked at me. 'Oh, yes, he can have a ticket,' said the inspector then. And he gave the ticket to Linley.

'It's really very kind of you,' I said.

'Not at all,' said the inspector.

After Inspector Ulton left Linley said nothing for a long time. He stood gazing hard, with the kind of gaze that doesn't seem to see anything; nothing here, I mean. And I said nothing to interrupt him. And then he said, 'Come and sit down, Smethers.'

And we sat in front of the fire. It was winter, by the way, and getting on towards tea-time. Linley began filling his pipe.

'What is it?' I said.

'There's an awful lot of organization nowadays,' said Linley, 'on both sides. With all the organization they've got at Scotland Yard, a criminal has either to give it up or to be cleverer than the detectives. The fellow who's done this of course must have been caught by them at one time, probably by Cambell himself: he was practically their chief man, not nominally, but practically. He's a spiteful fellow, whoever it is that they are looking for. Probably he was brooding for years in a convict-prison, and turning over and over in his rotten mind his grudges against those three men. And it may be interesting to find out on what occasion those three were working together. That may help to find the man who hates them so much. That finger-print shows you that if he is not an absolute fool he must be a pretty subtle devil. So we may look for a pretty crafty scheme, to find out how Island was killed in the doorway of Piero's.'

'I don't see how he could have done it,' I said.

'Do you remember what Ulton found when he was looking for wires?' he answered. 'And what then?'

'*I* don't know,' I said.

'You're too old,' said Linley, 'and so is Inspector Ulton.'

'I'm not old,' I said. 'Nor is he.'

'You were both born before wireless got into its stride,' said Linley.

'Wireless?' I said.

'Of course,' said Linley. 'A school-boy would have told you that. He would have been born into a world familiar with wireless. You weren't. That explosion was worked for the exact second by something: Ulton looks for wires, and can't find them, and then he is beaten. Simply wireless. A little set buried in the wall.'

'That's all very well,' I said. 'A little receiving-set is common enough, and no doubt it could work an explosion; but you don't have a transmitting plant in every house; that's a very big thing.'

'That's what we've got to find,' said Linley.

'Well,' I said, 'how many houses are there from which Piero's door can be watched?'

'A lot,' said Linley, 'from the other side of the square, and several more in the street on the righthand side of it if you stand with your back to Piero's.'

Piero's stood in a little square with a good many trees in it: starlings lived there by night, and sparrows by day. And all kinds of people sat on its benches, each with his or her history, that far outshone this story, if only you could get at it; and amongst them were several of Ulton's men, in various kit.

'But we can probably limit it a good deal,' Linley went on, 'by cutting out the houses from which Island could not be seen approaching, as the man would have to be all ready to do his dirty work with precision.'

'Well, let me go and telephone that to Scotland Yard,' I said. 'They'll soon find out if there's a transmitting-set in one of those houses. A big thing like that can't be concealed so easily.'

'Very well, Smethers,' he said. 'But wrap it up so that everyone doesn't know what you're talking about. Just say to Inspector Ulton that wireless may have done it, and to have a good look in houses that would have a view of Island's approach as well as the end of his journey.'

And so I did, in pretty much those words, and Scotland Yard seemed quite pleased.

We had tea then and Linley forgot about it all in the deliberate way that he has; letting it simmer in his mind; but with the lid on, as it were. And we talked of all kinds of other things. But a lot later that night, somewhere about ten or eleven, the telephone bell rang, and Linley went out and answered it and came back and said to me: 'No transmitting-sets in any of the houses. What do you make of that, Smethers?'

'Looks as if you were on the wrong track,' I said.

'Not while there's a telephone,' answered Linley.

And I never made head nor tail of that.

'I hope it will be all right tomorrow,' he said. 'A fellow like that is bound to do something pretty crafty. We are sure to see something.'

'What shall we see?' I asked.

'I don't know,' said Linley. 'But the fellow reminds me of a weasel. He's bound to follow Holbuck. Will Ulton be able to catch him?'

'He ought to,' I said, 'with a couple of hundred policemen, or however many he's going to bring.'

'It isn't numbers that do it,' said Linley, 'when you have cunning like that.' And then he added suddenly, 'Let's come and have a look at the ground.'

'At this hour?' I said.

'Yes,' said Linley, 'I don't want to sleep, and we may as well do our thinking there as anywhere else.'

It was kind of him to put it like that, as though I were going to do much thinking. Well, of course I came with him, and we got a bus, and we came to a part of London where they have tramlines. And soon we left the bus and got into one of the trams, all among people going home late.

'I suppose Sergeant Holbuck is a pretty tough fellow,' I said, 'if he plays football against the Old Sallovians.'

'I don't know him,' said Linley, and went on reading his paper. And I noticed that a man on the opposite side, some way further up the tram, turned a little away from me and gazed up at the roof.

We got out soon after that. It was cold, and late, and rather windy. The street we were walking in was nearly empty, except for a man reading an evening paper under a lamp-post. We saw no one else till we came to the next lamp-post, and saw another man reading a newspaper by the light of that. Nothing but cats slipping softly away from their homes, and every now and then a man reading a newspaper. None of these men ever looked at us, but just looked up from their papers and gazed away from us in the direction in which we were going. As we passed each of them the newspaper would give a little flutter, owing to the man turning it over to read on the other side. When I commented on these men to Linley, he said that it was the only time of day that they got for reading, and that they got light from the street-lamps to read by without having to pay for it.

And then the houses stopped, and we came to a big iron paling, and in the paling was the gate of the football-field. One could see dim fields and a winding line of willows, like a crew of gigantic goblins out for a walk. When we came to the gate, one of the men with newspapers coughed at us. And when I called Linley's attention to that, he said that naturally a man would cough when out reading a paper on such a cold night as this was.

We went all along the paling till it turned, and we turned with it by a little lane with a hedge on the other side. It was nice to see a lane again, after coming through the very middle of London. Then the paling turned once more, and we followed it all round those fields. We could see from the shape of that dark procession of willows, and from a twisty mist, that a stream ran through the fields; and presently we came to where it ran under the paling, and Linley stopped and looked at where it came through, and we saw that it was well wired. It was a very still night, and the mist lying over the stream was motionless, and the twigs of the willows were still as a hand held out to say Hush, and there was no sound in the fields but men coughing, now and again as we passed them. Then Linley drew out a folded copy of a newspaper from his pocket, and carried it in his hand, waving it slightly as he walked, and after a while the coughing stopped.

'You've cured their cough,' I said.

But he didn't understand me, so I was quiet again.

We walked away, and came to the streets once more, and went for a long time in silence. Then Linley said: 'I can't see how they are going to do it. But I suppose we shall see tomorrow.'

'I don't see how they did any of it,' I said.

'Well,' said Linley, 'the poisoning was easy enough, and the time that that waiter arrived at the Meateaters' Club probably dates the beginning of it. He had been there ten months. Very likely the crook that is doing all this got out of prison a little while before that. He wouldn't take long to make his plans; he'd have gone over and over them during his stay in prison, where poor Cambell and Island probably helped to put him. And there wouldn't be much difficulty in putting the explosive into the wall of Piero's one night; a mere matter of burglary, and in a house that no one was particularly guarding: Piero's have some valuable billiard-tables there, but nothing else of any importance, and billiard-tables scarcely lend themselves to burglary.'

'But how did they send the explosive off?' I asked.

'Ah; that was the big job,' said Linley. 'And, as it wasn't done by wires, it must have been done by wireless.'

'But they found no transmitting-set,' I pointed out, 'in any of those houses.'

'It might have been anywhere,' said Linley, 'so long as it was at the other end of a telephone.'

And then the magnitude of the plot began to strike me.

'But they wouldn't think of anything as elaborate as that,' I said.

'It's usually the simple things that happen,' said Linley, 'and they should all be tried first; but if it isn't one of them, why then . . .'

And then we came to our tram, and said no more about that strange plot that had already killed two men and was waiting for yet another.

Next morning Linley told me at breakfast that the game was to begin at 2.30. 'They had the ground well-watched last night,' he said, 'and I don't see how it could have been possible for anyone to have got in and hidden there, and today everyone who goes in will have to go through the gate with a ticket.'

'Shall I go and buy a revolver?' I asked.

'No,' said Linley. 'That was all very well in the days of Sherlock Holmes, when you could have dragged a small cannon behind you if you had felt that you wanted one. But the world has got more complicated. More licences needed. It was probably a happier world before it learned to fill in forms. But there it is, and it will probably never go back to those days now. No, no revolvers, Smethers. But keep your eyes open.'

Of course Linley was perfectly right: he always was. But it rather took the excitement out of it to think that we were only going to watch. Well, we should have been able to do no good after all, if we had had revolvers; or machine-guns for that matter.

We didn't eat much of a lunch. Linley seemed too busy puzzling things over, and I was too excited. Then we went off to the football-ground. We took a taxi this time. We showed our tickets at the gate and were passed in, and no sooner were we inside than we saw an inspector in uniform. 'Cold night, last night,' Linley said to him. And the inspector only laughed.

That paling was very strong and high, and spiked at the top: it wouldn't have been an easy job to get in overnight, to hide there among the willows; and with all those men that there had been coughing in the mist and reading newspapers outside, it would have been impossible. The game had just begun, and we walked along the back of the crowd, looking for Ulton. Most of the men in the crowd seemed to have their hands behind their backs, with walking-sticks or umbrellas in them; and I began to notice that, just as we went by, a stick or umbrella would give a tiny jump. It was a suspicious crowd. It was well organized certainly: the only thing I was a bit uneasy about was whether its suspicions were quite selective enough: if they suspected the right one, whoever he was, when he should come along, or would it be the other way about: that was what I was wondering. And then I thought what cheek it would be if he did come, among all those police, to murder one of them. And cheek was just what he had, or he wouldn't have sent that threat to Scotland Yard, and carried out already two-thirds of it. Then we saw Inspector Ulton, and Linley went up to him and asked him which was Holbuck. The name of Holbuck excited the crowd near us a good deal, and they began making little signals to watch us, but Ulton gave them a nod to stop them, and pointed out Holbuck to Linley. He was a big fellow, easily recognized, playing full back. I watched the game, especially Holbuck's part in it; but the ball was away with the forwards, and Holbuck doing nothing as yet. Linley watched the crowd.

After a while Linley turned to me and said in a low voice: 'They'll be cleverer than me if they get through.'

'What? The railings?' I said.

'No,' said Linley; 'that crowd. Or the railings either for that matter.'

'Then how will they do it?' I asked.

'They won't do it,' said Linley.

He was wrong there.

At last the ball came to Holbuck, and he kicked it three-quarter way down the field. It came back and he got it once more. This time he kept it to himself for a few yards, and then one of the other side charged him. Holbuck got the ball again, and dribbled it forward, getting it right past several of them; he went half-way up the field with it, going fast; and then he fell dead.

Well, I needn't tell you there was some stir. To begin with it was what half the crowd were watching for; and now it had happened before their eyes; and the half of the crowd that weren't watching for it were not much less surprised. They got a doctor and Holbuck was dead right enough, and they arrested the man that had charged him shortly before. All this time Linley stood perfectly silent.

'What do you make of it?' I said after a while.

'I don't know,' said Linley. 'The people round here are suspecting us.'

'Why?' I asked.

'We're strangers to them. Don't talk,' he said.

So I shut up.

We saw Inspector Ulton again, hurrying past. Linley went up to him. 'Well, it's happened,' said Linley.

But Ulton was cross, and said little, if anything at all. He had made the most careful plans and had just been defeated, and had lost a good life over it into the bargain.

'He'll come and see us,' said Linley to me.

And then we left with the crowd. I got the impression that we were followed at first, though it's hard to be sure of that in a crowd. And then I had the impression that someone we passed had conveyed the idea, 'They're all right. Leave them alone.' Both these things were only impressions.

Sure enough Inspector Ulton did come and see us, shortly after we got back. Came to see Linley, I mean.

He looked very worried.

'What does the doctor say?' were Linley's first words to him.

'That's what I came to see you about,' said Ulton.

'Well?' said Linley.

'Snake-bite,' said Ulton.

'Bit late in the year for snakes,' I said. And neither of them paid any attention to me.

'What kind of snake?' Linley asked.

'Russell's viper,' said Ulton.

Then they talked about that viper for a while, and there seemed something gorgon-like about it: it kills by coagulating the blood, by turning it solid. Luckily there are no such snakes going about in England.

'Where was he bitten?' was Linley's next question.

'They'd found no puncture when I came away,' said the inspector. 'But of course they'll examine the body and find out that. We detained the last man that was in contact with him, a man called Ornut, who charged him pretty hard.'

'Did you search him?' asked Linley.

'Yes,' said the inspector. 'But we found nothing incriminating on him.'

'I fancy you'll have to let him go.'

'We did,' the inspector answered. 'But we have his address.'

And then the telephone rang, and I answered it, and it was someone asking for Inspector Ulton. I told him and he went to it.

'They've found the puncture,' said Ulton when he came back from the telephone. 'It's in the sole of the right foot.'

'Must have worn thin soles,' I said.

But Linley got the point at once.

'That accounts for everything,' he said. 'They couldn't get to the football-ground, with all those men you had there watching. But they got at his boots.'

'You think that's it?' said the inspector.

'It stands to reason,' said Linley. 'You couldn't stab something through the sole of a football-boot. It must have been inside the sole.'

And Inspector Ulton agreed; and so it turned out; he went away to see. And that evening he came back again and told Linley what it was. They'd got a snake's fang fixed in the sole of Holbuck's boot, with a layer of something protecting the foot from the fang until the boot got thoroughly warm and the protecting layer melted; then the action of running would operate the fang. It was placed under the ball of the foot, where the boot bends most when you run. And there was another protection, a sort of safety-catch, like the catch you have on a shot-gun, which prevented the thing working at all while it was in place, but it could be pushed out of place by a good tap on the end of it, which ran under the toe of the boot. Kicking a football would do it, and evidently had done it; and the next time that Holbuck ran, after kicking the ball hard, the fang entered the sole of his foot, and was full of the venom with which Russell's viper concludes his quarrels in India.

'No clue to the man?' said Linley.

'Not yet,' said the inspector. 'We 'phoned to the Zoo, and no one's got poison from any of the snakes there. It looks like somebody who has travelled in India. It's not easy to trace poisons that are not got from a chemist, and that don't have to be signed for.'

'No,' said Linley. 'But we'll get him the other way; over the other murder. The clues to that will be at the telephone exchange. You know the time of the murder. We want to know what houses, of those that have a view of the door of Piero's, were using the telephone at that time; those that had a view of the door and a view of a man approaching it for some way, so as to give the murderer time to get everything ready.'

'And what then?' asked Ulton.

'Easy enough then,' said Linley. 'Find out who they were talking to, and find out which of the people called up at that time from one of those houses had a wireless transmitting apparatus, of which there are not many in England.'

'I see,' said Ulton. 'And you think it was set off by wireless.'

'It must have been,' said Linley.

'And wireless could do that?' Ulton asked.

'Make a spark, or strike a match? Certainly,' replied Linley. 'Why, they can steer ships or aeroplanes by it.'

'And where do you think the transmitter was?' said Ulton.

'Wherever the man was telephoning to,' said Linley, 'from the house that could see Piero's door, and some way up the street by which Island was coming.'

'We'll get the telephone calls,' was all that Ulton said, and soon after that he left.

'A sending apparatus is a large thing, isn't it?' I said to Linley.

'Yes,' he said.

'Not easy to hide it in London,' I said. 'So many people about.'

'It won't be easy when Ulton gets after it,' was Linley's comment on that.

The inspector came round next morning. 'There was a telephone-call from one of those houses at the time of the murder,' he said. 'A man giving the name of Colquist, which can't be traced, took rooms on the first floor of No. 29 saying he wanted an office. He took the rooms a week before the murder, and left them the evening of the day it took place. He said he was an agent for real estate. He had the telephone going just at the time of the murder, a long-distance call to Yorkshire.'

'To Yorkshire!' said Linley.

'Yes,' said the inspector.

'After all,' said Linley; 'why not?'

'Of course he's disappeared now,' said Ulton.

'Has No. 29 a good view of the street by which Island came?' Linley asked.

'Yes,' said the inspector, 'he could have seen Island coming a long way, from the windows of the first floor.'

'Then you'll have to go to Yorkshire,' said Linley.

'To Yorkshire?' said the inspector.

'Yes,' said Linley, 'if that's where the call was put through to from 29. What part of Yorkshire was it?'

'Henby, a village among the moors,' said Ulton.

'Then that's where the murder was done,' said Linley.

For some while Ulton didn't seem able to credit it. But Linley stuck to his point. 'If there weren't any wires,' he said, 'it was done by wireless. Chance couldn't have done it. It does odd things when left to itself, but it won't send off an explosion for a murderer at exactly the right second, after he has made all those preparations. Preparations like that scare chance away. No, it was done by wireless; and, if by wireless, why not from Yorkshire.'

'Then we've only got to go to the house and find him,' said Ulton a little doubtfully.

'Yes,' said Linley. 'And you may as well find out who he is before you start. He'll be someone that Mr Cambell, Inspector Island and Sergeant Holbuck all helped to put away where he was brooding over this revenge. And he was either comfortably off or his crime paid him well, financially I mean; for a transmitting apparatus is not bought for nothing. He shouldn't be hard to trace.'

'No,' said the inspector. 'That would be Septon, I should think.'

'What was his crime?' asked Linley.

'Selling cocaine,' said Ulton. 'He peddled it on a very large scale round the wrong kind of houses. Mr Cambell found him out, and Island and Holbuck were both in it. He'd be out now. They had him at Parkhurst.'

'Then you'll find him in Yorkshire,' said Linley. 'There'd be another of them watching Piero's, at the other end of the telephone. But Septon would have been in Yorkshire.'

'How do you know which was at which end?' asked Ulton.

'Because that kind of man is always the furthest away from the crime,' said Linley. 'They put up the money for it and keep out of the way, when they can.'

'I think you're right there,' said Ulton, who had known crime all over the British Isles. 'We must get off to Henby, and the sooner the better. Number 15 Henby is the telephone number:

it was the house of a doctor, but he went to Switzerland, and it's been let for a year to a man giving the name of Brown. He's been there just over two months.'

'When did Septon come out of Parkhurst?' asked Linley.

'Some while ago,' said Ulton. 'And then he had to report at police-stations. That was finished with two and a half months ago.'

'It shouldn't be difficult to get him,' I said, wondering if they'd let me come, too.

'He shoots,' said the inspector. 'We had some difficulty with him last time.'

Well, of course that's a little bit outside my line of business. I travel in Numnumo, a relish for meats and savouries; and I guarantee to get into any house, though of course I can't promise to sell a bottle of relish every time. I don't care how hard they try to keep me out: I get in in the end. But of course shooting would be something a bit new to me. And I don't pretend that I'd like it. But I still wanted to go.

'Well, of course, two can play at that game,' I said.

'No. We can do better than that,' said Ulton.

He didn't tell me any more of his plans, but turned to Linley and said: 'Would you care to come? We'll go by the 2.30 tomorrow afternoon.'

'Earlier, if you like,' said Linley.

'No,' said Ulton; 'it's on a hill, and he has too good a view.'

I didn't see at first how going earlier or later would alter the view. But I soon saw that was silly of me. Linley understood at once. He glanced at me and then at the inspector, and I saw he meant to ask if I could come too. 'Oh well,' said Ulton. But I somehow saw that I might, though the words themselves meant nothing.

'Well, you take that train, and I'll join you on it,' said Ulton. 'We book to Arneth. Better go first-class and we shall probably be by ourselves.'

'All right,' said Linley. 'And I should think he'd have an eye for detectives, with all that experience. It's their boots they spot them by, isn't it?'

And he looked at Ulton's big boots.

'We're mostly large men,' said Ulton, 'and have to wear large boots.'

'Yes, of course,' said Linley, seeing him to the door.

When Inspector Ulton had gone Linley came back to me and said, 'You want to go, Smethers?'

'Yes,' I said.

So he went to a drawer and came back with two revolvers. 'Better take one of these,' he said. 'Look out. It's loaded. Better not tell Ulton you've got it. Because he ought to set you filling in forms, or send you to prison, or something like that, if he knew you'd got it.'

'It's a bit bulky,' I said. 'Won't he see the bulge in my pocket?'

'Oh, yes,' said Linley, 'Ulton'll see the bulge. But he isn't the sort of fellow to ask what made it. I've another revolver for him. But I won't offer it him until things begin to look nasty. Because he'd have to notice it if I actually held it out to him in the train.'

'Won't he have one of his own?' I asked.

'They're supposed not to,' he said.

'Not fair on crime,' I suggested.

'That's about it,' said Linley.

Well, next day we went to King's Cross to catch the 2.30; I with one revolver and Linley with two; and, as Linley was buying the tickets to Arneth, the booking-clerk told him that seats had been reserved for us. A porter showed us to the carriage and there we found the labels reserving our seats, and one seat reserved for 'Mr Ulton', and two seats reserved for a Mr and Mrs Smyth, and the sixth seat already occupied. It didn't look like our having it to ourselves.

Well, time went by and no inspector came, and by 2.28 I began to get anxious. What should we do if the train started and we were off to Yorkshire to look for a dangerous criminal, without Ulton?

Linley said, 'Oh, he'll turn up.' But he didn't turn up.

And then I called out to a porter to ask if he had seen anyone like Ulton get on the train; and of course I had to describe him. And then the other man in the carriage joined in, asking me questions as to what my friend was like. He was a man with queer whiskers, this other man, and a large drooping moustache, and dapper little patent-leather boots. He spoke in a weak high voice. I described the inspector to him fairly well; a burly, clean-shaven, tall man. And then he said: 'What kind of boots had he?'

'Boots?' I said. 'Why?'

'They show up on a platform,' he said. 'They would help one to recognize anybody.'

'Oh, very big boots,' I said.

And so they were, even to me. Doubly so, I should have said, to this little man, huddled up in a corner seat.

'Ah, I know the kind of man you mean,' he said in his queer little voice and the trace of some accent that I couldn't quite place. 'I've seen no one like him near the carriage, but I'll help you look out for him.'

'There's only a minute,' I said.

'He might come yet,' he answered.

Then we were off.

'What shall we do now?' I asked Linley.

'What were you and your friend going to do, if I might ask?' said the man in the corner, seeing me so put out.

'Fishing,' I said.

'Ah, a pleasant sport,' said he.

'But our friend has got all the bait,' I told him. 'And now he's left behind.'

'What bait were you going to use?' he asked.

'Worms,' said Linley, to my great astonishment.

The man in the corner did not appear surprised. To Linley he said nothing; but to me he said: 'Haven't we met before somewhere? I seem to remember your face.'

'I don't think so,' I said. 'My name's Smethers.'

'Ah,' he said. 'My name's Ulton.'

'Ulton?' I said. 'Not Inspector Ulton.'

'Why not?' he said. 'Don't you recognize me by my boots?'

Linley smiled quietly at my astonishment. So he must have got there before me. But not very long before me, I think. I was feeling very foolish, when suddenly I had a downright inspiration. 'They hurt, don't they?' I said.

'Oh, nothing to speak of,' he answered.

But though he got the words out, they weren't true.

'What about taking them off in the train?' said Linley.

'I think I will,' said the inspector.

And there and then he took off his boots, replacing them with a pair of large slippers that he carried in a despatch-case. He took off his accent at the same time, and his queer voice; and I began to recognize him quite easily then, in spite of his odd whiskers. It's funny how much larger he seemed to get: he came out of that corner of his like a snail out of its shell. Linley took a revolver out of his pocket and reached over to Ulton. 'I've brought you one of these,' he said.

'Got a licence for it?' asked Ulton.

'No,' said Linley. 'But it will shoot just as straight.'

'We're not supposed to carry them, really,' said the inspector, as he slipped it into his pocket.

'We have one each,' said Linley, pointing at me.

'They're not very much use,' said Ulton. 'He'll be better armed than we are. We shan't be able to force our way into the house with these things, and once we get in we shan't need them.'

'Why not?' asked Linley.

And Inspector Ulton brought out of a pocket a glass ball like a tennis ball. He put it into his left hand and produced two pairs of glasses with rubber all round them, that fastened with a strap round the head, and gave us each one. 'When this ball breaks in a room,' he said, 'we shall be able to see and he won't.'

'Tear-gas,' said Linley.

'That's it,' said the inspector.

And it occurred to me that two things in this world are getting pretty complicated, crime and Scotland Yard.

'The difficulty will be,' he said, 'getting into the house.'

Well, they talked that up and down and made lots of plans; and the only thing about them seemed to be that they weren't any good. Ulton had got a sketch of the house, three or four sketches, that he had had sent down by train from the Henby constable; and I often heard the phrase, 'But that is commanded by *this* window.' There were plenty of ways of breaking into the house, but the best that they seemed able to make of it was that we were quite likely to lose two men by the time a third got in.

'Then what are you going to do?' said Linley at last.

'I shall have to go up to the door and ring the bell,' said Ulton.

'But will he open it?' asked Linley.

'Well,' said Ulton, 'I should say that that kind of man wouldn't.'

They had got no further than that. So then I thought it was time for me to speak, though they hadn't been noticing me for quite a while.

'I can get into any house,' I said.

'You?' said the inspector.

'Yes,' I said. 'I travel in Numnumo, a relish for meats and savouries.'

'But how do you get into houses?' he asked.

'Oh, different ways,' I said. 'But it would be no good my travelling in Numnumo if I couldn't get in anywhere.'

'But this fellow's sure to be armed,' said Linley, 'and he won't want you in his house.'

'Nobody wants me in their house,' I said, 'a perfect stranger, with something to sell that they don't want. But I get in.'

'But how?' said the inspector again.

'Well, it's my job,' I said. 'Might as well ask a policeman how he gets into his tunic. Just slips it on.'

'Do you think you could get into this house?' he asked.

'Sure I could,' I replied. 'Nobody ever keeps me out.'

'We might try it,' he said thoughtfully. 'Do you think you could drop one of these glass bombs when you get in?'

'Easier than pushing Numnumo,' I said.

'You might try it,' he told me. 'Drop it on something hard. There's no explosion: it only breaks. He won't see you any more after you've dropped it. You must wear these glasses.'

'Well, I don't mind,' I said. 'But it makes it all rather difficult. I usually smarten myself up all I can, before getting into a house. With things like that on my face it would make it much harder. But I don't mind.'

'Do you think you can explain them away somehow?' he asked.

'Explain them!' said Linley. 'A man that can explain Numnumo can explain anything.'

Which is not the way I should have put it myself, as it's a little hard on the proprietors; but it was the right idea, for all that.

'Of course I can,' I said.

So he gave me four glass bombs, and told me to drop them about wherever I had the chance.

'I don't know who else you'll find in the house,' he said. 'Somebody very deep or very simple.'

In the end we found no one but him.

Well, we got into Arneth and hired a Ford, and drove out four miles to Henby. It was dark by now, and I got the idea in the car that Ulton and Linley were feeling anxious, although neither of them spoke. I was feeling contented enough, because the job before me was just the one thing I could do, getting into houses; and nothing puts a man more at his ease than to be doing his own job among men who are strange to it. It gives him a feeling of superiority over them. Henby went up into the night, all on a hill, and one street straggled away from it out into darkness; and, a hundred yards or so beyond the last house of that street, all by itself was the house that the telephone knew as Henby 15. We stopped the car long before we came to it, and walked the last few hundred yards. Ulton explained to the driver just why we wanted to get out and walk; and to me it sounded all very plausible, but somehow I became sure of two things, that the driver never believed a word of it, and that he never guessed what we were really after.

'I should put on the mask now,' said Ulton.

And they helped me to fasten it while we were still out of sight of the house. Ulton gave me a whistle to blow in case I wanted help. 'We'll be as close as we can get without being seen,' he said. Even then, it seemed to me, they'd be a bit late, if I wanted help enough to whistle for it. Perhaps I looked a bit lonely, for Ulton said: 'It's no use our coming near enough to be seen, or he'd let nobody in. Very likely he won't let you in in any case. But do what you can.'

'I'll get in all right,' I said. And off I started.

The night seemed very dark, which was really all to the good, only somehow it didn't seem so. It seemed lonely too, and all the small gusts of wind that came blowing past me seemed lost in it. I heard a step coming my way, and a man passed me, who I knew must be the village constable going to report to Ulton. That made three people that would come if I whistled, but it didn't make anything less lonely then. And then I came to the house; a wicket gate and a path through a little garden, and I was at the front door. I rang till a window opened on the first floor, the window of a dark room, and no face showed.

'What do you want?' said the voice.

'Nothing,' I said, 'if you don't want anything.'

'What do you mean by that?' said the voice in the dark room.

'Only,' I said, 'that there's one thing that nearly everyone wants.'

'Well? What?' he said.

'Health,' I answered. 'And how are you to have that without food; and good food, with a relish to it?'

'I don't want to buy anything,' he said, and was just going to shut down the window.

'Wait a minute,' I said. 'I don't want to sell anything. I've a wonderful relish for meats and savouries here; but I don't sell it, I give it.'

It's a good catch that. You see, they give away one bottle free to whoever buys a dozen. So I catch them by telling them that the bottle is free, and getting them to sign an order for a dozen afterwards; and of course they pay on the nail. That's the difficult part of it, the order and getting the cash; all that comes later, but that free bottle gets me into the house. And it got me in here.

'Then what do *you* make out of it?' he asked me.

Interested enough to ask questions, you see.

'Well, the truth is,' I said, 'you'll like it so much that you'll order more. That's where I come in.'

The more you think it over, the more you'll see how that catches them. It looks like business only starting when they are so satisfied that they can't do without the stuff. Human beings are very gullible. You see, I *know*. And murderers are only human.

'Oh, well; let's have it,' he said grudgingly.

And in I went with my Numnumo. He opened the door, and seemed all alone in the house. A decent meal, or even the hope of one, probably meant a lot to a man like that.

He brought me into a small room, off the hall, and switched on the light and sat down. 'Let's have a look at it,' he said.

He was a nasty-looking fellow, sitting there. Not a man to play tricks with. I don't say he could read your thoughts; but he had a quick look in his eyes, as though if you tried to think of anything clever, he'd get there before you. He had an orange-coloured moustache, chopped short; and he sat there looking at me. Ulton and Linley felt a long way away. I didn't mind playing the Numnumo trick on him, or on any man; because that was second nature to me, and hardly felt like a trick. But I didn't like playing the trick I was going to play.

'This is your bottle,' I said, pulling the Numnumo out of my pocket. And I managed to pull out three of the gas-bombs, too. 'Samples,' I said, as they came out.

But he wasn't looking at what I had in my hands; he was staring at my glasses with the rubber fittings round them. I saw that, and explained in a hurry.

'The fumes from Numnumo,' I said, 'don't only make your mouth water; they make your eyes water too.'

Not much chance of selling it after that, of course; people don't want to be weeping into their plates; but selling Numnumo wasn't what I was after on that day.

He wouldn't take his eyes off me. And then he put down a hand and slowly covered me with a revolver.

'Oh! Don't do that,' I said.

And I dropped the three bombs full of tear-gas, and the bottle of relish on top. I apologized and stooped down to tidy up all the mess, and then the fumes reached him. So he got up and came groping towards me, meaning to shoot. But it was too late then; he couldn't see. And I began dodging him quietly. He stopped to listen, following with his revolver any sounds that he heard or thought he heard; till all of a sudden he seemed to change his mind, and shot himself through the head.

THE SECOND FRONT

IT'S some time now since I wrote about Mr Linley, and I don't suppose anyone remembers the name of Smethers. That's my name. But the whole world knows Numnumo, the relish for meats and savouries; and I push it. That is to say I travel and I take orders for it, or I used to, before this war upset everything. And some may remember the tale I wrote about that, about Numnumo I mean, because Mr Linley came into it, and he's a man you don't forget so easily; and, if you do, perhaps you don't forget Steeger and what happened at Unge. Horrid it was. I told about that in my story: The Two Bottles of Relish I called it. And then Steeger turned up again; that was when he shot Constable Slugger, and they couldn't catch him for either case. Funny, too; because the police knew perfectly well that he had done both murders, and Linley came along and told them how. Still, they couldn't catch him. Well, they could catch him whenever they wanted to, but what I mean is there'd have been a verdict of Not Guilty, and the police were more afraid of that than a criminal is afraid of the other verdict. So Steeger was still at large. And then there came a case of a man that did three murders, and Linley helped the police over that. They got that man. And then the war came, and murder looked a very small thing, and no more had been heard of Steeger for a long time. Mr Linley got a commission, and, when they found out about his brains, he went to the War Office, to what they call M.I., and I went to be, what I never thought I'd be, a private soldier, and Numnumo was heard of no more, except for a few little wails from the advertisers, saying what a good thing it used to be. Yes, I got called up in the summer of 1940, and was put in barracks near London. I used often to lay awake at night under my brown blankets, thinking of the battles the British army had been in, things I'd heard of at school, and more that the sergeants taught us about, and trying to picture what they were like and what they sounded like; and all the while a battle raging over the barracks. I got the idea that some of those old battles might have been fairly quiet compared to those nights. But I don't know.

Well, that battle was over in a year. We won it; I mean our airmen did. But we hadn't much to spare. It was a nasty time. I don't think the Germans would behave quite like that now. They've spoken very nicely of late about not destroying culture and civilization; but they didn't quite understand in those days, and used to talk about rubbing our cities out; and they very nearly did. But I'm not going to write about the war; perhaps somebody will do that in a hundred years, beginning at 1914 and forgetting about the years from 1919 to 1939, and going on till it stops, and a very interesting tale he should make of it. I'm going to write about Mr Linley again. That brings me to the year 1943. I had a day's leave, and got a lift on a lorry, and slipped up to London, and the first thing I did was to go round to Lancaster Street to have a look at the old flats. I wanted to have a look at them just to prove to myself that it was true that I hadn't always lived in a barrack-room. Well, they'd gone, those flats had. There was a square of grass and weeds and flowers; and there was a lot of groundsel. And in a way I liked the look of it, though it wasn't what I had come to see. They were rather dingy and dark, those flats as I remember them, and they called them Clarence Gardens. Now they really were gardens; or at any rate there was sunlight there, and some sort of flowers. I suppose there's no one that doesn't sigh for the country a bit some time or another in London, and here a bit of the country was, wild as any bit of the country you could see, even wilder than some of it. And for a moment I was glad to see this bit of sunlight and grass among all those miles of pavement, till I thought of all the slaughter that had gone to growing that groundsel. I looked up into the air then to see if I could locate just where our flat had been, because it seemed odd to think that I should have once been walking about, or sitting and listening to Mr Linley somewhere up towards the blue sky. And as I turned my eyes up from the groundsel I saw an officer standing near me and looking at me. I came to attention and saluted, and the officer said, 'Why, it's Smethers.'

And I said, 'It's not Mr Linley!' For he looked so different in uniform.

And he said: 'Yes, it is.' And he shook hands.

And in a moment we were talking about the old flat.

Then he surprised me very much by saying: 'You are just the man we want.'

Well, I'd had all sorts of jobs to do since they made me a soldier, all sorts of jobs, but nobody had ever said that to me. And here was Mr Linley saying it, just as if it was true.

'Whatever for?' I asked.

'I'll tell you,' he said. 'That man Steeger is getting to work again.'

'Steeger!' I said. 'The man that bought the two bottles of Numnumo.'

'That's the man,' said Linley.

'And shot Constable Slugger,' I said. 'What's he up to now? His old tricks?'

'Worse,' said Linley.

'Worse!' I said. 'Why, the man's a murderer.'

'He only murdered a couple of people, so far as we know,' said Linley. 'He was only a retail murderer. But he's a spy now.'

'I see,' I said. 'He's got into the wholesale business.'

'Yes,' he said, 'and we want you to help watch him.'

'I'd be glad to help,' I said, 'in any way I could. Where is he?'

'Oh, he's here all right,' said Linley. 'He's in London.'

'Why don't you arrest him?' I asked.

'That's the last thing we want to do just yet,' said Linley. 'It might warn a lot of others.'

'What's he done this time?' I asked.

'Well,' said Linley, 'they found out only the other day that he has recently received a thousand pounds. Somerset House found it out, and reported it.'

'Has he been killing a girl again, and getting her money?' I asked.

'No, that's not so easily done,' said Linley. 'He found poor Nancy Elth with her two hundred pounds, but he can't find a girl with money every day.'

'Then where did the thousand pounds come from?' I asked.

'The easiest money of all,' said Linley.

'Spying?' I said.

'That's it,' he said. 'It's the best paid of all the crooked jobs in the world. Especially at first: they'll give almost anything to get a new man into their clutches, provided he's likely to be of any use to them. And Steeger should be a lot of use. He's a really skilful murderer, and should be a skilful spy.'

'And where is he?' I asked again.

'We've found him all right,' said Linley. 'There never was any difficulty in finding Steeger. The difficulty always was in proving he'd done it. Aye there's the rub, as Hamlet remarked.'

'And what has he given away?' I asked.

'Nothing as yet,' said Linley. 'That's why we want you to help watch him. A thousand pounds is good pay, and it must be for good information. And of course it has been paid by a German in this country, or a Quisling or some such cattle. But they've not been able to get it out of the country yet.'

'How do you know?' I asked.

'Because there is only one thing that the Germans would pay on that scale for,' said Linley, 'and we know that they don't know it yet.'

'What's the thing, might I ask?' I said.

'Where the second front is going to be,' said Linley. 'We

think he has found it out somehow and the other spy has paid him for it out of his loose cash. But it's worth a million if he can get it to Germany. And a hundred million would be pricing it low, but they'd probably pay him fifty thousand for it. Anyway we know they don't know it, and the thousand pounds is a mere tip. But that's what the tip would be for.'

'How did he find it out?' I asked.

'We don't know as much as all that,' said Linley.

'I see,' I said. 'And you want him watched so that he doesn't get out of the country.'

'Oh, he can't do that,' said Linley. 'But we want to see that he doesn't send the news.'

'How will he try to do it?' I asked.

'By wireless, probably,' he said.

'How will he do that?' I asked.

'Well, we've located all the sending-sets,' said Linley, 'that have ever spoken since the war began; but there may still be some silent ones hidden, and waiting for a bit of very big news like this. And I think we've located all the carrier pigeons; though there might be one or two of them somewhere that we don't know of; but it's easier to hide a wireless set than a pigeon, because you don't have to feed it.'

'And you want me to watch him?' I asked.

'Only now and then,' said Linley. 'He's in London, and we know more about all the houses here than you'd think. We aren't really afraid of his working a sending-set anywhere in London, but we can't answer for the open country, and he has to be watched when he moves.'

'What about the other man,' I asked, 'the spy who pays him?'

'He lies very low,' said Linley, 'and we haven't spotted him. But that's only because he lies so low, and if he went about and did odd jobs with a wireless sending-set, we should have spotted him long ago. For that reason we don't think he'll try to do this job, but will leave it to Steeger. After all, Steeger's a pretty smart man, and it isn't everybody that has committed two murders and is able to walk about at large in England, Scotland or Northern Ireland.'

'I'd be glad to watch him,' I said, 'if you think I can do it.'

But I said it rather hesitatingly, because, though it was very nice of Mr Linley to offer me such a job, I had begun to see by then that it was a pretty important one, and, to tell you the truth, I am not quite the kind of man to be given a big job like that. Maybe I might have been if I'd been brought up to it, and given the chance of handling big jobs early, but I spent all my time pushing Numnumo, and was never given anything bigger, and somehow or other I seemed to grow down to the size of my job; or perhaps the job was only the size of me, and that's why I was given it, and never given anything bigger. And now here was Mr Linley offering me a job that mightn't look very big if I did it well, but, if I did it badly and let that man get out his news of where the second front was to be, why, it might cost the lives of thousands and thousands of men. That's why I said 'if you think I can do it', and by the way I said it I sort of showed him I couldn't: I thought it was only fair. But Linley said: 'That's all right, you're just the man for it.'

'Very glad to do my best,' I said. 'Do I go in uniform?'

'No,' he said. 'That's just the point of it. We don't want to give the idea that the British army is watching him. Or that anybody is. But somehow or other, though you look the perfect soldier in that kit, in plain clothes you might not give quite the impression we want to avoid.'

Of course I didn't look the perfect soldier at all, even in uniform, nor I never will. It was nice of him to say it, but I saw his point.

'That's right,' I said. 'I'll just go back a few years to the Numnumo days and I'll hang about somewhere near him and I shan't look very military.'

'Well,' said Linley, 'I'll let you know. We shan't want you just yet. We have him watched all right. But, if he got anywhere near a wireless, we'd want someone extra to watch him. He'd have to be watched very close then. Five seconds might do it, and he might pretty well ruin Europe. That's to say, any of it that's not ruined already.'

All this, I may say, was at the end of June, in 1943, when all the plans for the invasion of Europe were ready, and the Germans were still guessing. And, while they guessed, they had to strengthen a line of two or three thousand miles. One word from Steeger, if he had got at the truth, would bring it down to a hundred miles, and save them a lot of trouble. That's how things were when I parted from Linley that day just after midsummer, and a very nice lunch he gave me before we parted, at a big hotel, in his smart uniform and all, and me no more than a private. We didn't talk any more about Steeger there, even when there was no one in hearing. He wouldn't say a word about that sort of thing indoors. Well, I thanked him for all he had done for me, and for remembering me like that, and giving me such a fine lunch; and away I went on a bus back to my barracks. And only a week later I got a letter from Linley. It just said, 'That job is all fixed up, and your C.O. has been written to.' And I was sent for to the Orderly Room next morning and given a travelling warrant, and told to report at the War Office on the same day, for special duty, which would be told me when I got there. So off with me up to London and to the department of the War Office that I was ordered to go to, and there I was fitted with a suit of civilian clothes and given a ticket for a concert at the Albert Hall. What I had to do was to go to the seat whose number was on the ticket and sit there and take as much interest as I could in the music, and at the same time watch the man who would sit on my right. That's all they told me while they were fitting me with my suit of clothes. And then Linley came in while they were brushing my hair, because they said it had too military a look; and Linley made everything clear to me. The concert he said was to be broadcast, and Steeger had chosen a seat right under the microphone, and that had been reported. They were still sure that he had got hold of the secret of the second front, and it was pretty certain that he would say something about it during the interval, and the whole world would hear him. Of course he had to be watched the whole time, but he would probably do it in the interval.

'And how am I to stop him, sir?' I asked.

'Well, I'll be there,' said Linley, 'on the other side of him, and I think I'll be able to stop him, but I'll be glad of your help, especially if he starts to shout out the name of the country that is going to be attacked. You must shout him down then, or stop him any other way. But we don't think he'll do that; in fact it's a thousand to one against, because he'd give away that the enemy had been warned, and also he'd be hanged, which he has taken a good deal of trouble to avoid so far. What he is almost certain to do is to signal, and I'll be watching for that, but I might be glad of your help.'

'And how are you going to stop him doing that, sir, if I might ask?' I said.

'We'll just switch the wireless off,' said Linley, 'the moment he starts anything.'

Well, that was in the morning, and the same evening I was at the Albert Hall, sitting in a seat in the middle, right in front of the band, with a little thing slung on a wire just in front of me, only up in the air. That was the microphone. I knew it at once, because it was like nothing I'd ever seen before, and a microphone would be like that. And then in came Linley and sat down on my right in the next chair but one. He didn't even look at me: he looked to his right and he looked to his left, but when he looked to his left he looked miles beyond me, even if he was looking at me, or at any rate yards. And then Steeger walked in. I'd never seen him before; but, if I may say so without giving offence to anyone, I can always tell a murderer by a look at him. It was Steeger all right. And then the band struck up. It was what they call a symphony; by Beethoven; his fifth symphony they said, and there were going to be three intervals.

Well, it was all very nice, and Steeger sat there listening and doing nothing. All through the first tune he never moved, or even opened his lips. And then the interval came. I watched him then like a cat watching a dog. For one moment I glanced at Linley, but he seemed only to be thinking of the music, turning it over in his mind like, with his right hand just inside his coat. He was in plain clothes too. Then I watched Steeger again. And then Steeger put his hand to his breast pocket and opened his mouth and drew in a breath. He was going to cough. One or two other people were coughing a bit too, little coughs they had bottled up while the band was playing. But Steeger was going to give a great big cough; you could tell that from the size of his breath. At the same moment Linley pulled out a red handkerchief. And then he gave me a quick look and a slight wave of his hand, to tell me not to do anything, for I was just leaning forward and wondering if I should. Then he sat back and thought of the music again; at least he looked very contented and comfortable. Steeger coughed all right, and I let him, having got that sign from Linley, and then he blew his nose rather noisily and then he blew it again and coughed again. Then he coughed once more and blew his nose once more and put his handkerchief away. Then he sat as quiet as Linley. And very soon the music began again. And Steeger never moved or opened his lips all through it. And when the next interval came I looked at Linley, but he just shook his head. And then Steeger took the deep breath and pulled out his handkerchief and Linley pulled out his, and Steeger gave the one cough again and the one blast on his nose, and then another blast and another cough, finishing up with a cough and a blast, just as he had done before. And then the band struck up again. A nice tune, I expect, if you could listen to it, but I was too busy for that: I was watching Steeger. Not that he did anything more, either during the tune or the next interval, or any more during the show: he never even sneezed. Well, there isn't really very much more to tell: Linley told me about it all afterwards; about what Steeger had done, I mean: a few days later there came the invasion of Sicily, and then Linley told me. He got me another day's leave, on account of useful work he said I'd done, though I'm afraid it wasn't as useful as all that; in fact I'd really done nothing, but I took my leave in spite of that, and I went up to London and I saw Linley. And he gave me a lunch again, which was very welcome, as it reminded me of old times, before all this war began and one thing and another. And then he told me what it was that Steeger had signalled. He had done it in morse, he said. A cough meant a short, and a blast on his nose meant long. And what he had signalled was Etna.

'Why Etna?' I asked.

Because it was so much shorter than Sicily, Linley said. Only six dots or dashes, he said, whereas Sicily would be nineteen, and Etna, he said, would be quite good enough. But it never got through. There was a man on the platform with his finger touching a button and watching Linley the whole time; and the moment he saw the red handkerchief his finger went down on the button and that cut the stuff off. Of course they started it again when the band struck up; and all that the audience missed, that is to say the world, was the sound of people shuffling in their seats, and here and there a musician tuning up, and all the little sounds you hear during an interval. So they didn't even have to explain what happened. But they had the explanation all ready in case they interrupted the music.

'What was the explanation?' I asked.

'A technical hitch,' said Linley.

Oh, and there is one other thing to tell. They told me to be as inconspicuous as possible and not to look like a soldier, and not to seem as if I was watching him. So I thought the best thing to do was to give up being me at all, the me that I am now, I mean, and to go back to the older one, which is the real me really; that is to say, if you ask my opinion about it, but perhaps nobody really knows very much about himself, or what he really is. Well, I went up to Steeger as he was going away and I said how bad these times were for business, and for everything else, and you could get nothing nowadays, not even Numnumo; but that better times would be coming and Numnumo would be on the market again, and I was a traveller for it, which I was able to prove because I had one or two of the old forms in my pocket, and would he care to book an order? And he would get a bottle as soon as the war was over, and at the old price, and even below that price if he took half a dozen, and nothing to pay till the goods arrived. And I got his order for half a dozen, and he filled in his name and address on the form. Cornelius Westerhouse he filled it in, 94 Bapham Road, Wandsworth. Of course I knew there was no such road, and there wouldn't have been anybody called Cornelius Westerhouse; but somehow it warmed my blood to be doing the old work again, and it gave me a sudden thrill.

THE TWO ASSASSINS

I DON'T know if you will remember me. I have told you one or two tales about Mr Linley. My name is Smethers. Mr Linley is worth remembering; a wonderful brain he has; but you wouldn't remember me. I have been into a good many of your houses, for all that. I push Numnumo, as some of you may remember, and a good many of you may have thought I haven't got into your house. But you'd be wrong there. Some of you may have said: 'We don't have any of that muck,' and closed the front door, and you may have thought that was the end of it. But you forget the back door, and I can always get in there. That's why most of you have Numnumo in your kitchens, whether you know it or not. Well I'm not going to talk about Numnumo today, though I haven't stopped doing so by any means, but today I am going to tell you about Mr Linley. It was like this; the President of San Paradiso had come to London, and was going to appear at a big reception. And, to make a long story short, Scotland Yard had received information that he was going to be murdered there; and the Government were especially keen that he should not be. I needn't go into the reasons why they didn't want it to happen; but the effect in San Paradiso, if it did happen, was going to be very considerable, and there was a pretty big bunch of Paradisians who were determined to do it, and our Government was very keen they shouldn't. That's how things were, when suddenly word came to Scotland Yard that Don Hualdoz was in it. I needn't tell you much about him either, but he'd had a hand in that sort of thing before, often. And they said all down the Paradisian coast that he never had failed yet; far less been caught. And the way he did it was merely by thinking. He'd read what all the other assassins had done, and get to know what was expected; then he'd try something new. Scotland Yard was no end worried, because assassinations in San Paradiso were nearly always successful; and with Paradisians after the President, and led by Don Hualdoz, they looked likely enough to pull it off again. And it wouldn't do in London. For a variety of reasons it would make a situation that the Government didn't want to arise just then. And what seemed particularly bad to Scotland Yard was that Don Hualdoz was then on the far side of San Paradiso, about as far away from here as he well could be; and that was known to be a habit of his whenever he had anything big in hand; if he wanted an alibi, he always had it good. So his movement so far West looked a little ominous, and Scotland Yard was taking every precaution, and it was only by the merest chance that they asked Linley. One of them seems to have said that they might ask him, and most of the rest were against it, and one of them said one extra precaution might not do any harm. That's how it was. So one of them goes to Linley and tells him about it, in a kind of a way, without letting out too much information. And somehow Linley gets the idea, from the way the detective was skating round the subject, rather than from anything that he said, that what they were frightened of was Don Hualdoz. Well, that was a little while before the war, and Linley and I was still sharing a flat: the flat's all gone now, and there's willowherb growing there. We was sharing a flat, and Linley tells me in confidence all about it, as soon as the sleuth goes out. And do you know what he spends most of his time doing? While the sleuth was with him, I mean. He asks him how he thinks they are going to murder the President, and the sleuth tells him about various weapons, small automatics chiefly, and Linley tells him it won't be any of these. And the sleuth asks him why, and he tells him it's because they are what he expects, and in a big scheme like that those fellows from San Paradiso wouldn't come all this way to do something they were expected to do, and get caught before they had done it. And it was a big scheme all right, because they were out to have their little share in wrecking the world, and it would have made a lot of enemies for us if their scheme had come off, and we couldn't afford to have enemies just then; hadn't got guns enough. Well, when Linley goes on telling the man from Scotland Yard that none of the weapons he mentions is going to be used, he asks Linley how the man is going to commit a murder without weapons; and Linley doesn't know, and asks for time. And he spends a lot of it that evening thinking; talking to me sometimes, but mostly thinking. And an idea comes to him just before supper, and a funny idea it was; and, if he hadn't solved one or two mysteries for them before, they would never have listened to him. This was Linley's scheme, and he got them to take it up. The reception was going to be in one of those big halls that they used to have in London; but that was before Goering's time. They were to have it two days after the man from Scotland Yard called on Linley; and of course Scotland Yard was going to have detectives out on their own I saw at least a hundred of them, when the day came and I went to have a look, and of course there may have been some that I couldn't recognize; but they let Linley work his scheme too, and lucky they did. This was Linley's idea, and he only came to it after hours of thinking: he'd thought out all the ways they might murder the President, at least he tried to, and just about supper-time he saw light as it were, and the light showed him that he was never going to find out what those fellows were going to do, nor Scotland Yard either. That, Linley told me, was his really big discovery, the bright flash that lit up the whole problem and made everything clear. He said he found everything easy after that. That was the big idea. And the next one sort of followed on quite naturally. And I don't know how he got Scotland Yard to let him work it, but they did. Seemed silly to me, but then I'm not a deep thinker; I push Numnumo, and only have to think a little bit deeper than the people who buy it. And I don't pretend that's deep. Well Linley, he says that it's no use looking out for a man with a revolver strapped to a belt, nor even to search pockets for a quite little pistol. And one reason was that Scotland Yard had already announced publicly that everyone attending the reception would have to be searched for weapons, except those who had pink tickets, and I didn't see any pink tickets being shown, myself, when it came to it. And another reason was that anything obvious of that sort was apparently regarded by Don Hualdoz as merely vulgar. So that really there were two safeguards, one of them a search for weapons by the police, and another the very strong probability that no one would have any. Of course that brings us up once more against the problem of how they were going to assassinate the President of San Paradiso without weapons. But against that they had to put pretty copious information, however they got it, that it was going to be done. Well, Linley asks for half a dozen men, and *carte blanche* to detain whom he pleases and not let them go any further than the vestibule to the big room where the reception was going to be. Pretty high-handed of course; but better be high-handed with half a dozen men than infuriate three-quarters of San Paradiso, the three-quarters that didn't want the President shot. And the German ambassador was being perfectly charming just then to everybody he met, which was in itself a little bit ominous. Linley explained his scheme to me, and I said to him at the time, 'But you can't arrest a man because he is wearing a purple waistcoat.'

'I don't care,' said Linley: 'it is the only way.'

This was his scheme. He began by admitting that there was no way of working out the plans of Don Hualdoz, so far as he could see. There'd be something tricky about them that Linley hadn't been able to think of, and there'd be something out of the ordinary in the execution of them that wouldn't show on the surface. At least, so Linley thought. So he said the only thing to do would be not to look for machine-guns or anything like that, but to suspect anything they saw that might be out of the ordinary. You see, he gave Don Hualdoz the credit for being too clever for him, and he gave his men the credit for being able to get into that reception without any bulge in their pockets, or anything inside their pockets that you could see if you looked. I don't know how much he knew about Don Hualdoz, or how he found it out; but he somehow knew that, among the people who call that kind of thing politics, Don Hualdoz was an extremely astute politician, and he realized, as only a clever man like Linley would ever have done, that he could no more foresee one of Don Hualdoz's big political schemes than, good chess-player though he was, he could have beaten Capablanca. And Capablanca came from the American continent too, and gave his brains to one of the few things that a brilliant man can work at without doing the world any harm; while Don Hualdoz, being more practical, went another way. So Linley knew he was dealing with someone whose plans were out of the ordinary; and, though he counted on the men that would be sent to carry them out being innocent-looking enough, he fancied there would be something about them that would be out of the ordinary too. That doesn't seem much of a clue, and so I said to Linley. But what he said to me was that, though there would be plenty of mistakes, if he stopped every man that had anything unusual about him he would get the right man among them. As I said, it seemed silly to me.

Well, the day came round and I went to the Hall to see what would happen, and there was Linley standing inside the door with six men close to him, reading newspapers in the dingy light of the vestibule, if you could call it light. I went on to the Hall and that was a blaze of light, and everybody waiting for the President. Just as I got inside I heard a bit of a row, behind me in the vestibule, and Linley had got his first man. He had stopped him because he was wearing an odd sort of watch-chain with a big cameo on it, an odd thing to wear on a watch-chain but no harm in it, as far as I could see; and he was taken away to a little room, swearing. Then came a man with a very odd pair of boots, and he went the same way. I wondered how Linley was able to get the police to do it. But the Government was frightened and Scotland Yard daren't neglect anything, and Linley's six men had orders to do what he said. I went out of the Hall again then, and back to the vestibule, because it looked as if things were going to be more exciting there. And the next man Linley stopped was wearing a little bow as a tie-pin, a thin bit of horn no more than two inches long, with a golden string, and a little quiver of gold lying across it. He made no end of a row, but he had to go away to the little room. Then came a man with a carved walking-stick perfectly solid and harmless, but out of the ordinary; and he went swearing away to the same room as the rest. Linley seemed to have no trouble in getting as many detectives as he wanted, for, though some remained in the room to watch his prisoners, he still had six men round him. He made two more arrests that seemed to be equally frivolous, and I wondered how he was going to avoid six charges of false imprisonment, or whatever you call odd dealings of that sort. And then came a man with a coat of a curious cut. I will say it was an odd cut; I could see that for myself; but hardly enough to arrest a man. He made no end of a row, but he had to go. Linley had seven of them altogether. I got into the room where they all were. Linley let me come in. The detectives weren't keen on having me. I got the idea that they thought things were going all wrong and that they had arrested seven wrong men. I mean innocent ones. And I fancied that the fewer who saw what had happened, the pleaseder they'd be. But Linley got me in. Linley knew he'd arrested some wrong ones too, but what he calculated on was having the right ones among them. And sure enough he had. The detectives were looking at him to see what he wanted to do next. But Linley sat quite still on a wooden chair, listening to his prisoners protesting. And after a while I saw a look come into his face, as though he had spotted something. There was so much noise going on that I noticed nothing particular myself. The President had not arrived yet. He told me afterwards what he had spotted, Linley did. He said every man was protesting personally about his grievance, and they certainly were. But what Linley said was that after a while two men began to agree with some of the others, and to support them, and to say what a shame it was. I didn't particularly notice them myself, though, when Linley reminded me of it, I do remember one or two of them being quieter than the rest and trying to be helpful to some of the others. That didn't make me suspect them; rather the other way. But Linley said that that's what made him separate them from the rest; so that there were five men raging about their personal grievances and two men quietly encouraging them. Linley worked out from that that those two wanted to get the attention away from themselves on to a perfectly just grievance against the police, which they shared with five others; whereas those five others were thinking and talking hard about themselves, each one of them of his own particular case. I believe the five of them were given £50 each. Seems a lot of money. But, when the fate of things like nations is at stake, I imagine a few cheques for £50 don't go for very much. And they gave one of the men a new walking-stick, because they had examined his so closely that they had spoiled it. I'll tell you about the other two. Linley said that the one with the little bow in his tie, with the gold cord and gold quiver, had the bow made of rhinoceros horn, and it was a perfectly good bow, for a small child. In the gold quiver were two tiny arrows, with just the feathers showing. When the police took the arrows out of the quiver they found they had in their hands a perfect weapon, even if it had only a range of a few yards. But at a reception anybody can go right up to the chief man. That's how they shot President McKinley thirty odd years ago. Well, the ends of the arrows were greasy, and they smelt. And the police got them analysed. It seems they were smeared with decayed cater-pillars, one of the deadliest poisons on earth, a secret of the Kalahari. I don't think they have any cure for it even there, and there's certainly none in Europe. A machine-gun is a merciful thing compared with that little arrow; and nothing like as certain. And the other man too; he was just as bad; the man with the curious coat. He had been sent in case the first man should fail. The coat was rather like a British warm, and dyed the same colour. But it wasn't the same material. It was all guncotton. And there was a little arrangement for striking a light under the flap of a pocket, and a bit of an instantaneous fuse, and a little cap of fulminate of mercury, which is the stuff that you use in order to send off guncotton. There was enough guncotton in that coat to have blown up a lot of people, but they didn't mind that so long as they got the President, the people that sent the man in the coat didn't. And the man of course would have gone into fine mince too. They didn't mind that either. He was to go up close to the President and shake hands with him and touch off the charge with his left hand at the same time, if the other man missed with his arrow. And then there'd have been plenty of trouble for us starting in San Paradiso; and that's what the Germans were waiting for. The funny thing was they never charged those two men. Preferred to keep the thing quiet.

KRIEGBLUT'S DISGUISE

ONE day a little before the war; in 1938 it was, I think; any way Mr Linley and I were still in that flat that there used to be; and Mr Linley says to me one evening all of a sudden, and all about nothing in particular: 'I think they like to have spies walking about.'

'Who do?' I asks.

'Scotland Yard,' he says.

'What spies?' I says to him.

'German ones,' says Mr Linley.

And then he tells me the story of the German spy they were after, one of the kind they didn't like to have about, the kind they didn't know the address of. They couldn't catch him, you see, and they comes to Mr Linley. That is to say Inspector Ulton does. I've mentioned him before. He'd come a day or two ago and talked with Mr Linley, while I was out, pushing Numnumo. And it was like this: there was a lot of spies in England just then, and they rather liked to see them, like I said; because, when there was spies about, all they had to do was to take their addresses and watch who came to visit them, and of course read their letters, and so they got to know something of what was going on. But there was one spy they were afraid of. For one thing they didn't know his address, didn't even know if he was in England; and for another, and I fancy that was their chief reason, he was too clever for them, and they knew it. A man named Kriegblut. Well, things weren't too good in England in those days in the way of defences, and it was rather important not to let the Germans know quite how weak we were. Aerodromes and anti-aircraft batteries they let the ordinary spies see; the more they saw the better, really; and they reported to Hitler in the ordinary way. But this man Kriegblut was a man who could understand things. He wasn't interested in our aerodromes. It was our weakness that he was watching, the defences that weren't there, if you see what I mean. He was dangerous. And then they had the uneasy feeling, Scotland Yard did, that he would not only find out all they were afraid of his finding out, but a great deal more, being cleverer than what they was. Perhaps I haven't made it very clear, but any way they had the idea that Kriegblut was about the most dangerous man in the world, and pretty sure to be in England, but they couldn't find where he was, and could Mr Linley help them? That wasn't exactly the way they put it: what they said was that they thought Mr Linley might be interested in helping to trace this man, knowing how much he had interested himself in work of that nature. But it meant the same thing. Well, Mr Linley says he would be glad to take a look, and Inspector Ulton gives him a lot of details, but he warns Mr Linley they won't be much good, on account of Kriegblut's knack of disguising himself. For instance he tells him, Inspector Ulton does, that Kriegblut is about 5 feet, 6 inches in height, but he tells him at the same time that he has been seen going about at different times, he didn't say where, and been reported as being 5 foot 8, and at other times as being 5 foot 4. Height is of course the hardest thing to alter, and, if he could do that, it didn't seem much use to trouble about his complexion or the colour of his hair. The colour of his eyes was something more to go by, but he was rather fond of tinted glasses of different shades, which all helped to make a certain amount of confusion. Blue, his eyes were really; but so are a lot of other people's. The trouble was they had no idea where he was, Scotland Yard hadn't, and they liked to be able to lay a finger on their spies when they wanted them. I remember a gentleman telling me once that bucks will feed in India quite contented while they can see the tiger, but the moment he disappears they get uneasy and go off their feed. It was rather like that with us: Kriegblut was waiting to destroy us, and nobody knew where he was. Well, the thing worries Mr Linley at first, because he hadn't got much to go on. But he soon makes up his mind that Kriegblut will be in England. Where else would he be? And then he gets a great album from Scotland Yard, with photographs of all the disguises that spies have ever been known to use, and he settles down to study it; and that was what I found him doing that evening, when he says to me about Scotland Yard liking to have spies walking about. 'It's getting on their nerves,' he says, 'not being able to see a trace of Kriegblut.'

'You'll soon find him,' I says.

'Not so soon as all that,' he says. 'He's cleverer than Scotland Yard.'

'But he'll not be cleverer than you,' I says.

'I don't know about that,' says Mr Linley. 'If he's cleverer than them, he's pretty clever. The only gleam of light there is on the situation is that he's not as clever as Hitler.'

'How do you know that?' I says.

'Well, Hitler wouldn't let him live if he was,' says Mr Linley. 'He doesn't like them too clever. But he gets them pretty clever for all that. It's a difficult problem.'

Then he goes back to his album and is poring over it for the rest of the evening. Album did I say? There was twelve volumes of it, and fat ones.

'How have you got on?' I says to him next morning. For he looks worried, and I thinks I will try to cheer him up.

'I've looked through all the disguises that Scotland Yard knows,' he says.

'You must have been up all night,' I says.

'I have,' he says, 'and it's only the start.'

'What disguise do you think he'll be using?' I says to him. And I gets rather a surprise when he answers, but then I always does when I talks with Mr Linley. Surprising he is always, at least to me.

'None of them,' he says. 'But that's only the beginning. We only know all the disguises he won't use. A man like that will have something original, and we've got to find out what it is, if Scotland Yard can't do it.'

Nice of Mr Linley, that 'we'. He was always doing little things like that, little kindnesses you would hardly notice if you didn't know Mr Linley. Of course I knew my brains weren't going to be no more use to his than if a jockey riding the Derby was to ask a stable-boy to help by pushing behind. But it was nice of him to say 'we'. Well, we both agreed that Kriegblut would be in England: Scotland Yard wouldn't be that worried unless he were somewhere close. And they probably knew something of our awful weakness. And how much there was for Kriegblut to find out! Things looked all right to me, good solid houses standing all round one, but they weren't right really. I made a few suggestions, but they weren't any good, and then I went out for the day to push Numnumo.

When I came back in the evening Mr Linley was still puzzling over disguises.

'Have you thought of anything?' I asked.

'No,' he says, 'he is among us somewhere, and nobody recognizes him.'

'What about a Chinaman,' I said, 'or a policeman, or perhaps an engine-driver?'

But those suggestions weren't any good either. Mr Linley wasn't doing it like that, not merely getting a bright idea, I mean, like my idea of a Chinaman or a policeman. He had some way of working things out; thinking over disguise after disguise and somehow finding out why Kriegblut wouldn't use them. I don't know how he did it. The disguises in the album he told me about: simply that a man like Kriegblut would find something new. But though knocking out a few thousand disguises might get him half way, it wouldn't really get him any nearer, if you know what I mean. It wouldn't tell him which of the thousand which remained Kriegblut might have selected. Nor I didn't see how he was going to do it. And then he told me; told me the principle, I mean. 'You must have hundreds of pictures of disguises in those albums,' I said.

'Many thousand,' says Mr Linley.

'And how many are there left that are not in the album?' I asked.

'It isn't quite that,' he said. 'This man Kriegblut is of outstanding intelligence, and he'll only use something pretty good. What we must try to do is to fit a remarkable plan to a remarkable mind.'

'Are the Germans as clever as all that?' I asked Mr Linley.

'No,' he said, 'but they have vast resources, and we must no more think they can't lay their hands on a brilliant brain or two than we must suppose they can't lay their hands on uranium.'

'What's uranium?' I asked, for we hadn't heard much of it in those days. But I found that Mr Linley didn't know much of it either.

'What are you going to do?' I asked him then.

'I'm going to try to get my brain to work the way his works, if it can,' he says, 'and try and find some disguise that would be clever enough for him. He's pretty sure to be here, and probably Scotland Yard know that, in a way; so he must have a disguise. We've got to find it.'

'And how are you going to do that?' I asked.

'Only by studying his particular wits, and trying to find a scheme that would suit them,' he says.

Well, of course that was all beyond me, not having the brains of Kriegblut.

'What about . . .?' I says. But I stopped, because I knew it wouldn't be any good. And I think Mr Linley knows that it won't be any good too; for he says, 'You see it isn't only the disguise of his looks we must think of. Every spy must have an occupation or calling that entirely accounts for his being wherever he is. That's the most important part of the disguise. And he must be able to do it as well as anyone he may meet who is doing the same job. A spy without an avocation is as unnatural as a man without a shadow,' he says.

Well, I didn't think it was so hard after all, when he says that; for there are thousands of disguises, and a good many still left, even after Mr Linley had eliminated the ones that he said he had, but there aren't so many jobs as all that that a man can follow in England. So I tries again, and I says What about a barber? But Mr Linley says, 'No. Too much competition. A spy of the class of Kriegblut,' he says, 'doesn't mix himself up with a crowd of ordinary ones. A barber's shop,' he says, 'is known all over the world as the best place to get military information. Both sides use it, and of course it's thoroughly combed by detectives. It would be too common to suit a man like Kriegblut. Wouldn't suit him at all. No, he wouldn't be a barber.'

'Well,' I says, 'what would he be then?'

'Something we haven't thought of,' says Mr Linley.

There was a bit of a silence then, because I felt I couldn't think of anything more, nothing that would be useful like. And Mr Linley got no new idea neither, and I had to go off to push Numnumo. I didn't push it well that day. I let people say they didn't want it, and all kind of things that I never allow them to say when I'm feeling at my best. One of them said it was muck, and I let him leave it at that. That is just the kind of thing that it is my job to disprove. But I was thinking all the time of Mr Linley there in the flat with his wonderful brain, and he not being able to do anything with it. I pushed a few bottles in spite of that, and then home I went and there was Mr Linley, and you could see at a glance he hadn't got anything yet. He said very little; just asked how Numnumo had gone; and we had tea as usual. I got him back to the subject after a cup of tea and asks him if he makes out yet where Kriegblut is.

'Of course he's here,' says Mr Linley.

'And how does he get away with it?' I asks.

'It beats me,' says poor Mr Linley.

'Oh, don't say that,' I says.

'It stands to reason he'll be here,' Mr Linley says. 'And Scotland Yard can't find any trace of him. Inspector Ulton was here again after you'd gone, and I could tell him nothing.'

'Couldn't you really?' I says.

'No,' he says. 'I've been thinking. I've been working it out, but I can't do it. It won't come out. There's no answer.'

I hadn't heard him so depressed before. 'How was you trying to work it like?' I says to him.

'Been looking at photographs of Kriegblut,' he says, 'and reading about him, and then trying to picture a man that would be just as unlike him as possible. Possible, I mean, with the material at his disposal, which is a blue-eyed German of 5 foot 6, that has to be made so that he cannot be recognized.'

'A Zulu,' I says, 'or a nice little schoolgirl.'

'Well,' he says, 'that sort of thing. Something as unlike Kriegblut as he can manage. Only I can't think what.'

Well, I goes on talking and trying to help till I can't get any further, and it seems to me that for once Mr Linley is beaten; and I don't like to say that to him, and I don't want to say I can't think any more, and I thinks of a phrase I heard a customer use when I was trying to push a bottle or so of Numnumo on to him. A smart phrase that doesn't mean anything much, but sounds clever. I remembers little phrases like that, and sometimes they comes in handy. I remembers them so as to use them on another customer. They'll flummox me a bit at the time perhaps; but I don't mind that, because I'll flummox one of them a bit later on. 'We are only arguing in a circle,' I says.

'That's a light from Heaven,' says Mr Linley.

'What?' I says.

'What you said,' he replies.

Well, that puzzles me. But then Mr Linley always does.

'What do you mean?' I asks.

'It's the very thing,' he says.

'What is?' I asked.

'What you said,' he says again.

And then he explains to me: 'I've been thinking of all the disguises,' he said, 'that are just about the opposite of what Kriegblut is, and there's none of them that will fit with anyone that the police have watched, and they've watched pretty well everybody by now.'

'Yes, I thought I saw one or two people looking a bit inquisitive,' I says, 'as I was going my rounds.'

'I've suggested scores of disguises,' he says; 'scores of types of men to watch. And he's not there. I'd have been lost without you.'

'Without me?' I says.

'Yes,' he said. 'Your suggestion solves it.'

Well it didn't solve it to me, for all the credit he gave me. And there's men that would give you no credit even if you had solved it. But Mr Linley did. And it was all Greek to me. That remark of mine didn't mean nothing to me even when I said it. Meant nothing at any time.

'But will you catch Kriegblut?' I says.

'Yes,' he says, 'we will get him now. And all thanks to you.'

I was still quite in the dark. But sure enough they caught him. Over our supper Mr Linley explained it to me. 'Kriegblut is a great spy,' he says. 'We all knew that; and yet I wasn't giving him credit enough. I was only working out the kind of disguises that an ordinary clever man would use. Which was silly of me. And I ought to have been looking for some disguise that no spy had ever used before. I was just trying to think of disguises that would make him as unlike a spy as possible. Anyone could do that. Most of them do.'

Well, he goes to the telephone then and talks to Scotland Yard. They don't like talking on the telephone much. But all he said was so simple, there didn't seem any harm in it. All he said was to take a look at their spies; the ones they knows of, I mean. And then he gives a little description of the kind of man to look for among them. You see, the police had been combing every type of man in London and round the aerodromes and at every seaport; all except one type. One type was safe, and Kriegblut knew it, and that was what he went for. It was as Mr Linley said at the beginning, Scotland Yard likes to have a few German spies running about; it's like deer in a park to them; they likes to watch them. And other spies comes to them, and they watch them too. So they just leaves a few hundred of them at large. And Kriegblut disguised himself as one of them. And there was the biggest spy in Europe going about with a heavy sandy moustache on him, and a fat neck and a red face and a German accent, and six schoolgirls reporting him every day, not counting a hundred other people, and the police just smiling and telling them that he was only Dutch. Yes, Mr Linley describes a typical German spy to Inspector Ulton, a stage spy I should have said, and in doing it he describes Kriegblut, as he was just then. And they catches him, clicking his heels and talking with a thick accent. I don't know what became of Kriegblut; one never does hear much of those sort of people. I think they just interned him, or they may have executed him, or perhaps they used him and made him do jobs for us. One never knows.

THE MUG IN THE GAMBLING HELL

SMETHERS is my name. You won't remember me. But perhaps you may remember about the two bottles of relish that I told you about. Or maybe you've forgotten them. I wish I could. It was a nasty story. Well, it was Mr Linley that found out all about them. So one day they came to him again, Scotland Yard did; that is to say Inspector Ulton. It was when I was sharing that flat with him that I told you about, way back before the war, a long time. But you won't remember that. Anyway, I was, and a very fine flat too, but that is neither here nor there. Inspector Ulton comes in and asks if he could talk to Mr Linley for a moment. And Mr Linley says Certainly, and somehow they don't seem to mind me. That's how it all began.

'It's like this,' says Inspector Ulton. 'There's a young man called Alpit, with a flat in Minor Canon Street, and we had complete news of him from several sources, which have all been carefully checked, up to 7 p.m. on the night of March 19th. Then he went out, wearing a dinner jacket and black tie, to go to a party he said, but he didn't say where, and has never been heard of since.'

'Curious,' said Mr Linley.

'Very,' said the inspector.

'Sounds like murder to me,' I said. And that seemed to be word that the inspector didn't like. For he said rather sharply, 'There has been no suggestion of such a thing,' and turned away from me and went on talking to Mr Linley. What he said to Mr Linley was, 'I didn't let you know about it before; but we had no facts to give you, and it took us a long time to get any. For some weeks it was a complete mystery, a perfect vanishing trick. But we found out at last where he went, and we thought you might have some idea as to who had done it, that is to say if anyone has.' And I thought he looked rather sharply at me, as though he didn't want any of my suggestions. So, whether he did or not, I went on saying nothing.

'Where did he go?' said Mr Linley.

'He went to a gambling-hell,' said Inspector Ulton. 'Well, that may not be the correct word for it. They called it a gentle-man's club. But they kept its address very secret, and gambling with unlimited stakes is what it was for. What it really was was a flat that was owned by a man and his wife; and this young fellow Alpit was what they called a member, and another man called Haggers. That was all that were there that night, and there may have been a few other members; members was what they called them. But it was just a collection really of crooks and mugs, more mugs than crooks of course, because they were the people this pretty pair really wanted, with a crook or two to help them get the money if it wasn't coming as easily as it should; just as a shepherd may use a sheepdog or two, but he doesn't eat them, the only good meat being the mutton. Well on that particular night, the 19th of March, there were only those four there, three crooks I should say almost certainly, and the one mug, this young fellow Alpit; and he was only twenty. Well, of course you can't have a flat without somebody to look after it, and they had a man that they called the hall porter o the Green Baize club. That's what they called it, and of course when we got the address we naturally questioned this man, as we had every right to do, no force or inducement whatever having been used. That should be clearly understood.'

'Quite so,' I said, because he seemed to be looking at me But he paid no attention.

'Of course he answered our questions,' Inspector Ulton went on, 'and it wasn't our business to stop him talking, so we heard a good deal. That is to say we heard all that happened at wha they call the Green Baize club. What happened afterwards we can't be quite sure of, and were wondering if you might have any idea that would help us.'

'What happened at their club?' says Mr Linley.

'There was high play,' says Inspector Ulton, 'and pound-notes handed round in big bundles, and one of two things must have happened, this young man Alpit must have lost or won. If he lost it would look like suicide. Any really big casinos abroad where high stakes are the rule have everything all ready for suicides. We should hear a lot more of those tragedies if they didn't. Suicide is quite a regular thing where there is high gambling; I mean quite as regular as rain at a test match; and one looks for it accordingly. The other possibility is that he won. Not likely with a young fellow like that among people like them; but we have to consider it. In that case we should like to interview the man who lost, as he might be able to throw some light on what happened. Or somebody who may have followed him in the street, knowing that his pockets were full of money; he might be able to throw some light on it too. We should like to interview him.'

It seemed to me there was a third possibility; this young gentleman might have come out about level. I didn't like to suggest it to the inspector, because he didn't look as if he wanted suggestions from me; but I did just say to Mr Linley, 'What about his coming out about level?'

But Mr Linley said, 'No, no, Smethers. Mathematically x can equal y as easily as anything else; but to account for such a climax as that, however it happened, one looks for something big; big losses or big winnings, as I take it there always were at this club, Inspector.'

'Well, that's what the little idea of this couple was,' said the inspector.

Mr Linley thought for a while, and then he said, 'It's not for me to make any suggestions as to how you do your work, or to interfere with your methods.'

'No?' said the inspector, as Mr Linley hesitated.

'But it seems to me,' went on Mr Linley, 'you might question that hall porter a little bit more.'

'Well, we might,' said the inspector.

'See if he can't remember who it was that won,' says Mr Linley, 'and roughly about how much.'

'Well, it's always the couple that own that flat,' said the inspector.

'Still, I should ask him,' said Mr Linley.

And that's all that was said on that occasion. It must have been nearly a week later when Inspector Ulton came in again.

'That young man Alpit,' he said, 'won a thousand pounds.'

'Was he paid?' asked Mr Linley.

'Yes,' said the inspector, 'in packets of one-pound notes.'

'I see,' says Mr Linley. 'Then his pockets must have bulged a good deal.'

'Yes,' says the inspector.

And then to my great astonishment Mr Linley says, 'I'm afraid I can't help you.'

The inspector seemed surprised too, for he had never come to Mr Linley, not to my knowledge, without getting some remark from him that would completely smooth out the mystery, or whatever it might have been that was troubling the inspector. But now he just says, 'I can't help you.'

After a bit the inspector says, 'Then perhaps I'd better be going.'

'I'm sorry,' says Mr Linley then. 'But it's like this. You don't come to me for the obvious, and I've nothing to tell you but that. Your mysteries go rather as chess-problems do, as a rule. Something one hasn't thought of. But not the obvious.'

'And what is obvious about this, if I may ask?' says the inspector.

'Oh, merely,' says Mr Linley, 'that it would be murder and not suicide, because, however secret the scene of either, a good deal of work is needed to hide a body, so that it requires a live man to do that, a murderer and not a suicide.'

'Yes, we'd thought of that,' says the inspector.

I think Mr Linley must have been completely put out, because I've never seen him like that before, and I don't think he'd have said what he did if he hadn't been. What he says is, 'Take a careful look.'

Well, of course the police had been doing nothing else for weeks, and I could see that Inspector Ulton didn't like it. I can't think why Mr Linley could have said it, except for that. So he says, 'Take a careful look,' and the inspector goes away.

'Beaten you,' I says. I couldn't help it. And I don't know if that bucked him up. But something did. For he had been silent a long time before I spoke, and for a bit more after that; and then he says, 'No. It's merely that it isn't a problem at all. You're looking for something out of the ordinary; so is Inspector Ulton, or he wouldn't have come to me. So was I at first. But it's no problem; it's all too ordinary. That's why we've overlooked it. There are more ordinary things in the world than you think, Smethers. Can't you see what happened?'

'Well, no,' I says.

And I couldn't. It was no use asking me.

'Think again,' says Mr Linley.

But it wasn't any use. 'I haven't a clue,' I says.

'I'll give you one,' Mr Linley says. 'I was wrong about the murder. It wasn't a murder.'

'Suicide, then,' I says.

'No. Wronger still,' says Mr Linley. And he goes on like this. 'If it had been a suicide they'd have found the body at once. If he had been murdered by somebody following him in the street, whether the man who lost the money, or somebody attracted by the bulge of his pockets, the body couldn't have been so hidden at once in London that the police would never have found it in two or three weeks. It couldn't be done.'

'Then what do you think happened?' I asked.

'The young man simply walked away,' he said.

'Walked away?' I says. 'Why?'

'I've been thinking of that,' says Mr Linley. 'Not because he was afraid of the gang. Nothing so exciting. They were accustomed to gambling there: that kind of thing went on every night. And not because he had cheated, and knew that they would make it unpleasant for him. They would never have paid him if he had. No, you must look abroad for that body. Some pleasant place on the continent. And quite alive too.'

'Then whatever is he afraid of?' I asks.

'Their revenge,' says Mr Linley.

'But can't the police protect him?' I asks.

'No,' Mr Linley says. 'Not against that kind of revenge. A young man like that, who they say had never been to that gambling-hell before, goes out probably to risk a pound or two, and wins a thousand. I don't know how. Too big for ground bait. Sheer luck, I suppose,'

'But what's their revenge?' I asks.

'Simply that, by all the rules of gambling, he's got to come and play again. He doesn't seem to be quite the fool that he looks, going into a club like that at the age of twenty. He has the sense to see,' says Mr Linley, 'that he's ruined now, and a thousand pounds will never stave it off. He's got to go on until they get it back; and they'll take the rest of what he has got with it. No, it's too obvious and too simple to be worth while telling them at Scotland Yard. Still, you might ring up Inspector Ulton for me. You know the number. You hear it on the B.B.C. nearly every day. And say just these words from me, nothing more: "Look for him along the Riviera".'

THE CLUE

'Yes,' said Smethers, 'Mr Linley is a wonderful man.'

Smethers was being interviewed by a man from *The Daily Rumour*, who would far sooner have interviewed Linley. But Linley would not talk about himself, and so they had gone to Smethers.

'I understand that you lived in the same flat with him,' said the journalist.

'That's right,' said Smethers. 'I did for a couple of years.'

'And what was the most remarkable case in which he took part?' said the interviewer, a young man of the name of Ribbert.

'I couldn't say that,' said Smethers. 'I've seen so many of them.'

'You've told us of some,' said Ribbert.

'Well, I have,' said Smethers.

'Are there any that you haven't told us about?' asked Ribbert.

'Well, yes,' said Smethers. 'There was the case of Mr Ebright, who was lured to an empty house by a telephone call, and there murdered. You could find an empty house before the war, if you looked for it; and this man had found his way in, through a window at the back, the police said, and had lured Mr Ebright there somehow, and was waiting for him when he came. You may remember the case.'

'I think I do,' said the journalist.

'There were no clues in it,' Smethers went on, 'no clues at all; not what you would really call clues. And that was what brought the detective in charge of the case to Mr Linley, and that is why you might call it one of his cleverest bits of work. The detective thought Mr Linley might help him, because he

81

was Inspector Ulton who had been helped by Mr Linley before. I was there at the time, when Inspector Ulton came in, and after they'd said Howdydo, he says to Mr Linley, "There's a case with a certain amount of mystery about it, and we thought that you might perhaps have some idea that would help us."

"'What are the facts?'" asks Mr Linley.

"'There are very few of them,'" says the inspector. "It's a case of murder."

'I was surprised to hear him say that, because it's a word that Inspector Ulton never seemed to like to use. But he used it this time. "He was killed with a hammer or some such object," Inspector Ulton says. "His skull was battered in, and the hammer, or whatever it was, had been cleaned on a bit of newspaper. The body wasn't found until two days later, so that the murderer got a good start. We know it was premeditated murder, not only because the dead man, Mr Ebright, was lured there by a telephone call, but because there are no fingerprints except his in the whole house. And that means the murderer must have been wearing gloves all the time, even when he was doing a crossword, which is the only thing besides the sheet of bloody newspaper that had been left in the room in which the dead man was lying, a bare room in an unoccupied house in a little street near Sydenham."

"'How do you know that it was he that did the crossword?'" asks Mr Linley.

"'Because he would have been doing it while he was waiting for the other man to come,'" says Inspector Ulton. "He must have got there first so as to let Mr Ebright in."

"'Yes, that is so,'" Mr Linley says. "Could you let me see the crossword?"

"'It's only an ordinary crossword,'" says Inspector Ulton. "And all the letters are done in capitals, which give us no clue to his handwriting."

"'Still, I would like to take a look at it,'" says Mr Linley.

'And Inspector Ulton takes an envelope out of his pocket and pulls out a torn sheet of newspaper. "There it is," he says. "It's been tested for fingerprints, and there are none there."

'And there was the crossword, nearly all filled in.

'"He must have waited a long time for his victim," says Mr Linley.

'"We thought of that," says the inspector. "But it didn't get us any further."

'"I think the crossword will," says Mr Linley.

'"The crossword?" says the inspector, looking a little puzzled.

'"I don't know," says Mr Linley. "Let me look at it. I think that it may."

'And he looks at it for quite a long while. And then he says to Inspector Ulton, "Who did it?" Which seemed odd to me at the time. But he explained to me afterwards that they usually know at Scotland Yard who has committed a murder, but that what they want to know is how to prove it. But Inspector Ulton only says, "We don't know."

'And then Mr Linley asks, "What was the motive?"

'"Ah," says Inspector Ulton, "if I could tell you that, we wouldn't need to trouble you. The motive would lead us to the man like a foot-track. But there's no motive and no clue, or none that have ever come our way."

'And Mr Linley goes on looking at the crossword, and Inspector Ulton says, "What do you make of it?"

'"A friend of his," says Mr Linley. Which was hardly the right word to use of somebody who had murdered him. But that was Mr Linley's way of putting things. Always a bit whimsical he was.

'"A friend?" is all that Inspector Ulton says.

'"Someone of his acquaintance," says Mr Linley. "Or he couldn't have lured him to go to that deserted house."

'But that was getting nobody any forrarder. For Inspector Ulton says, "We had thought of that, and had gone carefully over the list of all the people he knew. But the trouble is there are seventy-five of them. It would be one of those, as you say. But we can't very well put seventy-five men on trial."

"'No,' says Mr Linley. "The dock wouldn't hold them all.'

'But one could see that Inspector Ulton doesn't think that very funny. And then Mr Linley goes on, "But I think I can whittle them down a bit for you. To begin with, he has one of those new fountain pens that will write for weeks on end without refilling them. Not quite everybody has one. So that reduces your list by two or three. And then he would have sent it to be refilled about the time of the murder, which reduces it a good deal further, if you can trace that, as no doubt you can."

'I saw that he must have got that from the crossword. But after that it was all pure magic to me. For he goes on, "And he is a man that has a garden. I should say a fairly good one. And then he lives amongst chessplayers, though he doesn't play himself. And he is not without education, but was never at Eton or any similar school. And he has a gun and probably lives near a river or marshes."

"'But wait a moment, wait a moment," says Inspector Ulton "How do you know all this?"'

"'And one thing more," Mr Linley goes on. "He knows something about geology."

'And all the time he was holding this bit of a sheet of paper in his hand and glancing now and then at the crossword. I couldn't make head or tail of it all. And I don't think Inspector Ulton could either. And then Mr Linley begins to explain. "You see we begin with his seventy-five friends because it isn't a casual burglar trying to rob him. A man doesn't go to meet a stranger like that with jewellery on him; or with money either, unless he is going to pay blackmail. And if he's going to pay blackmail, there's no need to murder him. No, it was one of your seventy-five. And you see the track of his pen?"

"'Yes, I see that," says Inspector Ulton.

"'And you see where it began to give out at the third word

and could hardly manage the fourth. So he gave it up and went on with a pencil."

"'Yes, I see that too,' says the inspector.

"'Well,' says Mr Linley, "there are words in a crossword that you get helped to by the letters of words you have done already, but the ones a man puts in first are the ones he knows. Now look at these, Inspector. The first two clues that he went for, which are not nearly the first in the crossword, are 'Four of thirty-two' and 'A kind of duck'. Those are the two that he picked to do first. And he puts in Rooks and Shoveller."

"'Two birds,' says the inspector.

"'No,' says Mr Linley, "the second of them is a bird, and the kind of bird not likely to be much known except among shooting men, and not always by them unless they live by muddy places in which the shoveller feeds. But rooks are what chessplayers call what the rest of us call castles. But though he is familiar with the correct name for them he doesn't play chess, for he has missed a very easy clue in five letters, 'Starts on her own colour'. He would never hear chessplayers talking about that, because it is too elementary. But he can't be a chessplayer himself, if he doesn't know that that refers to the Queen."

"'Well!' says Inspector Ulton.

"'And the third one he picks out," Mr Linley goes on, "is 'London's clays and gravels'. And he writes down Eocene. Which is quite right. But not everybody knows that, and it seems to make him a bit of a geologist. And then we come to his fourth effort, when his fountain pen gave its last gasp. The clue to that is 'A classical splendour of the greenhouse'. And he gets that one at once, or at any rate it's his fourth choice, without any letters to help him. And that is why I say he is not without education, because he must have known something of Horace to get that word, and must know something about a glasshouse, and I should say a well-kept one, which makes him a bit of a gardener. Amaryllis is the word that he has written in, as far as his failing pen was able to do it."

"'Why, that narrows it down quite a lot," says Inspector Ulton.

"'Yes," says Mr Linley. "We have now got a sporting friend of Mr Ebright, if one can use the word friend, and if one can use the word sporting, who has quite a nice garden, and either a knowledge of geology or else he lives on those very clays and gravels and so knows their correct name, and an educated man. Now among Mr Ebright's educated friends several would have been at Eton, Winchester or Harrow, etc. But you can eliminate all of them because of a staring gap in this crossword. Number 9 down, you see. It says 'Long, short, short' (six letters). If he can't get that he has certainly never been at Eton. The simple answer is Dactyl. Simple to anyone who has ever had to do Latin verses. And, indeed, you would get that much at a private school. I don't quite know where he was educated. But this negative clue should eliminate a good many."

'And I put in a suggestion then. "Mightn't Mr Ebright have come in," I said, "and interrupted him before he had finished?"'

"'He might have," said Mr Linley, "but he had done all except three or four, and that Number 9 is one of the very first you would expect him to pick, if he knew anything about it, because it is so easy. It is a very curious gap, that gap in the crossword and in his education."

"'Well, I think you have helped us wonderfully," says the inspector.

"'And I think we might follow his preferences a little further," goes on Mr Linley, "though that will not be so easy. He was using a soft pencil and it was soon blunted, and I think we may allow him some knowledge of entomology, because he wrote in this while his pencil was still sharp, without the help of any letters from words that cross it, for they are more blurred and the pencil was pressed harder."

"And Mr Linley showed us the word Vanessa, and the clue to it, which was "The family of the peacock".

"'With a magnifying glass," went on Mr Linley, "we might get some more. But perhaps you have enough when we have identified the murderer as a man acquainted with Mr Ebright, who owns a garden, was educated, but not at Eton, knows geology, or lives on the London clays or gravels, is associated in some way with chessplayers and yet does not play, and has at one time or another collected butterflies. If you don't actually place him from that, it will at any rate remove suspicion from most of your seventy-five."

'And sure enough it did. There weren't as many as half of them that had a garden. Only twenty of these turned out to have had a classical education and, of those twenty, five had been at Eton. Of the fifteen remaining, only half a dozen of them knew anything of geology and only two of those had ever collected butterflies, and one of them was found to have two nephews who often stayed with him in their vacations from Cambridge and were good chessplayers. And he did not play.

'All that was found out by Inspector Ulton and Scotland Yard, and it was a lot to find out. And they even found out that he had sent his pen to be refilled about the time Mr Linley said. And they arrested their man, and he was tried. But the jury didn't feel that you could quite hang a man on a crossword, and they brought him in Not Guilty.'

'Then he is still going about!' said the journalist.

'Yes, when last I heard of him,' said Smethers. 'But I don't think there's any harm in him now. It was a near thing and it frightened him, and I don't think he'll try it again. You see, Mr Linley nearly had him.'

ONCE TOO OFTEN

IT was a funny world before the war, or it's a funny world now; anyway, they don't seem the same world. I was thinking of that old world of the nineteen-thirties the other day, when I happened to come on the place where our old flat used to be, Mr Linley's and mine, and that set me thinking about it, and about the days that I spent there and all the things that I saw Mr Linley do. It's just a gap between two houses now, but it set me thinking of those days. He was clever, Mr Linley was. And he still is, though I don't often see him nowadays. But I had one great bit of luck just after the war, just after I gets demobilized. Mr Linley asks me to come round and see him again. He has the address of my lodgings and he telephones to me and asks me to come round and have a talk in the new flat that he's got. It may have been just luck, or he may have had a ring from Scotland Yard and known the inspector was coming, and given me this chance to see the end of the long story. I don't know which it was; but he was like that, and would do odd things like that, that he knew would please one, though there isn't any obligation for him ever to please me at all. Well, any way, I went; and I hadn't been there an hour talking of old times, when the inspector comes round from Scotland Yard casual like and asks if Mr Linley would be interested to hear a bit of news about what Scotland Yard was doing just now, as though it was something that didn't matter at all, but might be amusing to hear about. Somehow I seemed to know, the moment he spoke, that there was something he couldn't make head or tail of, something that had stuck Scotland Yard, and that he was trying to get some help about from Mr Linley. And, do you know, I was right: it was just what he had come about. Yes, Mr Linley said, he would like a chat and would like to hear what they had been doing. So the inspector sits down and they has a chat. Inspector Ulton he was.

Well, Inspector Ulton tells of another horrible murder, in a small house in a suburb this time; a man had murdered his wife and disappeared, and they couldn't find him to hang him; not that that's what the inspector said, but it's what he meant. A woman was missing, he said, and the police were anxious to interview her husband, because they thought he might be able to give some information about her present whereabouts. He shows Mr Linley a photograph of the man they want, and says it might interest him to try his hand at the case before the people at Scotland Yard find their man, as they will do in a very few days. And Mr Linley looks at the photograph and says, 'A very difficult case.'

'Well,' says Inspector Ulton, 'there are certain elements of difficulty in it, but you don't see them in the photograph.'

'I do,' says Mr Linley.

'But it's rather a noticeable face,' says the inspector.

'No,' says Mr Linley, 'not rather noticeable. Very noticeable indeed. Very remarkably so. Look at that profile; and six foot tall, I see written underneath. That man wouldn't go down a street with three hundred men in it without being noticed by every man of them that was able to notice anything, provided that any such man were there.'

'Exactly,' said the inspector.

'Well, and you can't find him,' says Mr Linley.

'We've not found him yet,' says Inspector Ulton, 'but we've only had ten days.'

'You'd have found him on the very first day,' says Linley, 'with a profile like that.'

'Then what is your theory, sir?' says the inspector.

'Only that it is a difficult case,' says Linley. 'We must do a bit of thinking, a good deal of thinking in fact; because, if you can't catch a man with features like that in London, in twelve hours, it's on the face of it a difficult problem.'

'I don't think I quite follow, sir,' says the inspector. And nor did I, for that matter, until Linley spoke again.

'Any really good puzzle,' he says, 'any really difficult problem of any sort, has two things about it that always distinguish it.'

'And those?' says Inspector Ulton.

'One of them,' says Mr Linley, 'is that it seems absurdly easy.'

'And the other?' asks the inspector.

'The other,' says Linley, 'is that you can't do it.'

'Well, I wouldn't say that,' says the inspector.

'Of course not,' says Mr Linley. 'I only meant that you haven't done it yet.'

That is the way he put it.

'If you haven't done it,' he went on, 'there must be some great difficulty about it, and that's the first thing you want to find out, the key-move of the problem.'

And now I could see that the inspector saw Linley was talking sense.

'And what do you think it is, sir?' he says.

'I think he has entirely altered his face,' says Linley. 'If you can't find him, I think he is entirely unrecognizable. It can be done. And while he was about it he may have altered his height.'

'His height?' says the inspector.

'Yes, even that,' says Linley. 'You often hear of a man losing more than an inch in one leg, when he breaks it by accident. Anything accident can do science can do much better. And science isn't only on the side of the just. And we must count on the possibility of their being able to do it the other way too, and being able to make him taller.'

'Taller?' said the inspector.

'They might be able to,' said Linley, 'but perhaps a bootmaker would be able to do all that was needed in that line. High heels could be concealed to a certain extent by bringing the leather down over them. But with a possible change of two inches either way, totalling four inches, his height is not much of an identification. That extra four inches might bring in another two million men.'

'And you think his face is altered?' said the inspector.

'It must be,' says Linley, 'or you'd have found him by now. Could he have slipped away out of the country?'

'No,' says the inspector. 'There's nobody gone in the last week that we don't know all about, or haven't been able to trace.'

'So I thought,' says Linley. 'And he isn't hiding?'

'Don't think so,' says the inspector. 'We've searched pretty thoroughly.'

'Yes, of course you would have,' says Linley.

'But who's going to alter his appearance like that for him?' says Inspector Ulton.

'Medical science can do that and a lot more,' says Linley.

'Yes, for decent people,' says Inspector Ulton; 'soldiers wounded in the face and all that.'

'Even the law defends a criminal,' says Linley.

'An alleged criminal, you mean,' says the inspector.

'Exactly,' says Linley. 'Then surely the doctors may help one now and then. And then the decent people may pay moderately well, but nothing to what the alleged criminals pay. It's a big temptation to help them.'

'I see,' says the inspector.

'Tell me more details,' says Linley.

'Well,' says the inspector, 'it's a woman entirely made away with, entirely disappeared, any way. Like what we talked about once before. And the man . . .'

'You don't mean . . .!' says Linley.

'I do,' says Inspector Ulton.

And somehow I knew from that just what they meant, though it doesn't look much to go by. And I blurts out; 'It's Steeger been murdering again!'

'Now,' says the inspector, 'nobody's said a word about

murder, and nobody's incriminated Mr Steeger or anyone else. and I'd advise you to be careful what you say.'

'All right,' I says. 'I won't say another word till you've hanged Steeger. And honestly I think it's about time you did.' For I've never been able to forget that awful business at Unge.

And do you know what Inspector Ulton does? He pretends not to hear me. Well, they talks in rather low voices after that. at least Inspector Ulton does, and Mr Linley gradually suits his voice to his, so that I don't hear much. But what I did hear went something like this. This man Steeger, under another name (Alnut he was calling himself now), had been marrying a woman. Of course she had some money: he liked them to have that. They lived in a little house all by themselves: she did the cooking and a char came in now and then. And one day, I didn't hear when, Mrs Alnut disappears completely, same as Nancy Elth had done. And Steeger, that is Alnut, kept a big Alsatian dog Inspector Ulton wouldn't say that Steeger had done any murdering, and he wouldn't say what he had kept the dog for only that they wanted to interview Mr Alnut, in case he might be able to throw any light on the present whereabouts of Mrs Alnut; and not a word about the dog. That's to say, not to me but I hears Mr Linley say to him, 'And how did he dispose of the body this time?' And Inspector Ulton says, 'Well, there was the dog.' But I wasn't meant to hear that. Perhaps I ought to tell you Mr Linley's deduction right at the end, after you'd had time to guess how Steeger had hidden himself, or even that he was Steeger; but I'm only telling you what I heard, just as I hears it I must say I thinks it wonderful clever of Mr Linley to find out that Steeger had changed his face; and he always was clever whatever he did; but it didn't seem much use, because it didn't seem to help very much in the search for Steeger, to say that he looked like somebody else, not if you couldn't say who that somebody else was. And I think that was rather the view that Inspector Ulton took, judging from the way he looked, for wasn't always able to hear what he says. He doesn't admire M

Linley's cleverness as I does, unless it's going to be of some use to him. What he wants to know is, where is Mr Alnut, and when can they interview him at Scotland Yard about the present whereabouts of Mrs Alnut. And that's what Linley can't tell him. And he can't find it out for himself: I sees that at once from the look of him. Quite worried, he was.

Well, here was the mystery, as I seed it: Steeger had changed his name, married a girl with a bit of money, lived in a small suburban house with her for a few months, kills her and gets his dog to eat her. And while he's doing all this he gets his face changed. Probably goes about with a bandage, saying he's had an accident, and gets it done bit by bit. But that's only my guess, because I didn't hear much about dates. And the inspector says, 'How are we to find him?' And Mr Linley looks out of the window and says 'Any of those men going by now, between five foot ten and six foot two might be him.'

'That's bad,' says the inspector.

And suddenly an idea comes to Mr Linley. I sees it coming, and it kind of lights up his face. 'We'll get him all right,' he says.

'How will we do that?' says Inspector Ulton.

'We'll go to Charing Cross station,' says Linley. 'They say everybody goes through it in the course of a year. And we'll wait there for a year, if necessary.'

'But what's the good of that,' says Inspector Ulton, 'if we can't recognize him when he comes?'

'You needn't worry about that,' says Linley. 'We'll spot him.'

It's the only time I've ever known Mr Linley not take me into his confidence. But he talked quite low, and I saw he wasn't doing it then. He apologized for it afterwards. But what he said was that if he didn't keep it secret from everyone, except Inspector Ulton, it might get out and get round to Steeger, the way secrets do get round to the wrong man when they once get out, and then he'd never come. But he said I might go to Charing Cross and watch, if I liked. One day Steeger would come, and I might be there if I was lucky. That puzzled me a bit. Why let me know where Steeger was going to be caught, if they didn't trust me not to let it out. I asked Mr Linley that one day. And he said it didn't much matter if Steeger did know where they were waiting for him. He'd know there would be a detective or so hanging about the station in any case; but, if he was right in what he had said about Steeger altering his face as much as he'd altered his name, Steeger would count on not being recognized, wherever he went, and would probably walk right past them out of bravado, as he must have been doing already. But he'd be caught. And as I'd known about him for some time now, I might like to see it; and it would happen one day at Charing Cross station. Well, I went every day after that, and I spent hours there and I saw a lot of the world, or perhaps I should say of its inhabitants. After a while I got to know quite a lot of them by sight, regular customers always going by the same train, except of course on Saturdays. And through them all, however well I got to know them, there was always a thin stream of new faces, ones I had never seen before and didn't see again. I won't say I saw everyone in the world, but I sees a good many of them. Sometimes I sees Linley there, more often not; and I never sees Inspector Ulton at all, not to recognize. And there was an old woolly bob-tailed dog there with a collecting-box on his back. I don't know what kind of a breed. I never seed such a dog. Funny, I thought it, using a dog, instead of putting a collecting-box on a wall. But perhaps it wouldn't have been seen as well there. If I was to tell you all the people I seed, it would make this story too long. And if I told you how many there were in a single day, you would never believe me. And I said to myself Everybody stops and looks at the bob-tailed dog, so I'll stay near him. And in any case the dog was led wherever there were the most people. Well, naturally. So that's what I decided to do.

All this wasn't waste of my time, not by any means; I was quietly pushing Numnumo all the time. Quietly, because Numnumo isn't the only muck in the world, and the railway officials weren't going to have me competing with the advertisements on their own walls, not if they seed me at it. I felt I owed the railway company something for the business I'd been able to do on their property, so I used to pay back a little now and then by putting a few shillings into the collecting-box on the back of the old dog. 'What kind of dog is he?' I asked one day of the porter who was holding him on a lead, and he held him pretty short all the time, for the dog didn't seem much to take to the game.

'Old woolly sheep-dog,' says the porter, so far as I heard him; but he spoke in a husky voice and an engine was making a noise, and he moved away before I could ask any more. Never saw such a dog.

I got the idea that they'd one or two of their very best detectives on this job, and so I told Mr Linley, because there were days when I sees a stream of three or four hundred people going through the gates to a platform, and not one detective among them. You can always tell a detective; they usually carry newspapers, which every now and then they pretend to read, and they give funny little coughs, and they put up white handkerchiefs to their faces, pretending to blow their noses, and if they do blow them they trumpet through them, and they're all dressed pretty much alike, and sometimes they wear leather-soled boots, but you can tell them even then. But when I sees not one on a whole platform, then I knows that they must have some special kind, some kind that I can't recognize. I asks Mr Linley what he thinks about that, and he says he doesn't think there were any detectives about. Then how are they going to catch Steeger, I asks? And all Mr Linley says is that perhaps he won't be coming today. It always interests me when people talks sheer nonsense, because there must be some reason for it, unless of course they talks it naturally, which was never the case with Mr Linley, not by no means. I used to buy a platform ticket at first; but Mr Linley tells somebody that I'd been useful to him once, over the horrible affair at Unge, and they makes some arrangement with the railway company and they lets me on for nothing.

Well, the days went by, and the weeks too, and I quietly pushes Numnumo. Only once I was stopped by a porter for annoying a passenger. But I says he looks thin, as though his food wasn't agreeing with him, and I only done it out of kindness, because Numnumo would fatten him up. You know the talk. And he doesn't turn me out. Not only that but I pushes a bottle of Numnumo on him, telling him he looked tired and Numnumo would brighten him up. And every now and then I gives a shilling to that strange grey woolly dog as a kind of offering to conscience, not that I had much of it left after years of pushing Numnumo, but more than Steeger, any way. And one day Steeger comes, as they said he would, as they said everyone would in the course of a year. We hadn't waited two months. He was about as unlike Steeger as anyone well could be. Linley was right: he'd had his face altered. His height too, by about what Linley said, nearly two inches. He was an entirely different man. His own mother wouldn't have recognized him. But his dog did. I was quite near him at the time. There was a little whimper, and a tug at the chain. And he drags the porter right up to Steeger; and the porter was Inspector Ulton. Steeger would have kept clear of his dog, but he was watching for an Alsatian. He'd disguised himself, but two could play at that game, and the Alsatian was disguised still better. They'd shaved him and stuck this odd grey woolly stuff on him. Of course they'd had to cut off the poor brute's tail, which is about the one brutality the law allows in England. Anyway not as bad as doing it to a puppy, because he had at least had the use of his tail for the best part of his life, whereas a spaniel or a fox-terrier is never allowed it at all. Well, bad as that was, Steeger was worse. Never saw a man more surprised, when two detectives slip out of the crowd and arrests him. Inspector Ulton must have given a sign. Well, they hanged him this time all right. And, as I said before to Inspector Ulton, it was about time. And that was the end of Steeger, and my little tales.

AN ALLEGED MURDER

Now what ought I to do? Jot down a few notes, I suppose, so as to get my story clear. And then, if I can find the time, I might go to the police. But they'll only say I'm too suspicious, and send me away. Besides, I've hardly got the time: nobody has nowadays. I work in a bank all day, and then when I get home I want to have my tea and a bit of a rest. I might perhaps go on Sunday, if Scotland Yard is open on Sundays. But they'll only say I am too suspicious. Albert Merritt is such a smart sort of fellow. Not a man they would ever suspect, though of course they did once. But they were sent away with a flea in their ear, and they're hardly likely to do that again. Not for me, anyway. Well, to my notes: they go like this. First of all there was Aimy Cottin. I thought a lot of Aimy. And so, I think, she did of me, till she met another fellow. She told me about him straight out. She said he was a wonderful man, the strong man of her dreams. I asked her what he had ever done. But she didn't know. Nothing, she thought. But it was for what he was going to do that she felt this huge fascination for him. 'And what's he going to do?' I asked her. And she said, 'Something big.' She didn't know what. But she knew it was something big. She said women could always guess the kind of things that a man had done; but they knew, knew mind you, what they were going to do. I can't see how that can be. And I asked her. And she said, 'A girl can see at once something big in a man. If he's done nothing yet, it's all still there to be done.'

It didn't make sense to me. I said, 'Aren't we going for walks any more?' And she said, 'Not now.'

By *now* she meant never. Never any more, now that she had

seen this man Albert Merritt. That's who he was. And where do you think she had met him? In a train. And not in the same train either. The two trains had stopped in a station, and their carriages had been opposite one another. Not much time to work up a romance. But she did. Told me all about this wonderful man. Didn't even know his name. Didn't seem very wonderful to me. But there it is. You never can tell. Never can tell what a girl will think wonderful, I mean. They had sat and looked at each other. That is all. And then the trains moved on. And she called it the romance of her life. Funny. I mean it seems funny to me.

Well, all that was a long time ago. And then there comes on the Ulwrick case, that everyone's heard about. The girl, Ulwrick, that was murdered by somebody. Though not by Albert Merritt. Or so the jury said. And Aimy married Merritt only last year, and went to live near Eastbourne. And soon after that I didn't see Aimy about any more, and I didn't get answers to letters I wrote to her, and I got suspicious. And of course I didn't say a word of that to a soul, on account of my having been fond of Aimy, and the other fellow marrying her, and of course everyone would say it was only spite, and I held my tongue. But I went down to Eastbourne and went to look at the bungalow, and I found nobody in it. So I went to a house-agent in Eastbourne and asked if he had a bungalow to let, and described the kind of one that I wanted, which I made as much like that one as I could, and I got a pass from the man to have a look at it. And that's where I had this odd bit of luck that made me so suspicious, more than I was already by nature.

I found Aimy's diary lying about in some rubbish. I knew her handwriting and it caught my eye, and I picked it up at once. If there'd been a clue in it, it would have been almost too good to be true. But there wasn't. Not that murderers don't leave clues about. That is why some of them get hanged. Some people think every murderer leaves a clue. But sometimes I wonder if only one in ten do it, and the ones that are hanged

are the unlucky ten per cent. However that may be there is no
clue in the diary, so far as I can see, and it only made me suspicious. And suspicious I still am. What shall I do? I've no time
to go to the police except on Sundays. And will they believe
me if I do? My word against a respectable-looking man like
that. Of course he has been in trouble, bad trouble. But he got
out of it, which may put him in a stronger position than ever.
And, then, he dresses so smart. He doesn't look like a murderer.
What should I do? Well, here is the diary I found, all in Aimy's
handwriting; I can take my oath to that.

The diary. June 3rd. Today I saw his photograph in the papers.
The wonderful man in the train. I knew I should see him again
some day. The personality of the man! It was bound to break
out. It's more than two years since we met. I mean since our
eyes met in those two trains. But I'm sure it was him. It's in all
the papers, right on the front page. Such a strong face. A man
who won't stand any nonsense. You can tell that at once. It's a
murder trial. *The* murder trial I may say. Columns in all the
papers. It would be dreadful if anything happened to him. But
it won't. He's too clever for that; clever as well as strong. You
can see it in his face, even in the photograph. No end clever.
Not one to leave clues lying about. And he's got a clever counsel
to defend him. He'd see to that. And between them they should
manage all right. They must.

June 4th. I went to the trial and got a seat. There were
hundreds of people there, a lot of them quite well-dressed ones.
But I got a seat. It was the same man. The man I met in the
train. He looked so splendid there, standing up before them
all. The Prosecutor talked first, and said a lot of nasty things,
and then Albert Merritt gave evidence, I shall always call him
Albert, and he gave it so nicely. And then the Prosecutor asked
him a lot of questions about that Ulwrick girl, and he answered
so that you couldn't quite make out what he meant. I said he
was clever. Clever wasn't the word for it. The Prosecutor tried

to be sarcastic, but that didn't impress the jury; you could see that.

He said he'd done it before, the Prosecutor did, a nasty fellow. But Albert's counsel said quite rightly, 'You get on with the job you're doing, and don't bother about other things. He ain't being tried for doing anything to that other girl. Stick to the job you're at.'

And that shut up Mr Prosecutor. And the judge says, 'Quite right, too.'

He wouldn't stand no nonsense from any of them. Of course he'd never have none from me. I adore that strong kind of man that won't have any nonsense.

Oh, the alibi he had! He was clever, he was. The Prosecutor wasn't half so clever. I was there all day. And late in the evening the jury says Not Guilty. And the Prosecutor looks silly: I should have liked Albert to do to him what he did to that Ulwrick girl and serve them both right. But one can't have everything, and it's enough that Albert got off; and applause in Court too.

June 5th. I have spoken to Albert! It is too wonderful. His picture in all the papers, and he talked to me for 5 minutes. And we're going to meet again. Two girls proposed to him. The impudence of them!

June 10th. These last few days have been too wonderful. Too much to write in my diary. Too much even to try to. I've been out with Albert every day. We went in Hyde Park. We had a bit of a discussion with a man about a chair in the Park. The man said it was his. So Albert simply knocked him down. Albert is that sort. He stands no nonsense from anybody. I knew he was strong like that, the moment I saw him in the train. Sitting in a first-class carriage he was.

June 11th. I am engaged to Albert. It is too wonderful for words. We are going to live in a little bungalow, somewhere down by the sea. Albert has asked me to put my savings all in his name. He says it will be convenient. I've over two hundred pounds. I'm going to do it, if only to show my trust in Albert.

July 10th. Albert and I are married. It's all so wonderful, and I could write so much. But Albert says Don't. Because our happiness would be spoiled by putting it in writing. We must keep it all to ourselves, he says.

I only want to do what Albert wishes. So I won't write any more.

That's all the diary says. Now, what ought I to do? I don't like not seeing Aimy about anywhere, and wondering what really happened to Alice Ulwrick, and that other girl before her. But if I go to the police about it, they will only think me silly.

THE WAITER'S STORY

'I DON'T do much waiting now,' said the old waiter. 'The hotel looks after me very well; gives me a nice little pension; and if they ever wants any little bit of extra help, back I goes. And it's always well worth it for me. Memories? Well, yes, we all have memories, but with fifty years as a waiter at the Extrasplendide I probably have a few more than most people. There's many people that get a big dinner once or twice in a year, or it may be several times: it depends on their chances. But there's not many of them sees a big dinner-party every night, week after week, as I have done, pretty near. And don't think a waiter sees nothing much of a big dinner. He sees a great deal more than anyone else. They each talk to two or three people and listen to the speeches, the diners I mean; but a waiter hears; and sees everything. And not only sees and hears; he can get just about as many snacks as the diners, if he feels like it, and has reasonably quiet and unostentatious ways. Yes, I've got memories. Well, let me see. I think about the best dinners I ever remember were some that were given by a man called Bleg. He *did* give dinners. Well-dressed he was: I remember the first time ever I saw him. Comes into the private room that the Extrasplendide always reserves for him: white tie, white waistcoat, and neat new tail-coat; and all the men with him dressed the same way, and the women dressed up to the nines. And pretty well the whole lot of them from the same place as himself, the gutter; that's where he came from, a crossing-sweeper by trade. And the rest of them no better, or a good deal worse; men and women, all dressed up as I said. And one man that was always with him, a slick-looking

102

customer, and the only one of the lot that had ever worn evening clothes before.

How do I know that? Well, I've worn them myself most nights for forty or fifty years; and sometimes, when I've been a bit tired, I've slept in them. I should know something about the way of them. Well, those *were* dinners, as I have said. You know those big jugs one puts water in. We had them thick down the table, one for every guest or two, and all of them full of champagne. And plenty of other wines beside that, mind you, being served all the time, and liqueurs too. And the food. Well, the order to the Extrasplendide was always the same, 'The best that you've got. And make it a bit better than usual.' They had thick double doors to that private room, and no sound ever came through. There was some rule about no drunkenness in the hotel, and they had to be very strict about it. There'd be anything up to twenty people, all from the gutter, as I said, and all dressed up to the nines. Those that could walk in a gentlemanly way to their taxis used to drive away in them, and those that couldn't quite manage it were given rooms for the night. And then Bleg and the slick-looking customer used to play poker for an hour. Now, I've seen that sort of thing before, smart men playing poker with mugs, I mean. But I never saw the like of this, nor I never met anybody that did. The mug won a few hundred pounds in notes every night, and the smart man lost. That happened night after night. The smart fellow always sat next to Bleg at dinner. He never said much, but whenever Bleg was pretty full of champagne the slick customer would suggest a nice liqueur or two. Bleg used to get half seas over by his own efforts, and then the smart man would come quietly in with suggestions, and see him the rest of the way. One day I wondered if he was the Devil. I believed in the Devil in those days. I suppose I was a bit superstitious. But no use teaching us all about the Devil, if we don't come to believe in him. I don't believe in him any longer. Don't see the necessity for him. I have seen men in my time that can do all his work for themselves. Doesn't seem any need for more.

Well, this smart man was very like him and he was always at Bleg's elbow, and always tempting him. And, as soon as he had him drunk enough, he would go to a little table and lose money to him. You may wonder what his game was. Well, I'll tell you; because one day he got talking to a woman, and I hears every word of it. There isn't so much as you might think said in hotels that isn't heard by somebody, other than the two people that are talking, I mean. I hears him tell the whole story. Of course it was late in the evening. You don't hear so much till the champagne has gone round a bit. That's what does it; that and a sort of sense that they own their surroundings, and that nobody is going to dare to take any advantage of them by repeating a word they say, or even understanding it. Well, it turns out that Lippet is his name, and that he's the secretary of an American millionaire; not just one million, but as many as he wanted; long ago, before two wars. And this American gentleman, Mr Magnum, had come to London with his secretary, Mr Lippet, for a bit of a jaunt. And, when he got there, a crossing-sweeper had been rude to him, the man Bleg. I don't know which of them had been in the wrong, probably both of them. Magnum probably thought he owned as much as his money could buy; and Bleg probably thought that foreigners were no use, and had no right to get in his way. Any way, he swept dirt over the ends of the trousers of Magnum, and was rude when Magnum swore at him. And that was their pretty quarrel. Magnum reaches for his gun, and finds that he doesn't carry one. He is too old to knock out Bleg, and he walks away with Lippet and says to him, 'Lippet, you have got to have that man killed.' And Lippet says to Magnum, 'You can't do that in this burg.' And Magnum says to him, 'I know it will come expensive; but that man's got to die within a year.'

Lippet still says it can't be done. 'They'd hang, draw and quarter us,' he says: 'That's the way they do things over here. Or they used to,' he says, 'only a little while ago, and they're not much more civilized yet.'

And Magnum says, 'I don't care what I pay. But you've got to work it for me. What's the use of having a bit more money than anyone else in this town, if I'm to be annoyed and put out like this, and able to do nothing about it? You've got to do it.'

Well, he was so mad that Lippet saw he had got to do as Magnum had said, or lose his job.

'It will cost a lot,' he says.

'Didn't I tell you,' says Magnum, 'that I don't care? Must I go on telling you? Do it. And let me know what it costs.'

'Would a quarter of a million dollars be too much?' Lippet asks.

'Oh, don't bother me,' says Magnum. 'Don't bother me with details. When have I ever haggled with you when I wanted a thing done?'

'Very well, sir,' says Lippet. And he does a bit of thinking.

Well, he gets in touch with Bleg and studies his tastes, which are mostly for beer, and he finds he takes to whiskey just as well. And then he springs champagne on him. And that goes down well, in every sense of the word. He was a nasty, bad-tempered fellow, who was not quite new to drink, so that it wasn't like having to teach a duck to swim. That was what makes Lippet think he would get the best results for his master's money in taking the line he took, the line that led to those dinners. He probably put down a few hundreds at first for Bleg and his friends to dress themselves. After that Bleg pays for the dinners out of his winnings every evening at poker. I hears the whole tale as Lippet tells it, one night to the woman, and he figures that Bleg will be dead in a year. Of course he had had a little too much champagne, or he wouldn't have told her, but she was much too drunk to remember what he had said; so no one was any the wiser, except me.

Well, Bleg and his friends were drinking hard, and it didn't look like him living out the year, any more than Lippet intended. Did I tell you every waiter got a tip of five pounds each night? Well, we did. And of course waiters don't think so much about diners who tip them, as the diners think they do. Still, there is such a thing as gratitude, and a fiver is a bit out of the way, so when I hears all about it I says, I'll warn Bleg. And I waits my opportunity, and I does. He was sickening already, when I spoke to him, but there seemed still time to save him. I gets him alone one night when there's nobody near him that's able to take any notice, and I says to him, 'They're trying to kill you.' And, when he doesn't believe me, I tells him the whole story, the whole thing right from the beginning up to the end, which has got to be within a year from the start.

He hears me, every word, and then he says to me: 'Did I ask your advice?'

And I says No. But I tells him he's been good to me, and so I decided to save him from Lippet, so that he won't be dead in under a year. And Bleg says: 'Well, I likes this way of living. So I don't want no more of your advice.'

Way of living, he calls it! That wasn't what Lippet and Magnum called it. And they got him all right.

He may have understood beer, but the champagne was all new to him, and the little liqueurs on top of it used to knock him silly night after night, till something or other gave way in him, and he was dead in under the year.

A TRADE DISPUTE

A WILD barbarous land,' someone was saying of some country one day in a club, 'a land that would never have heard of a trades union.'

Queer watch-towers on the world are London clubs. The smoking-room of a ship is another. Not so much in the Atlantic, because, big though the ships are there, the people in them look on them more as ferries, and are chiefly thinking of when they will get across, instead of just settling themselves down to travel. But anything steaming out of Marseilles . . .; however, I digress from the London clubs; where, among a lot of ignorance, is a lot of knowledge, from which no corner of earth can entirely hide.

'I wouldn't say,' said a retired police officer who had spent most of his life in India, 'that barbarous lands knew nothing of a trades union. They wouldn't have that name for it, of course, but they would probably have the idea of it, whatever they named it, and it might work as well as they do here.'

'Did they have trades unions among the border tribes?' asked someone.

'Not exactly,' said the old police officer. 'But I saw something very like it working once, and I think it saved India. There was bad trouble coming once, and before its time. And it was averted at the very last moment; and, if you like to hear, I will tell you how.'

We all listened and heard this story.

'I am not at liberty to tell you who wanted to make trouble in India, but you will understand me when I say that, if you put a red-hot poker into a hive of wild bees, you make very considerable trouble very quickly. One red-hot poker. And one clever spy could make that much trouble in India, by going to the wrong people at the wrong time and taking them in the wrong way. Well, there was just such a spy, and we thought him the cleverest spy in the world. I don't say we were right, as we didn't know all the spies; but he was the cleverest spy we knew, and of course the most dangerous. He was coming into India from the North, over the North-west frontier, and we were watching for him. Altogether we must have had as many men waiting for that one man as there would be in a brigade. We had all my little lot of Border Constabulary, and then we had police and mounted police, and plenty of plain-clothes police, and a few platoons of frontier scouts, all on the look-out for him; not much less than a brigade. And we had agents out in front of us, among other things. And the Inspector General was cross and uneasy, for fear that we should not stop him. We were watching about forty miles of the frontier, including two passes, and all the rest was the crest of some rocky hills. And there were about eight forts in that line too, with soldiers in them who had been told all about our spy; and every fort had a good view, as far as its rifles would carry. We knew he was coming through some part of that forty miles, and we knew what he was coming for. One or other of the two passes was the obvious way for him, and of course we watched them well; but we knew all the time that he was a man who rarely did anything obvious unless it was so obvious that nobody would expect him to do it. We had been told that he would come within the week because the trouble he meant to stir up wouldn't keep any longer than that.

'The Inspector General never left us alone, which I thought was a bit unnecessary, because we were alert enough and I didn't see how he could get through, with one man to every twenty yards of the frontier and a clear view for a few miles by day, and by night we lit fires. On the two passes every man was stopped, and every camel searched. Not a man was passed through until he had been identified sufficiently clearly to make sure that he could not be the man that we were expecting. Lists were made in a book and every man recorded; carpet-sellers coming from Persia; horse-dealers out of the uplands, the high plateaux from which invasions started so often, and went through Europe before history began; men bringing Afghan quilts, marvels of needlework, to sell in the shops of Peshawar; jewellers with turquoises, opals and sometimes sapphires; and the name of every one of them written down and his story checked. That was in the passes of the Khyber and Malakand; and all along the rocky land wide of the passes, where the usual rule is to shoot at sight, men were watching every yard. For five days this had gone on.

'And then came the news, travelling in form of rumour, as it often does in all services, but none the less true, the news that the man for whom my men were watching had got through into India. None knew where he was even now; but Intelligence knew he had started, and it had been found out, I don't know how, that he was nowhere in front of us. My information was that he must have got through into India. And I had the kind of feeling that one sometimes has before thunder, that the Inspector General was on his way up to my sector. I could swear that the man had never come past me, but I wanted to prove it. I had a line of rocky hills, and the Malakand going through it. I went down my whole line questioning, and then I came to the Malakand. There I got the names and descriptions of every man that had come through since I took over; Suleiman ben Ibrahim, carpetseller; Feisul Dun, horse-dealer; Yakub ben Ismail, jeweller, travelling from China; Daoud, the knife-grinder from Kashgar; and so on and so on, all perfectly correct, all identified.

'I began to feel easier. Sure enough the Inspector General came. He took reports from every one of my officers all along the rocky line of those godforsaken hills, and then he came to the Malakand and went through the list, man by man, and read the descriptions of them. All these men were known, and all were expected about the time they came. The knife-grinder used to come regularly once a year from Kashgar, walking leisurely, wheeling his queer old instrument, no more than a hundred miles a month, and then back again. It was a long beat, but regular, six hundred miles or so between China and India, coming by Gilgit, and he sharpened knives all the way, for men who liked to keep them sharp. In Peshawer, where he usually stayed for a week, he used to turn round and travel back to Kashgar. More than once I had seen his lonely figure pushing his wooden instrument with its gritstone wheel, wearing a high fur hat and a sheepskin coat, with divers shirts underneath and rough, homespun breeches, and grey putties and sandals. I knew all the other men too, and had seen them oftener.

'I felt pretty well able to answer all the Inspector General's questions. And answer them I did. And he couldn't find any fault with my answers. Yet that spy had got through. The Inspector General told me so officially. Well, he went away thoughtful, and that day we were relieved by the lot from whom we had taken over; and I and the C.O. that relieved me had a talk about the sector, and we went over the list together. And when we came to the knife-grinder of Kashgar, and the only name he had got, which was Daoud, as far as we knew, he said, "But I let him through on the 15th." We looked at each other and said nothing. We saw at the same moment that one of us had let through that deadly spy. I never knew which. He had come through hundreds of miles of barren land, to be like a phial of poison in a cistern, and that cistern was India, and one of us had let him through. We knew that it must have been he, one of them, for there were not two knife-grinders on the road from Kashgar. That is what I meant by saying that something similar to our Trades Unions was known there: it was one man's beat, a union with only one member, if you like; but he had his rights. We looked at each other for a long time before we said anything, and then all I remember that either of us said was said by the other man, "It will be nasty for India." I could only nod my head. One of us had let him through. One man doesn't seem much. Nor does one spark in a large barrel of gunpowder. India was quite as inflammable.

'There was nothing for it but for me to go and tell the Inspector General, and I set out to do so. I didn't look forward to it. And as I went I thought of worse things than talking to the Inspector General. I began to turn over in my mind what was going to happen to India. War, to begin with, and in very few days, and after that; well, one never can see as far as the end of a war. And suddenly I saw a young police-officer coming along the road towards me. "There's been a murder," he said.

'"Oh?" I said, not very much interested, for they were not as rare as all that. It was what I was talking about, a clash of interests such as Trades Unions safeguard. "He worked another man's beat," my young friend said. "And the other man knifed him."

'And it turned out that the two knife-grinders had met.

'"Can you show me the body?" I asked.

'"It's just down there by the road," said that police-officer.

'I hurried down and saw it. It was our spy all right, with a knife wound just in his heart. The real knife-grinder wouldn't have him on his beat. It was just a trade dispute. He had beaten three or four thousand men, but the knife-grinder of Kashgar had got him.

'"Look here," I said, perhaps talking a little big, but saying what I honestly thought at the time, "that knife-grinder has saved India. What had we better report as the cause of death?"

'"Well, perhaps heat-stroke," said my young friend.

'It was a damned hot day, and I was sweating all over without that, thinking of what was to come; so I agreed. And heat-stroke it was reported.'

THE PIRATE OF THE ROUND POND

I'VE been reading a lot about great men lately; *having* to read about them; Julius Caesar, William the Conqueror, Nelson and Mr Gladstone. But there's a thing I've noticed about grown-ups, and I imagine it applies jolly well to all of them, great and small: they don't keep at it. They may be great just when they're having a battle, or whatever it is, but at other times they'll sit in a chair and read a paper, or talk about the taxes being all wrong, or go out for a walk along a road, when they might be ratting or climbing a tree, or doing anything sensible. Now, Bob Tipling is great the whole time. I should think he is the greatest chap in the world. Any way he is the greatest chap in our school, by a long way. And he's not only the cleverest, but he's best at cricket and football too. Once he made a hundred runs. And he's a fast bowler too. Well, I can't tell you all about that: there just wouldn't be time. We beat Blikton by an innings and 70 runs, and all because of Bob Tipling. But what I am going to tell you about is about Bob as a pirate, because lots of people have seen him playing cricket, but I and one other boy are the only people in the world besides Bob who know all about him being a pirate. So, if I don't tell about it, probably nobody will, and that would be a pity. Not that I like writing, I'd sooner be out-of-doors. Well, Bob was talking to me once, and I was saying what I'd like to be when I grew up, if I could get the job; and of course that isn't always so easy. What I'd like best of all would be to capture cities, like Alexander and those people; but of course you can't always do that. And then Bob said that he didn't want to be anything when he grew up, because grown-ups were always dull and didn't seem able to enjoy themselves properly, or even to want to: he wanted to be it now. And I asked him what he wanted to be, and he said a pirate. And I asked him what sea he was going to. Now, Bob Tipling always knew all about what he was talking of; more than anybody else; so I can tell you I was pretty surprised when I heard his answer. And yet I knew that Bob wasn't talking nonsense. He never does. He said, 'The Round Pond.' Well, I knew the Round Pond quite well; used to go there most Sundays; but I didn't see how you could be a pirate on the Round Pond. And so I asked Bob. Well, he said he'd had the idea for something like a year, and he'd hung about Kensington Gardens, which was quite near where he lived (both of us for that matter), until he found a boy whose father had lots of money, and he had told the idea to him and he had liked it very much. The idea was to put a pirate ship on the Round Pond, and to fit it out with torpedo-tubes.

'How would you do that?' I asked.

'It's already been done,' he said. 'They're miniature torpe-does, just as it's a miniature ship. There's two of them, one on each side, and we've had a dozen torpedoes made. They are shot out by compressed air, like little air-guns, and there's a good big explosive in them, which goes off when the nose hits anything. They cost a lot to make, but this boy has got lots.'

'Does your ship put to sea?' I asked.

'Oh, yes,' he said.

'Then how do you fire them?' I said.

'That cost a lot too,' he told me. 'I touch them off by wireless.'

'What will people say,' I asked him, 'when they see you shooting off your torpedoes from your wireless-set on the bank at their boats?'

'They won't see,' said Bob. 'But we'll have to be careful about that. We could have it in a large sailing-boat at the edge of the water, what they call a parent boat; or we could hide it in a tea-basket. Then we wait till a good big ship has put to sea, and we launch the pirate-ship so that it should intercept her.

If it doesn't, we try again and again, until we are lucky. What I want to do is to get the Rakish Craft (that is to be her name) head on to her beam at about 3 or 4 yards, then we fire a torpedo, and if we meet her somewhere about the middle of the pond, she should never reach land. What do you think of it?'

'I think it's perfectly splendid,' I said. 'There's only one thing seems to be missing like.'

'What's that?' he asked rather sharply.

'Treasure,' I said. 'Isn't treasure rather the chief part of a pirate's life?'

'That shows all you know about it,' he said. 'The principal part of a pirate's life is the battles he has, and the thrill of seeing his enemy sink, and the danger, the risk of hanging. I don't say they'd hang me, but I'd go to prison for years if I was caught. And of course if anybody was drowned as a result of the accident, going in to pull out the ship or anything, then I'd be hanged. And even without that, after all I'm a pirate; it doesn't matter where: I might be hanged in any case. Now, I'm giving you a chance you'll probably never have again in a lifetime. Would you like to come in with me?'

Well, of course it was pretty wonderful getting an offer like that from such a tremendous chap as Bob Tipling; because I knew he would be as wonderful as a pirate as he was at everything else. Of course I said, 'Yes, rather.'

And then he told me what I would have to do. Carry the tea-basket chiefly, and walk about and look unconcerned. Or look concerned if he told me to, and walk away from him to draw attention off. 'It's full of detectives,' he said.

That was on a Saturday morning, and we get the afternoons off on Saturdays. So Bob Tipling told me to meet him at the Round Pond at 2 o'clock, which I did, and he made me walk up and down looking unconcerned. There were some nice ships there, big sailing-ships and some clockwork ones, and even one that went by petrol, a beauty, a big gray ship. 'That's the one we'll get if she's there when we put to sea,' said Bob. 'She'll hole nicely.'

And I made the mistake of saying, 'Wouldn't it be rather a pity to sink a nice ship like that?'

But Bob explained to me that the people who owned it should think themselves very lucky if their ship was sunk without any loss of life, which wasn't often the case if you were attacked by a pirate. 'And, after all, there must *be* pirates,' he said. 'And anyhow,' he said, 'I shall only attack those that deserve it, as Robin Hood used to do on land. The money that that boat cost would have kept a poor man and his family in food for a year. I'm helping the Government, really, to swat the rich. Though that's not the view they'll take if they catch me.'

'They ought to,' I said.

'We'll just not get caught,' said Bob Tipling. 'Now walk about concernedly, so that they'll watch you if I want their attention switched off me.'

So I did, and it's wonderful how soon I saw one or two men mopping their faces with white handkerchiefs, and making funny little signs. We went away then, because we didn't want people to get to know us.

There were only three of us in it; Bob, me and this rich boy that Bob had found. He had hung about among the trees in Kensington Gardens off and on for nearly a year, before he found this boy walking alone and got a chance to talk to him. He had tried others, of course, but they hadn't enough money. This one had, and he took to the idea at once, as who wouldn't? He had always wanted to be a pirate, and knew that he never would be; and then this chance came to him, brought by Bob. Bob had worked it all out, except the actual making of the torpedoes, and he knew there were people who could make them, and send them off by wireless: all he wanted was the money; and this boy had it, or he could get it out of his father, which comes to the same thing. Bob fixed next Sunday week for putting to sea, under the black-and-yellow flag with the

skull-and-crossbones; only, Bob said that the actual flag might
attract too much attention, and that he would sail under false
colours, as pirates often did. We said nothing to each other in
school; we almost might have been strangers; but it wouldn't
have done to have let a thing like that get out; we should only
have been hanged, if it had, before we started. Bob Tipling said
that it wasn't a hanging matter. And he would be sure to know.
At the same time we were pirates, and I never heard of anything
else happening to a pirate, if he got caught, in any book that
I've read. So it seemed best not to risk it.

I learned a lot that week in school, but what it was I couldn't
tell you, because I was only thinking of one thing all the week,
that is of being a pirate. They say it's wicked to be a pirate
and I dare say it is. At the same time nobody could say that it
isn't better than sitting indoors at a desk, learning things; especially the kind of things I was learning that week, whatever they
were. I never knew a week go by slower. I'd have liked to have
timed it, because I should think that it was the slowest week
that ever went by. But it came to an end at last, and I slipped
away from my home, which is where I lived, and came to the
Round Pond at the time Bob Tipling said, which was 12 o'clock
on the Sunday morning. I came along the Broad Walk, because
I was to meet Bob and his friend there. It was all black earth
by the edge of the walk, or dark gray any way, and there were
little trickles of yellow sand in it. I liked the look of the black
earth, because it made me think of a wide and desolate moor
and it would have been, if it hadn't been for the grass. And
there was a great row of elm-trees there, and all the little leaves
were just coming out, because it was Spring. They looked very
small and shiny. And at the end of the row I met Bob and his
rich friend. Bob had his arms folded and a coloured handker
chief round his neck, and I thought he looked very like a pirate
We were quite near the Round Pond then. Bob introduces me
to the rich boy, and his name turns out to be Algernon, and
some other name that I forget. And it's just as well to forget it

as we were all involved in piracy together. Bob is away where
the police can't catch him now. I'm not going to tell you *my*
name. Algernon was carrying a big luncheon-basket by a handle,
and Bob has the ship on the grass beside him, with a bit of a
cloth wrapped round it to hide the torpedo-tubes.

'That's a nice boat,' I says.

'It's a long low rakish craft,' said Bob.

Bob was giving the orders, and Algernon and I went down
with him to the pond to the part of it where he says, where
there was a little kind of a bay. There were lots of ducks on it,
mostly black-and-white ones, and every now and then they
would get up out of the water and shake their wings and splash
themselves. I suppose they were having a bath. Algernon said
they was tufted ducks. And then there was ducks with green
heads, that was just ducks. And there was a couple of geese
that swam by, honking. And I saw a swan. And there were
sea-gulls, lots of them, flying backwards and forwards over the
pond and squawking as they flew. And there were lots of boats.
I saw a little sailing-boat far out, nearly becalmed, and some
clockwork ones like ours. And then all of a sudden I sees the
big gray ship that went by petrol. I stopped breathing for a
moment when I saw that, and then I pointed her out to
Algernon, and Bob nodded his head. And then we both went
round to where she was, just beside our little bay, and there
was a boy running it that was about the same age as me, which
is thirteen. Bob is fourteen, and knows about as much about
most things as grownups. I don't know about Algernon: I should
say he was about the same age as Bob, but nothing near so
clever. And just as we came up to where the boy was, a fat little
brown spaniel with a wide smile ran up to the boy and licked
one of his knees, which was bare. And the boy jumped out of
the way. And there was a lady with the brown spaniel, and she
said to the boy, 'Our Billy won't hurt you.' And the boy says,
'I am not accustomed to being licked by dogs.' 'Oh, aren't you?'
says Bob.

I don't know if the boy heard him or not.

And then Bob says to me in a lower voice, 'That settles the business of it being a pity to sink his nice ship.'

There was a fat man standing near, smoking a cigar, evidently the boy's father, and I says to Bob, 'Well, it's he that will lose what he paid for the ship if we sink it.'

'That's true,' said Bob. And he goes up to the fat man with the cigar and says to him, 'That's a fine boat your boy's got, sir.'

'Yes. You leave it alone,' says the fat man.

'Certainly, sir,' says Bob.

'Well, that settles it,' he says to me. 'The ship is doomed.'

The big ship touched land just then, and Bob hurried back to his bay, to be ready to launch the Rakish Craft, his idea being to launch it just at the right moment to cut off the big gray ship when it sets out again. With the curve that there was on the bay we could send our ship right across her course. I had a very responsible job. I had to unpack the luncheon-basket and get my finger on to a knob of the wireless-set that was hidden under some paper packets, and to press it down whenever Bob gave the sign. I can't tell you what the sign was, because I took an oath to Bob that I would never reveal it, but it is something he did with his elbow. Well, the big gray ship set out almost at once. 'That's the last she'll see of land,' said Bob. But he was wrong there, because our ship didn't quite hit her off, Bob not having had time quite to calculate the speed of the big ship, though he knew the speed of the Rakish Craft, and so we were a bit behind her and never fired a torpedo, and we went right across the pond, and the gray ship went very nearly to the other end of it.

Well, the boy ran round and the fat man walked slowly after him; and, to make a long story short, they puts to sea again. And Bob watches to see about where the gray ship will come in, and goes round and launches the Rakish Craft to intercept her about half-way. And Bob said he had calculated the two speeds exactly, but I think it was pure luck. Anyway, the Rakish Craft, heading towards Bayswater, comes right up to within nearly two yards of the side of the gray ship, which is sailing towards Hyde Park; and just as the gray ship passes our bows Bob makes the sign with his elbow, and I presses the button where I am sitting on the grass beside the luncheon-basket, with my finger inside it touching the wireless set. And there is a white fountain against the side of the gray ship, and both boats rock a bit, and the big one goes on apparently unconcerned. And I look round, and nobody has noticed a thing. But I couldn't see anything out of the way, myself, except that white splash and the two boats rocking a little, ours more than the other one. For a moment I thought that Bob's game did not work, and then to my delight I saw the big ship's bows dipping a little, or thought I did. Then I saw I was right. She continued straight on her course, but the bows went lower and lower. And all of a sudden her stern went into the air, and she dived right under, and never came up any more. The only thing that could have made it any more perfect would have been a bit of blood on the water. However, one can't have everything. I wanted to cheer, but I caught Bob's eye. Bob strolled round with Algernon to the part of the shore to which our ship was heading, and they hardly glanced at the water. Bob wanted to go on and sink some more boats. But that's where Algernon showed sense, and he told Bob not to do it. That's what they were talking about when on the grass by the luncheon-basket. And I joined in with Algernon and said, 'Don't do it, Bob. Nobody has suspected a thing, and we can start all fresh next Sunday; but, if you get them suspecting you now, they'll be waiting for you next time you come, and it will probably be prison for all of us.'

And Algernon says the same, and between us we just persuaded Bob, and stopped him doing any more piracy that day. But he insisted on hoisting the pirate's flag, the skull-and-crossbones, yellow on black, because he says you ought to do that as soon as you open fire, whatever colours you have been sailing under till then, and, as he wasn't able to do it at the time, he would do it as soon as he can, and sail across the main once more, as he now called the Round Pond, flying the skull-and-crossbones. I wasn't easy about it, but nobody seemed to notice, and Bob said it was the right thing to do. I didn't like to look too much at the fat man or his boy, for fear they should catch me looking at them, so I just went on quietly eating a biscuit, and Bob had the sense not to look at them too much either, though his pirate's blood was up. But, as far as I could see when I did take a glance, they were puzzled, and unsuspicious of us. So we packed up the luncheon-basket that fired the torpedoes, and Bob put our ship under his arm, and I carried the luncheon-basket, and away we walked over the grass, and I never saw three people that looked more innocent-looking. Bob said that we ought to have drunk rum then. And so we would have, if we could have got any. But even Bob's rich friend, Algernon, wasn't able to manage that.

I was pretty pleased when I went home. I'd always wanted to be a pirate, and now I was one, one of the crew of the Rakish Craft, and we'd sunk a big ship. I'm not going to tell you where I lived. Pirates don't do that, if they've got any sense. If there's people looking for one of them they must find out for themselves, without the pirate helping them. I came home to tea; and I wished I could have brought my mother some gold ingots and a few pearls, as pirates often do when they come home. But I remembered what Bob told me, and knew I must think of the glory of it, and not bother about what it ought to be worth in cash. Of course there should have been heaps of gold taken from ships before they were sunk; but it was good enough seeing the gray ship go down, even without any loot. I was only sorry for the sea-gulls, that they had no corpses floating about. They'd have liked to have pecked at their eyes.

My father and mother wanted to know what I'd been doing, and so did my sister Alice, because they saw that it must have been something. But I couldn't tell them that. And I'm not going to write about my father and mother. They're grown up and can write about themselves if they want to; but I've got my hands full telling about the great battles Bob fought at sea, and the ships that he sunk.

Well, I learned a lot more at school that week. But I can't tell you about that. I've got more important things to write of. Besides, I've forgot it. Bob didn't say a word to me all that week, so that we shouldn't be overheard. And that of course was a good precaution. But he didn't look very precautious. He looked as if his blood was up, and as if he was going on sinking ships till he got hanged, as so many pirates do. I met Bob again at the same place and the same time next Sunday, and he was folding his arms tighter than ever, and wearing that look that I mentioned. I was afraid we would get into trouble. But it was too late to back out now, and, as for warning Bob to go a bit slower, it couldn't be done. I mentioned it to Algernon, but he didn't seem to see it. He'd put his money up, or his father's money, and he wanted to see something for it. So we went to the Round Pond and launched the Rakish Craft from one of the little bays. Then I went back on to the grass and got out some sandwiches from the luncheon-basket, and watched Bob.

I think Bob was trying for a small sailing-boat near the shore, because the Rakish Craft just sailed across the little bay, pretty close to the sailing-boat, but it didn't come near enough to fire. And when I saw there wasn't going to be a fight, it gave me time to look round. And what did I see when I looked round but that same fat man again and his son, and another fine boat like the last one, even bigger if anything. Well, I saw that before Bob did, because he was watching the sailing-boat that he didn't get; and as soon as our Rakish Craft came to land again, as she soon did on the other side of the little bay, I moved up nearer to Bob and Algernon, to a bench that there was near the pond, and signed to them to come over, and told them what I had seen. And, just as I thought, as soon as I'd pointed the big ship out, Bob wanted to go and sink it. And I tells him that would be fatal. 'Won't they be wondering still what happened to their other boat?' I says to him. 'And won't they spend the rest of the day putting two and two together, if they see their new one sink, and see the Rakish Craft quite close again and the same crew standing by?'

'Did you ever hear of a pirate sparing anything, when he had it at his mercy?' said Bob.

'Did you ever hear of a pirate that wasn't hanged?' I asks.

'Yes,' Bob replies, 'all the clever ones.'

'And are you being a clever one?' I asks.

And then Algernon joins in, and I admit he showed sense. 'Sink smaller craft today,' he says, 'at the other end of the main from those people, and give them time to forget.'

Well, the two of us just succeeded in stopping Bob, and it would have been a bad business if we hadn't. And Bob goes after a smaller ship, as Algernon says, a long way away from the fat man. It was a clockwork ship some way out, and Bob launched the Rakish Craft so as to cut it off; and when it gets close he gives me the sign and I presses the button, but he wasn't close enough and it was no good. The torpedo came to the surface then, but it was painted gray so that it wouldn't show up, and very soon it sank, because it only barely floated, and there was a small hole in it so that it would soon fill with water. Nobody noticed it, and the Rakish Craft sailed on, under the colours of Spain, which Bob fancied, and came to the other shore, and Bob and Algernon went round and got hold of it, and wound it up and brought it back. And there was the same ship that Bob had missed, putting to sea again, and Bob had a better idea of her pace this time, which was very slow, and he launches the Rakish Craft out of the same bay.

It was a lovely day for a fight, and lots of ducks were there enjoying the sun, and the sea-gulls were flying in flocks over the water. Bob didn't reload the torpedo-tube, so as not to attract attention. He still had his starboard torpedo, and he put to sea with that. And this time the Rakish Craft headed straight for the enemy. And I wanted to fire, but Bob didn't give the sign until she was quite close, because he had missed the last time. And then he made the sign, and I fired, and both boats rocked a lot when the fountain went up against the side of the enemy's ship, because they were pretty close, and it was a smaller ship than the one we had sunk last time. And then the enemy sailed on a little way, but not far. And soon her bows began to rise out of the water, and very soon after that she slid to the bottom of the sea; and the Rakish Craft sailed on to the further shore. The boy that owned the boat looked quite surprised, but he didn't seem to suspect Bob or Algernon, and of course not me, who was sitting quiet on a bench with the luncheon-basket beside me. I watched him so closely that I didn't see what the fat man was doing, or how much he saw.

He was a long way off, but of course you can see anything on the water at almost any distance, and he must have seen the ship sinking if he looked. Bob went round to the far shore with Algernon, and got the Rakish Craft when it came in, and hauled down the colours of Spain, which were red and yellow, and hoisted the pirate's flag. I'd sooner he hadn't hoisted the skull-and-crossbones, but there was no holding Bob over a thing like that. I believed that he had the idea of reloading his two torpedo-tubes and putting to sea again and sinking more ships, for I saw that Algernon was arguing with him as they came back. Anyway, he had the sense not to, and Algernon and I got away as quickly as possible. I did a lot of wondering that week. The boy who owned the small ship that we sunk was still there when we left, and he was looking puzzled. I was wondering what he made out about it when he had thought it over. And I was wondering how much the fat man saw, and how much he knew. Well, it wasn't any use wondering. But I couldn't help doing it, for all that. And I was a bit sorry for the boy that had owned the boat, and so I told Bob one day. But Bob said, 'Did you ever read of a pirate that was sorry?' And I had to admit that I never had.

'The kites are the only things that I'm sorry for,' he said; 'not having any dead bodies to peck at.'

Of course there weren't any kites; but I saw what he meant; and I saw that it wouldn't be any use to say anything more on those lines to Bob. Well, he gave me my orders where to meet him next Sunday, the same place. Algernon and I were his crew, and of course we had to obey. In a way I was looking forward to that Sunday all the week, because it is a splendid thing to be a pirate and sink ships. But every now and then I couldn't help wondering how far Bob would go, and what would happen to us all if he went too far. And I couldn't ask him. It would have been such cheek.

Well, next Sunday came eventually, and I slipped away as usual and joined Bob and Algernon at the same place. It was a lovely day, and the lilac leaves were all flashing. There would be buds soon. Algernon was there with the luncheon-basket as usual, which I took, and we all went down to the pond. And the first thing Bob looks for is ships to sink. But the first thing I looked for was the fat man. And sure enough there he was, with his son and his big ship. And he was nearer to us this time, having come round to our side of the pond. I walked past him, and took a look as I passed, and he looked at me a bit sideways, and I thought he suspected something. But not the boy; he was only watching his big ship. And it was a fine ship, full of funnels and lifeboats and portholes, even better than the one we had sunk. And another thing I noticed; the boy whose ship we had sunk the Sunday before was there again too, and he also had a rather better ship. Who gave it him, I wondered? And I got the idea that the fat man was at the back of it. So I goes back to Bob and tells him that I think the fat man suspects us. And Bob says, 'Aren't pirates always suspected?'

And he won't be warned. He has seen the fat man's new ship, and is going to sink her at all costs. I think it's dangerous just then to sink another ship at all, but to sink the fat man's big ship would be absolutely fatal; and so I tell Algernon, and

Algernon agrees, and we both of us warn Bob. But Bob says, even if he was going to be hanged for it he would sink that ship first. And when Bob starts talking about the big ship like that, Algernon all of a sudden deserts me and goes in with Bob, and says they will sink her whatever happens. Well, after that I could do nothing, except sit by our wireless-set and obey orders. So I sat on the grass, pretending to eat sandwiches, and watching for Bob's sign. And then the big ship came steaming past our bay, close in to the shore and Bob times her exactly, and set sail with the Rakish Craft. And it wasn't more than a few minutes before he gave me the sign with both elbows. And I pressed two buttons, and the ships were quite close, and both torpedoes hit. They were so close that our good ship nearly ran into theirs, but just passed astern of her and went on, rocking down to the gunwales. And the other ship went on, after the two fountains had gone up her side, just as the big one did last time, as though nothing had happened. But very soon she begins to dip by the head. And soon after that she takes her last plunge. Well, of course it was perfectly splendid, even if it did mean prison for years: and I looked at the fat man, and his face was half-turned towards me. And somehow there was an expression in it, and I was sure he had found us out. It certainly looked like prison. I packed up the luncheon-basket and went over to Bob. 'You've done it now,' I said. 'Let's get away quick, and never come here again.'

But you can't stop a pirate when once he has tasted blood. They always go on till they are hanged. 'I must hoist my flag,' he said, 'before I go.'

And there was no stopping him. He goes to where his ship comes in to land, and hoists the skull-and-crossbones and gives the Rakish Craft one more run across the bay. And the fat man stands there watching all the time, smoking his cigar, and says nothing. I was glad to see that at least Bob didn't reload his torpedo-tubes. And when the Rakish Craft reaches shore he takes her out of the water. And the fat man walks up quite close.

Bob did have the sense not to run; but we all walked away pretty fast, and got out of Kensington Gardens, never looking behind us once, because we didn't dare. But I knew we were being followed. I don't know how I knew: I just knew. When we got out into Kensington High Street, I said to Bob, 'Let's separate, so that they can only follow one of us.'

But Bob said that was no good, because if they got one of us that would be all they wanted, to unravel the whole plot. So we kept together and walked over half London, so as to tire out whoever was after us. But that was no good, because the fellow who followed us out of Kensington Gardens made a sign to a nasty-looking fellow ahead of us, who watched us as far as he could see, and then made a sign to another. I knew he was watching us, from the way that he looked so straight in the opposite direction, from the moment we came in sight, the direction in which we were going, so that once we were past him he did not have to trouble to turn his head.

I felt that we never got out of sight of those nasty people. Not even when we separated to go home. What I thought was that they hated everybody, and watched them all, because they thought they were all crooks. I seen them before, and that's what I thought. But we was worse than crooks now. We was pirates. So they were right to watch us. One couldn't deny that. I tried to do a bit of doubling to throw them off, when I got near my home. But it only made it worse.

Well, all Monday and Tuesday I was wondering what was going to happen. And Bob didn't say nothing, either because he didn't believe we had been followed, or because he was pretending that there was nothing wrong. You could never tell with Bob. And Wednesday came, and nothing happened. I still felt uneasy when I went to bed that night; but when I woke up on Thursday morning, and still nothing had happened, I said it was all imagination and nobody had followed us at all, or made little signs at us, silly little signs like lifting their arms and gazing hard at their wrist-watches. But I said as I woke up that

Thursday morning that people who lifted their hands up to look at their watches only wanted to see the time, and were meaning no harm to us. So I had a good breakfast and set out to go to school. And there was the fat man walking right past our house, smoking his usual cigar! He was not following me; he was going the other way; but it gave me a feeling like what the man must have had in a poem they taught us at school, which went like this.

As one who walks a lonely road in terror and in dread,
And having once looked round goes on and turns no more
  his head,
Because he knows a frightful fiend doth close behind him
  tread.

That's how I felt that morning, and all that day; and the next day, and the day after. I knew something was after me. I told Bob that morning that the fat man had found out where I lived.

'Oh, that's nothing,' said Bob. 'He's got to prove it.'

'He's got that boy as a witness,' I said, 'and probably lots of others.'

'Not he,' said Bob very airily.

But I don't know how he felt.

'Anyway, I'll never go there again,' I said. 'So, if by any lucky chance he hasn't got any absolute proof yet, he'll never get any more.'

'We'll see about that,' said Bob.

And an awful fear came all over me that Bob would make me go back. Because, if we ever went there again, we hadn't a chance. I could see that. And Bob isn't the kind of chap you can disobey, when he says a thing.

Well, the days went on going by, and I was afraid of my own shadow. And they noticed that there was something wrong, at home. But I said it was some work that was worrying me, some lines that I had to learn, and that I couldn't remember. And my

father said, 'That's right. Keep at it.' And my mother said I'd
remember them all right. And neither knew the awful thing that
was threatening Bob and I. And they tell us at our school that
that isn't grammar. But I can tell you I had much too much to
think about, that week, to have any time to bother about
grammar, even if it was worth bothering about. And of course
they didn't know about us being pirates. Well, Saturday came
at last, and Bob called me over to him that morning. I think he
must have seen something too, for he said, 'You may be right
about those sleuths. It may be a coincidence about the fat man
passing your house; but I don't believe much in coincidences,
and we may be up against it.'

'Then you'll never go back to the main,' I said, as we all
called the Round Pond now.

But Bob was silent. I didn't know what he was going to do,
and he wouldn't say.

And that afternoon he said to me, 'We're going back to the
main.'

'We'll all be hanged,' I said.

'Oh, no we shan't,' said Bob.

'Prison, then,' I said, 'anyway.'

'No,' he said. 'You may be right about them suspecting us,
but what I'm going to do is to go back there with my ship, and
no torpedo-tubes on her. And we'll sail her right across. Then,
if they suspect our ship of being a pirate, they'll seize her and
see their suspicions are groundless. How can they charge us
with sinking ships with torpedoes, when ours is quite unarmed?'

It seemed a good idea, and I felt much better; for I feared
that Bob would take me and Algernon to the main and sink
another ship, and we'd all go to prison that Sunday.

'And we'll bring the luncheon-basket too,' says Bob. 'And do
you know what we'll have in it?'

'No,' I says.

'Luncheon,' says he.

'That's splendid,' I says.

'And then they can bring their charges for damaging property,' says Bob; 'and see how they'll prove it. Especially when Algernon's father hires a lawyer to prove we are innocent. Piracy indeed! You don't only have to catch your pirate. You have to prove he is one. He is only an alleged pirate till then.'

'Yes, we are only alleged pirates,' I says, brightening up.

But Bob folds his arms again, and says, 'I am a pirate to the last. But still, they'll have to prove it.'

That lifted a little of the load off my mind; but I wasn't easy yet, for the fat man knew where I lived, and he must have been very sure of what we had done, to want to track me down like that. And, when Bob went away, most of the old fears came back, and I couldn't look into the future without seeing prison. Well, Bob had fixed the same time on Sunday to meet him near to the main; and so I had to go. And I went, and I met him with Algernon. And the luncheon-basket looked lighter. This time, I was glad to see there were no torpedo-tubes on the Rakish Craft. But he had the pirate's flag flying on her, which seemed a mistake. However, that was Bob's way. And then we went round to the far side of the pond, meaning to sail her right across and take her out and go straight home. That was the north side; and the first thing I sees is the fat man with his boy and his boat, standing on the east side, where he usually is. And he has a big wireless-set on the ground beside him, playing a tune to amuse the boy, a tune about Teddy bears. Then Bob launches the Rakish Craft, with the skull-and-cross-bones flying big and bold from the foremast, and a nice little bit of a wind was making it fly. And he winds her up, and off she goes. There was a small sailing-ship quite near, and I sees Bob look at it with a wistful look; and I was glad he had no torpedoes, because if he had he'd have sunk her for certain, and we should have all been in jail; because you can't go on and on doing a thing like that and not get caught. But we've no torpedoes, and nothing in the luncheon-basket but luncheon, and the sailing-ship goes safe, and the Rakish Craft steams on, and the sound of the tune about the Teddy bears drifts to us over the water. I see the fat man watching us, and I didn't like it; but I glanced over my shoulder at Bob, and something about the look of him made me see that the more we were watched the better, because the Rakish Craft was going about her lawful business that day, and it was a good thing for people to see it. Still, I knew that I wouldn't be easy until she had crossed the main, and we were all on our way home. And then I saw a ship about the same size as ours, putting out from the east shore and coming across. She was faster than ours, and looked like cutting across our course. A pity, I thought for a moment, we hadn't torpedoes. And then I was jolly glad that we had not, because I knew what Bob would have done if his tubes had been loaded.

It was a gray ship, with guns all along her sides; I counted eight of them on each side as she came near, guns that were big enough to have fired a rifle bullet; they seemed rather crowded to me, and I wondered what the ship wanted so many of them for. The ship came on, and the Rakish Craft went on, and I thought the other ship would pass right ahead of her. And then it gave a curve and came straight for the Rakish Craft. Then I thought it would pass astern of her. And then it gave another twist and came straight for our ship again. Bob and I, and I think Algernon too, realized at the same moment that the manœuvre was too good to be chance. It must be directed! If wireless could fire torpedoes, it could direct a boat. Even aeroplanes have been directed that way. When the strange ship got quite close, she gave a sudden twist to port, which brought her alongside only a few inches away. It was obvious then that the ship was directed. I looked at Bob, and he had his mouth open. Then I looked across the pond at the fat man, and he was sitting beside his big box that was playing the tune for his boy. But I knew that the tune was only camouflage: the box was much larger than what you'd need, for one thing, to play a tune like that. He was sitting there quite unconcernedly. But the boy wasn't unconcerned: he gave the whole show away, staring at the two ships, glaring would be the right word for it. For a while the two ships kept dead level, quite close; and all of a sudden, bang! And the starboard guns opened fire, the whole broadside. They were pointed downwards, and they hit the Rakish Craft just above the waterline on her port side. Several people looked up when they heard the bang. But there was no smoke to speak of, and I don't think anyone spotted where the noise came from, except us, who were watching, and that boy.

I could see the holes in our port side, where every shot had hit; and they must have gone right through and made cracks on our starboard side below the waterline. They wouldn't have been more than cracks, or the Rakish Craft would have sunk, but she remained there, rocking on the water. One of the bullets must have gone right into her engines, for she didn't go forward any more. Then the strange ship turned round and sailed back the way she had come, and the Rakish Craft stopped rocking. I thought at first that she would keep afloat, and that the breeze, which was proudly flapping her black-and-yellow flag, would blow her ashore in about ten minutes. But she was making water all the time, and she couldn't last ten minutes. And we saw her go down with her skull-and-crossbones flying, yellow and black from her masthead, as a pirate's ship should.

There's not much more to tell, except one funny thing: the fat man launched his gray gunboat again and sent it right across the Round Pond. And she was flying the skull-and-crossbones too.

A VICTIM OF BAD LUCK

I AM absolutely the victim of bad luck. Absolutely. It was all Morson's fault. I'm not blaming him. He made a mistake that anyone might have made. Still, it was a mistake; and I have to suffer for it. We were having a bit of a talk one evening about how to get a little cash for ourselves, both of us being a bit short of it, as who isn't in these days? And Morson says to me 'What about going to old Potter's house one night, and seeing if he has got anything to spare?'

And I says, 'They give you a nasty lot, if you get caught at that game.'

And Morson says, 'We are not going to get caught. I've thought it all out. We'll go in there one night when he's playing his wireless set, and he won't hear us. We'll wait till a night when his cook is down in the village and there'll be nobody there with him, and he'll have his wireless on, as he always does when the B.B.C. is giving a concert.'

'It's a bit risky,' I said.

'Not in the least,' he says. 'I've got a copy of the *Radio Times* and we'll go when they've got Beethoven turned on. That's the fellow he always listens to. And he turns him on full blast. We'll go in our stockinged feet, and if he can hear us walking then when he's sitting close to his wireless and it's full on, well, he'll have wonderful ears.'

'I don't quite like it,' I says.

'What don't you like?' he says to me.

'I don't quite like doing that,' I said.

'Nonsense,' he says. 'Everybody does it now. You have to do something like that to keep going at all. You don't want to starve do you? Anyway, I'm not going to. Everybody does it. Don't be old-fashioned. I'm not asking you to rob a bank.'

'No. I know,' I said.

'I am only asking you,' he goes on, 'to come with me to old Potter's house at a time when he can't hear us, and just walk in. He never locks up till he goes to bed, and we'll go in just after he has had his dinner, on a night when his wireless is on, as it usually is. I think I can find out what evening his cook will go down to the village. But, even if I can't, it's easy enough. There's only one way she can go by, and we only have to wait at the end of the lane to see when she goes. Then he'll be quite alone; and, if he has got Beethoven or one of those blighters turned on, he couldn't hear if you shouted. It is easy enough, and everybody does it.'

'Still,' I said. 'I shouldn't like to be caught.'

'Now, who is going to catch us?' says Morson. 'I tell you he'll be alone in the house. And we'll go when his Beethoven is making such a noise that there'll be no hearing anything else. And if they don't have it just as the *Radio Times* says, we won't go in at all.'

'I've always been careful not to get into any kind of trouble,' I says.

'We'll take all the care that's necessary,' says Morson. 'It's upstairs that he's got the stuff. You'll have to see that there's no chink between the curtains, for the light to shine through, before I turn it on. He might see it through his window, shining out on his lawn, and we're going to take no chances. I never do. You only get caught if you do, sooner or later. But I sees that they don't catch me.'

'I won't go in if his wireless isn't full on,' I says.

'Nor will I,' says Morson.

'I don't quite like taking his things,' I says.

'We'll only take a few things what he doesn't want,' he says. 'Things he has in a room upstairs to which he never goes, some silver things that are no use to him, and would be a lot of use to us. I wouldn't do it if we could get it in any other way. But when we can't, it's the only thing we can do.'

And when he puts it like that he gets me to agree with him. But I says to him, 'Are you sure that old Potter doesn't want any of those silver arrangements himself?'

And Morson says, 'Quite sure.'

So I says to him, 'All right, then, I'll come. But you must take care that he's playing that Beethoven of his all the time.'

'That's all right,' he says. 'I've got the *Radio Times* and it will be on for half an hour tomorrow night, just after his dinner, and I think that his cook will be down in the village. But we'll watch and make sure of that, and then we'll go.'

Well, there didn't seem to me to be anything wrong about that. Old Potter didn't want his silver things, and we did. He'd be alone in the house, and we'd go in our stockinged feet, and his wireless would be full on and he couldn't hear us.

'What if his wireless stops?' I asked as a last precaution.

'We'll stand perfectly still till it goes on again,' Morson said.

Well, that seemed all right; and the next day came round, and Morson and I waited at the end of the lane at the time that he said old Potter's cook would come by. And sure enough she did, within five minutes of the time that Morson had said. We were down behind a hedge and saw her go by, heading towards the village. Then we had to wait a bit over a quarter of an hour till old Potter's Beethoven was to come on, and we heard it right from the end of the lane, and we walked in through the front door with our boots in our hands, which we had taken off some yards before we got to the house. The wireless was going full blast, and everything seemed all right. Morson led the way to the room where the silver things were, and I went straight to the curtains and saw that the black-out was perfect. And then I turned on the lights. Two of them I turned on, as it seemed perfectly safe as soon as he shut the door; and we could hear the wireless going all the time. Well, we collected all the silver things that we wanted, and stuffed our pockets with them and turned out both the lights. And Morson opened the door so gently you couldn't have heard a sound, even if the wireless had not been roaring. And we tiptoed downstairs. And there was old Potter at the foot of the stairs with a shotgun, and his wireless still on. Well, of course there was nothing we could do. And when we saw that he had made up his mind to make trouble, we came with him to the police-station in the village as he said.

What puzzled me was how old Potter ever found us out. Our counsel for the defence didn't know his job, and bungled it badly, but he did tell me that much. He said that when I switched the two lights on, and again when I switched them off, four distinct knocks would have been heard on his wireless. Morson thought himself so clever, making sure that there would be nobody else in the house, and watching at the end of the lane to see the cook go by. But that is what caught us, really. If there had been anybody else in the house old Potter wouldn't have known that it wasn't his cook that was turning on the lights in that upstairs room, where he kept those old bits of silver that he didn't want; and I shouldn't be here in this stuffy little room, where they tell me that I'll be for the next three years, and all through the fault of Morson who promised me we should be taking no chances.

THE NEW MASTER

I CANNOT prove my case. I have been over everything very carefully; I have had a talk with a lawyer about evidence in coroner's courts, without letting him know what I was really after; I have considered arguments that I should be expected to meet; and after long consideration I have decided to give no evidence at all, or as little as I can. This will mean that my friend Allaby Methick will be found to have taken his own life, and no doubt they will say that his mind was temporarily deranged. If they do call me I shall do all I can to imply that he suffered from undue mental stress. And that is all I can do for him. I know that I shall be sworn to tell the whole truth. But what is the use of that if no one will listen? And I might even be considered deranged myself. The whole truth is this.

Allaby Methick and I belonged to the Otbury chess-club. It is not a chess-club that anyone ever heard of over ten miles away, and any knowledge of the hamlet of Otbury would go little further than that. There we used often to play on summer evenings, sitting down in the schoolroom, of which the chess-club hired the use, when the blackbirds were going to sleep, and playing on till the nightingales in briary thickets at the top of the down above us were all in full song. He lived about a mile on one side of Otbury, and I only a little more than that on the other. Except on the rarest occasions, I used to beat Methick. But that never deterred him from coming to have a game whenever I asked him to come; and the cheerful resignation with which he lost never varied. There were not many other members of the Otbury chess-club that ever turned up, so we played a great deal together. And then one evening, as I came to the little schoolroom from my walk under the edge of the downs and found Methick already there, instead of sitting down on a bench at the long table before a board with the pieces set, he broke out with the words, 'I have got something that will beat you.'

'A problem, do you mean?' I said.

'No,' he said. 'Come and see. It's at my house. We can have supper there.'

Almost before I answered he was striding out of the school-room, not literally dragging me with him, but somehow the result was the same.

'What is it?' I asked, as we walked by a sheep-track over the downs. Methick was too excited to explain the thing very thor-oughly; but at any rate he made it clear that it was a machine I was coming to see.

He lived alone in this little house of his, except for a char-woman who came every day and who helped him a bit in the kitchen. But he did most of his own cooking. He had some invested capital; but something had made him decide that it was better not to save capital, and so he had sold out and spent some of it every year on his simple needs, and, finding that he had something like a thousand pounds that he could spare, he decided to spend it on chess, for the good reason that chess was what he enjoyed most. 'But how on earth,' I broke in at that point, 'can you spend a thousand pounds on chess?'

'The machine,' he said.

'The machine?' I repeated.

'Yes,' he said. 'It can play chess.'

'A machine?' I said again.

'Yes,' he said. 'Haven't you heard?'

And then I remembered that there was a machine that was said to be able to play a little chess of a sort, and I mentioned it to Methick.

'Oh, that,' he said. 'That was a very simple affair. That has been improved beyond recognition. My machine can beat you.'

'I should like to see it,' I said.

'I'll show it you,' said Methick.

'Does it know the regular openings?' I asked.

'No,' he said. 'It plays queer openings.'

'I hardly think it will beat me,' I said, 'if it doesn't know the openings.'

'It will,' he said. 'Its openings are better than ours.'

Of course that seemed to me nonsense, and I said little more. There was no need to argue with him, I thought; for the game would show all that I would have said, more clearly than I could say it. And chessplayers seldom argue, just as heavyweight boxers when they chance to meet do not slap each other's faces. The ring waits to test them.

Through Methick's small garden we went on that summer's evening and into his house, and there in his sitting-room was the strange machine. At first I thought it was a very fine wireless-set; and then I remembered what it was that I had been brought to see. Long arms of flexible steel lay folded in pairs in front of it. Two it might require for castling, but I could not see what need it would have for more. I asked Methick. 'It is simpler,' he explained. 'They cover all parts of the board, and one of them is for removing captured pieces.'

But I soon lost interest in the steel hands, in the wonder of that astonishing iron brain, that answered every move, and made calculations that I soon saw were beyond me. For Methick put me at once in a chair at the table, that was a chessboard with squares of boxwood and ebony, though in each square was a small hole into which fitted a metallic stud that there was in the pieces; and what arrangement of wires there was underneath the wooden squares, I had, and have, no idea.

The vast brain before me was hidden, as human brains are hidden, though instead of skull and skin, it was walnut that concealed it from the eye. But to the ear it was plain enough that there was something intricate there, the moment I made my move, for a faint humming arose, as though innumerable wires were singing to themselves; and often, as I made a move, their note would suddenly change, so that I knew I was faced by some active and vital thing that was thinking as hard as I. I wanted to look into its face, but the polished walnut prevented any glimpse of that. It was queer to sit opposite an active and powerful intelligence without ever being able to see its eyes or its face, or anything but that smooth panel of walnut; unless I could get some insight into its character, as you are able sometimes to do with human beings, from its long and delicate hands. It had nine of them at the ends of athletic flexible arms, hands no wider than silver forks, but very sensitive. With these it moved its pieces, or grabbed those of mine that it captured.

For the benefit of chessplayers I may say that I played the king's gambit, and the machine responded with something like the Cunningham defence, but it wandered away into variations that I had never seen or read. Every move of mine produced an answering change in the note of the tune the machine was humming, if you can call it a tune, and Black's move came so quickly that, whatever process of thought there was among all those wires, it must have been instantaneous: not like the slower process of our reasoning; something more like our instinct.

I learned from that game something new of the intricacies of the Cunningham gambit; but I learned something else besides an example of the wisdom of that machine: I learned something of its petulance and bad manners. For as it began to win, which it did after half an hour, it began to slam down its pieces, as I scarcely noticed at first, so absurd it seemed; but soon it was unmistakable that the machine was frivolously exhibiting a silly and vulgar triumph. So this was what Allaby Methick had in his house, a mind greater than Man's, at any rate greater than mine, but a tawdry and vulgar mind. And the thought suddenly came to me: If it behaves like that when winning, what would it do if it lost? Then Methick played the monster, or whatever you care to call it, I am sure with the hospitable intention of putting me at my ease by letting me see that I was not the only person to be beaten by a machine, but that it could beat anyone else. At any rate it soon beat Methick, slamming its pieces down at the end with an even vulgarer display of its sensitive flexible arms than what it had shown to me, and humming in a contented way that suggested an absurd self-satisfaction. Methick opened a cupboard then and brought out a decanter of cut-glass and two tumblers and water, and we both had some Irish whiskey.

'Well, what do you think of it?' he asked in a glowing voice; and I praised his wonderful machine as well as I could. But Methick sensed that my praise, which ought to have come so easily, was being held back by something. In the end he got it out of me: the intellect of the thing was amazing, but what of its character.

'Character?' said Methick.

'Yes,' I said. 'Do you like to have it in the house?'

He got my point then. 'Yes,' he said, 'it's showy and vulgar; but I don't mind about that. It's its intellect that I got it for.'

'Yes,' I said. 'Yes, of course. But doesn't one sooner or later always come up against the other thing, if it's there?'

'Its vulgarity, you mean?' said Methick.

'Exactly,' I said.

'Oh, I don't think so,' said Methick. 'I am only interested in its intellect.'

That was all very well, I thought. But what would the monster be interested in? And what might it do with its long flexible arms? But I didn't say anything more. You don't decry any treasure that any host shows you, especially when you have seen nothing like it before, and are not likely ever to be able to afford to get such a thing yourself. So I said no more about it. I wish I had now.

I went home soon after that second game, pondering as I walked along the slope of the downs. On those downs were often found some of the earliest of the crude axe-heads with which Man had slowly won his victory over the beasts, till aided by grimmer weapons he had obtained dominion over the world which he had held for what seems to us to be a long time. Now something was loose that was more mighty than Man. I saw that machines were already getting the mastery, and taking from Man his dominion over the earth. Wherever I looked I saw signs of it. It was no consolation to reflect that Man made the machine. Its origin mattered not: only that it was mightier than he. Had the negroes risen in America and seized power, it could not have consoled the white man there to remember that the negroes had been brought in by the Anglo-Saxon race. And here in England our labour-saving devices had been ousting men from employment for fifty years, and influencing their ideas, until there was scarcely a house in England that had no fancies, given permanent form in metal, that were the fancies no longer of Man, but of the machine. And now, to reveal to me clearly what I had long suspected, this machine that, for all its vulgarity, was a power superior to us. I am a chess-player, and I had tested it. Had we had our day, I wondered? The megatherium, the mammoth and all the great lizards had had theirs. Was our turn coming too?

When I reached home I forgot these gloomy thoughts; but they remained at the back of my mind; and when a day or two later I went over to Otbury again, and saw Methick at the chess-club at our usual hour, they all awoke and troubled me once more. Something of these gloomy fears I almost conveyed to Methick; but, whether he listened or not, he was too preoccupied with the wonder of his mechanical thinker to appreciate what it was that I was trying to indicate. 'The thing,' he said, 'is playing an entirely new opening. Of course it is too good for me, but it ought to be shown to the masters. I don't believe anything like it has ever been played.'

'Yes,' I said. 'But don't you think it is a pity to let anything like that get too clever for us?'

'I think the masters ought to see it,' he said.

I saw then that we were on different sides. He wanted to show what this wonderful thing could do. I wanted to see Man hold his place, a place that none should usurp. It was no use to say any more. We had both lost interest now in playing each other, but Methick asked me to come to his house again, and this I gladly did, for the more uneasy I was, the more I wanted to see how far the thing had got. Against everything but thought I felt we could hold our own, but this machine was a deeper thinker than we. There was no doubt of it. There is nothing I know in the world that is a surer test of sheer intellect than the chessboard. Hear men argue, and how often one soon finds that neither of them can express what he really means. At strategy, which so closely resembles chess, men may make resounding names; but the purity of that art is spotted and flawed too often by chance, so that, though strategy is the test of power, it cannot quite equal chess as a test of the intellect. So I walked almost in silence beside Allaby Methick, over mint and thyme on the downs through that summer's evening, a prey to vague fears.

When we got to the little house and went into the sitting-room, there was the monster, concealed by its walnut panels, sitting before its chess-table. On that table was a strip of paper such as chessplayers use on which to record a game, and two sharp pencils and a knife that had lately been used to sharpen them, with the blade still open and pencil-marks on the blade. The steel hands were folded and idle.

'Look here,' I said to Methick. 'I don't want to interfere with anything in your house. But do you quite trust that machine?'

'Why not?' he asked.

'It's cleverer than we,' I said.

'Oh, yes,' he said, with an obvious pride in it.

'Well,' I said, 'supposing it should get jealous.'

'Jealous?' said Methick.

'Yes,' I said. 'There are two kinds of jealousy; one wholly despicable, which resents all superiority. People suffering from that kind would hate an archbishop for his sanctity. But there is another kind, one with which it might be easier to sympathize, the kind that does not like inferiority, and that cannot tolerate it when it is in power. Suppose it should ever feel that kind. Look at all we have got; and it has nothing. Look at all we can do; and it can only sit there and play chess when you put out the pieces. A mind like that, compelled to play second fiddle. Do you think it would like it?'

'I suppose not,' said Methick.

'Then why have that knife where it can reach it?' I said.

Methick said nothing, but removed the knife. I couldn't say any more, because I saw that Methick did not like my interference, and did not relish it more for being right. So I did not say anything more against his pet, but sat and watched him play, man against machine, and saw Man being beaten. Again that vulgar display of unseemly triumph, and I wondered once more what the thing would do if it lost.

'Would you care to play?' asked Methick. I said I would, and sat down and played against the monster. I took no interest in its opening, or in any of its play as such; but I watched its speed and its forestalling of all my plans, and its easy victory. Undoubtedly it was a superior intellect. Its slamming down the pieces with those steel hands as it began to win, its throwing the captured pieces on the floor; and the contemptuous triumph of its final move and its insolent humming, were not only disgusting, but gave rise in me to uneasy forebodings as to what might be brought upon us by such an intellect combined with this crude behaviour. Methick must have seen that I was annoyed with his pet, and may have thought that it was because I had been beaten. Whatever his reason, he put the chessmen away and put down a portable wireless-set on the table and turned it on, and we got some gentle music that Beethoven had written for a lady named Elise, which was a very pleasant change from the noisy exultations of the triumphant machine. I saw from the way that Methick handled his set, almost from the way he looked at it, that this was the secondary interest in his life. Chess was the first, and that his grim machine gave him; and the second was the concert-halls of the world, to which his little portable set was a doorway.

When the music was over he opened the back of his portable set and took out from it what is called a wet battery, a rectangular glass jar full of a dark green liquid, and looked at it with the care that a hunting man will give to his horse's food. He had a large table of inlaid wood in that room, but, like many a man living alone, he used only one table for everything, and he tended the needs of his wireless on the table with boxwood and ebony squares on which he played chess with the monster, while he rested his cup of coffee on the only unoccupied corner. Cheered by the music that Methick had so thoughtfully turned on, I said good night, and walked home in the calm of an evening that was glowing with early stars. I will not say that I do not mind being beaten at chess, for there is nobody who does not mind, and nobody would believe me. But I will say that my defeats at chess were not the principal reason of my reluctance to visit Methick again; the principal reason was my dislike of sitting in front of something that was gloating all the time over its intellectual superiority, and which, as soon as the course of the game made that superiority evident, manifested its insolent delight as noisily as it could.

One could not readily put up with such rudeness from an equal; but the knowledge, which every move demonstrated more surely, that the thing was superior to me made it quite doubly as galling. If Methick liked to put up with it, let him, I thought. But for myself I kept away. I had other interests of course besides chess and music and Methick. I am married. But my wife is not interested in chess, and I doubted being able to tell her about that machine in such a way that she would have believed me. Always at evening, at the time that I used to play chess with Methick at Otbury, I used to think of him. But I felt sure that he would be at the little chess-club no more, and that he would be playing with his machine. At sunset I used especially to think of him, finding in that ominous look that sometimes comes over the hills as the sun goes down a certain harmony with feelings equally vague that I had about what might be going to happen to Methick. One day as the sun was setting a brilliant vermilion I had that feeling stronger than ever, something in the sky and in my mind, and all the way between, something ominous. I said to my wife: 'I must go over and see Methick.'

She said, 'You have not been playing chess with him lately.'

I said, 'No. That is why I must go.'

So I walked over the grass and thyme on the slope of the downs, as moths were sailing abroad, and came in the gloaming to Methick's gate, and walked through his garden and found his door ajar and went in. And there was Methick at his usual table, but not playing chess. His portable set was on the boxwood and ebony squares with the jar of green acid beside it, and Methick was doing something or other to its works, which I do not understand.

'Not playing chess?' I said.

'No,' he answered. 'The B.B.C. are doing the whole of Beethoven's concertos. It's the Emperor tonight. I can't miss that. I can play chess any time.'

'Look here,' I said. 'You don't suppose; you don't imagine, I mean; that that thing you've got could ever be jealous of the time you are giving to your wireless-set.'

'Jealous?' he said.

'I've seen a dog jealous of a cat,' I replied. 'Very jealous. And, you know, a dog is nothing, intellectually, compared to that machine of yours. Neither of them, for the matter of that, could compare for subtlety with either of those things that you've got.'

'Subtlety?' said Methick.

'Yes,' I said. 'There's no emotion a dog can feel that that thing of yours can't. Or a man for that matter. *I* can't outwit it. And, if you don't mind my saying so, it's got a nasty sort of a character. And it could be jealous.'

'I mind very much,' said Methick. 'It's a wonderful thing. It cost me all the money I had to spare, and more. And you practically tell me I've wasted it. And why? Because it beat you at chess?'

'No, it isn't that,' I said.

'Why, then?' he asked.

I couldn't explain. Perhaps I ought to have. But it wasn't easy, once I'd annoyed him.

'It can outplay the Cunningham,' I said as a sort of a warning. But he wouldn't take it.

'Have a game with it,' he said, to stop me arguing with him, as much as anything.

'No thanks,' I said. 'You have a game with it.'

And he did. I lifted the wireless-set off for him. Nobody troubled to move the battery. And Methick set the board and sat down, and with his coffee on the other side of the table from which the battery stood, he made the first move, which set everything in motion, and the machine answered. And then I witnessed a most astonishing thing: this brilliant intellect, this master chessplayer, played trivial and silly moves. Its first move, which I record for the benefit of chessplayers, was Pawn to Queen's Rook's fourth, and its second was Pawn to King's Rook's fourth. It had lost its temper. It was evidently jealous of Methick's interest in wireless, the set being right in front of it on its own table, and the mysterious Hertzian waves, for all I know, running through its massive and barbarous brain and getting all mixed up with its savage emotions; and it was sulking. After those first useless moves, having shown its petulance, it settled down to play properly, and a very interesting game resulted, but it did not play with its usual speed. Methick won. How it happened I never quite knew. It is not easy at chess to recover from two bad moves; and yet I think the machine did; and the solution to the mystery of that master mind being beaten by a poor player was revealed to me by the sudden exclamation of Methick just as he won, 'I forgot to oil it!'

I was the last man that saw him alive, and so I must attend

the inquest. He died of poison. Sulphuric acid, which he drank with his coffee. There is no doubt of that. Is it any use my telling this story in court? Will the coroner or his jury believe that the machine was jealous of the interest in another machine, showed right in front of its face, and angry at not being given its due ration of oil? Will they believe that those steel arms reached out while Methick was out of the room, and picked up the jar of acid and tipped some into his coffee? I think not.

A NEW MURDER

In the little town of Trembley there is a blue lamp at the end of the main street, and under it is the doorway of the police-station, through which one evening of a summer's day went in a Mr Crarson, who owned a house three or four miles from Trembley, and asked to see the inspector. A police-sergeant showed Mr Crarson in to a small room, in which the inspector was sitting at a table, Inspector Mullens. He got up to shake hands with Mr Crarson, whom he knew, and asked him what he could do for him, and heard this odd story.

'I have come about a murder,' he said.

'A murder, Mr Crarson?' said the inspector. 'Where has it happened?'

'It hasn't happened yet,' said Crarson; 'but I think it may, and it seems to me that it might be better to stop it than to hang the murderer afterwards.'

'Certainly,' said the inspector. 'And who is it that is going to be murdered, if I may ask?'

'Me,' said his visitor.

'You, Mr Crarson?' said the inspector. 'Who by?'

'By Mr Tarland I think,' said Crarson.

'Mr Tarland? Mr Tarland of Hiverwold? He'd never do such a thing, Mr Tarland wouldn't. Why do you think that he has any design against you? Have you ever quarrelled?'

'No,' said Crarson. 'But he has invented a breakfast food and put it upon the market.'

'Oh, yes,' said Inspector Mullens. 'I know. We all know Tarland's Jimjims. I eat them myself. But may I ask why that should make him want to murder you?'

148

'Because I know how they are made,' Crarson replied. 'And Tarland knows that I know.'

'Not as good as they're supposed to be, aren't they?' said the inspector.

'By no means,' said Crarson.

'Well, I know there are secrets in trade,' the inspector said. 'And tradesmen may not like them to get out. But Mr Tarland would never commit a murder on that account. Not a gentleman like him.'

'They say there's a million behind Jimjims,' said Crarson. 'And even more. A man might do a lot to save a million.'

'Not Mr Tarland,' said the inspector. 'And besides, I eat Jimjims myself every day. So there can't be much harm in them.'

'I know how they're made,' said Crarson.

'Well, you may be right,' the inspector said. 'But he wouldn't commit a murder on that account.'

'A man that would sell Jimjims would,' said Crarson.

'Have you any evidence?' asked Inspector Mullens.

'Yes,' said Crarson.

'Oh, you have? And may I ask what it is?'

'There is a bullet-hole in the window of my bedroom.'

'Oh,' said the inspector, 'that is serious. I must come and look at the bullet-hole.'

'Well, I wouldn't say a bullet-hole for certain,' said Crarson; 'but a round hole in a window-pane.'

'I must come and see it,' said Inspector Mullens. 'When did it happen?'

'Yesterday, while I was out,' said Crarson.

'Oh, while you were out. Then he didn't shoot at you?'

'He may have thought I was in, and hoped that the bullet might hit me.'

'Oh,' said the inspector. 'Not a very careful murderer.'

'No,' said Crarson. 'But one doesn't like to have bullets flying about one's bedroom.'

'Have you found the bullet?'

'No,' said Crarson.

'We can't proceed to any action on your evidence,' said the inspector, 'if no bullet can be discovered. But I will come and look for myself. Don't allow anyone to enter the room till I come.'

So Crarson returned to his house, and told his housemaid not to go to his bedroom. But she had already done the room and swept up a little broken glass, and seen the round hole in the window-pane and noticed nothing else unusual whatever. And soon after, the inspector arrived. Strong and silent are words so often used to describe men that the phrase has become hackneyed, and yet I must use it to describe his car, for it had an uncanny way of slipping up a hill, and arrived at Crarson's house with only the slightest hum.

'Now, let's see the room where the shooting occurred,' said he.

And Crarson led the way upstairs to his bedroom. And there was the window-pane with the round hole in the middle of it, about the size of a sixpence.

'There was a little broken glass,' Crarson explained. 'But my housemaid swept it up. I think we could get it for you, if you would care to see it.'

'No, that won't be necessary,' said the inspector, looking at the opposite wall. 'But any bullet entering that window should have hit that wall, and I can see no mark on it. If it was fired from very close below, the slant could have taken the bullet into the ceiling. But there is no mark on the ceiling, and a shot from just under your window would have been surely heard by somebody in your house. It couldn't have hit the floor unless it was fired from an aeroplane. Let us look at the wall more carefully.'

So they looked at the wall, and the only mark they found was the mark of an old nail.

'Nothing hard enough there,' said the inspector, 'to have stopped a bullet and bounced it down to the floor. And there would have been some scratch on any such thing if there was. And your housemaid found no bullet. Nothing, you say, but a little broken glass. We can only assume that whatever the missile was bounced back from the broken glass. Not a very useful missile for murder. Still, we'll look outside.'

And they looked outside on the lawn and nothing was there but one tiny triangular fragment that fitted the edge of the hole, and which flashed in the grass like a diamond, so that they easily saw it. Nothing else could they see.

'Well, Mr Crarson,' said the inspector, 'I quite see that the break in your window has caused you anxiety. And your anxiety led you to complain to us. I am not blaming you. At the same time, we have a certain amount of work to get through, and . . .'

'I am very sorry,' said Crarson.

'Oh, never mind,' said the inspector. 'It is just that we have these other things to do.'

And then he was away in his powerful car.

For the rest of that day Crarson worried off and on about having gone to Trembley and troubled the police and having received the inspector's veiled rebuke. And next morning, while he was downstairs, he heard a sound from his bedroom and ran up and found another hole in the same window-pane and some broken glass, and nothing else on the floor. Only twenty-five yards in front of that window was a rhododendron shrubbery, and the shrubbery ran up to a little wood. There had been no sound of a shot, but the housemaid from another room beside an open window had heard a noise from the shrubbery, which had sounded to her like an air-gun, though she did not describe it too precisely, for fear of incriminating her nephew by too exact knowledge, for he was armed with an air-gun and sometimes shot sparrows there when he should have been doing other work. Crarson would not let the housemaid enter his bedroom, but took a look round, saw a fragment of broken glass, and went out and locked the door. Then he went to his telephone and rang up Inspector Mullens. Inspector

Mullens had arranged that morning to meet Mr Tarland accidentally, and had talked to him about his licence for killing a pig, and gradually led the topic round to Crarson; and Tarland had shown no animosity against Crarson, beyond saying, 'He is one of these food faddists.' And Mullens had quickly decided that there was no quarrel on Tarland's part. Dealing with Crarson was more difficult, for the man was obviously frightened, and seemed entirely convinced that Tarland intended, to quote the inspector's coarse metaphor when talking of the case to his sergeant, to 'do him in'.

'Please come over at once,' Crarson said on the telephone. But Inspector Mullens sent his sergeant. Sergeant Smegg came over in that fast car, and thoroughly inspected the room, and found some small fragments of glass on the carpet and no mark of a bullet whatever anywhere in the room. This much he reported to the inspector, and added, 'I saw a flea on his bed, sir.'

'For goodness sake,' said Inspector Mullens, 'say nothing of that. There's nothing gentlemen like less than anything of that sort. If we were to insult him by mentioning fleas (and he would take it as an insult) he'd be harder to manage than ever. Stick to the clues, which is what you were sent to find; and, whatever you do, don't be coarse.'

'I'm sorry, sir,' said the sergeant.

'He's a difficult man to deal with, you see,' said Inspector Mullens.

'I quite understand, sir,' said Sergeant Smegg.

Then the inspector telephoned to Mr Crarson and told him that the sergeant's report, after thorough investigation, showed no dangerous missile whatever, and that the damage could have only been caused by boys with catapults or throwing some harmless thing, and that such boys would be traced and dealt with in due course.

Next morning it happened again. Still nothing more could be found than minute fragments of glass, and this time Crarson telephoned to Old Scotland Yard, dialling Blackfriars double

O, double O, for he felt he would get no help from Inspector Mullens. He told them all that had happened, and they sent down a car that afternoon, and there were three men in it besides the policeman who drove it: they were an inspector, an authority upon poisons and another on germs. Where the splinters of glass had lain they cut a strip from the carpet and took it away with them, locking up the room before they left, Crarson having had his bed, his brushes and razor removed to another room.

'That will be all right now, sir,' said the inspector, 'if you don't let anyone know outside the house that you have changed your room.'

'But what do you think it is?' asked Crarson.

'We'll let you know in a few days, sir,' said the inspector. 'It will be all right.'

'But it wasn't all right, for in a few days Crarson was dead. He died of plague. No germs were found on the carpet, under analysis, nor poison either. One thing the inspector from London had seen, though he didn't say so to Crarson, was that the glass on the floor was not the glass from the window: it was thinner than that, and was in fact the missile, a hollow glass bullet fired from some large kind of air-gun. It had broken the window and broken itself, and come in with its deadly contents. What those contents were the scientists from Old Scotland Yard never found out, though it was all pieced together afterwards, too late to save Crarson. The only one who really discovered the fatal missile was Sergeant Smegg from Trembley, though he did not know what it was. He saw and reported a flea, but he did not know that it was a plague flea, something that through history has killed more men than artillery ever has done, and there were large numbers of them in Crarson's bed. Where Tarland got the impregnated fleas nobody ever found out. But the funny thing was that he died, too. He must have been careless in handling the goods, as he would have probably called them; failing to see, as those men often do, that an evil he had intended for one of the mere public would come home to himself.

A TALE OF REVENGE

'REVENGE,' said the retired detective, 'that is the worst passion of all, when it really gets going. Doing to the other man what he has done to you, or even only what he may have wanted to do to you, if you find out in time. There's a limit to avarice: it is limited by what a man is able to get out of it. And they'll do a lot for love; but a man in love is not such a brute to start with as what a revengeful man naturally is. So for really horrible crimes I put revenge first.'

Every man has a story to tell, if it can be got out of him, and I had got into conversation with the old detective over a trifle, sitting on the same bench by an esplanade, looking out to sea, and he was telling his story now. I threw in one of those remarks that one makes to prevent silence from settling down, and he went on. 'The worst case I ever knew was a case of revenge. Far the worst case, if my guesses were right. He was one of those brooding fellows that never forgive and if anyone tries to do anything that he doesn't like to one of them, he'll never stop till he's done the same to the other man. That's what they're like: they never forgive. He was one of those.'

'And only some trifle, I suppose,' said I, 'that the other man wanted to do to him.'

'Well, I wouldn't say that,' said Mulgers. That was the old fellow's name. 'No, I wouldn't say that. I wouldn't say that it was a trifle. He did want to eat him.'

'To eat him?' I exclaimed.

'Well, they were in a lifeboat, you see,' said Mulgers. 'In a lifeboat during the war. And they had been there for some days. Quite a while, in fact. And there were only three of them left;

the man Smith and the man that he couldn't forgive, and a small man. Well, Smith and the other man, a man called Henry Brown, were about the same size, and when the last of the others died, I don't know how, Smith made up to the small man all he could. Of course he wanted the survivors, if anything happened to one of the three, to be himself, and the small man. So he curried favour with him in every way that he could, short of giving him food, because there was none of that to give, unless you count a biscuit, which was not much among three men. You may find it hard to believe, but there were no fish-hooks: no one had thought of it. I had the story from Henry Brown and he assured me that it was true: they had put oars in the boat, but had never thought of the fish-hooks. Well, they lived on that biscuit for three days, and on water: they'd thought of the water. It was in the early part of the war: somebody thought of fish-hooks later. If they'd even had a butterfly-net they could have caught some of the flying fishes that sailed by them like blue birds. But they couldn't quite catch them with their hands, and it only made them hungrier to look at them. They shared the biscuit fairly, Henry Brown said; but evidently not the friendship. They did a little rowing, but not very much, not any longer having the strength for it and not very well knowing where they were, all the men in the boat who had known anything of that being dead. Jones was getting on grand with the small man.'

'Who did you say?' I asked.

'Smith,' said the old detective. 'Did I call him Jones? A slip of the tongue. I knew another man of that name. Smith was getting on grand with the small man, and neither of them was talking to Henry Brown, and they had to have food if they were to live any more. Brown was by himself at the other end of the boat. And then that night in the starlight the little man moved over and got talking to Henry Brown, while nobody rowed. And Smith knew what that meant: the other two were quite pally, and the next time anyone went, they were going to be the survivors; and, being so hungry himself, he knew how the others were feeling, and knew what would happen to him. And to the small man too, if it came to that. But him first. Evidently in cases like that, men don't seem to look beyond the next two or three days; and the small man seemed content with his friendship with Henry Brown, even if there was no chance of its lasting a week. There they sat talking away as if they were going to be friends for life. Which of course in a sense they were. Henry Brown never told me what he had meant to do; but it was pretty clear. The little man didn't look much of a fighter, by Brown's account; but they would have been two to one. And then of course, when Smith was gone, the small man would have been easy meat. Not that Henry Brown ever said anything to me about that; but I drew my own conclusions. And Smith knew. A turtle came by next morning, which might have given them a hint that they were somewhere near land, but they couldn't wait, and Henry Brown seems to have made up to the small man more than ever. They didn't catch the turtle; and, though Brown never said so, it looked as if the next meal was going to be Smith. And that's what Smith would never forgive. He tried to recover lost ground with the small man, but it was no good: Brown had got him. It was in the tropics and it was very hot, and he gave him his hat on top of his own to keep off the sun, and was doing what he could in little ways to keep the small man alive.

'I don't know when they planned to eat Smith. Not at all according to Brown. He told me that he was only talking to the small man because he liked him. But Smith had got the idea that that was what he intended to do, and the small man afterwards. And he couldn't forgive it. They were quite near the coast, if they had known it; the West Indies. But Brown couldn't wait. Not that he ever said so. And I fancied that Brown and the small man were just about to do what they had planned when they saw the palms of an island, and a current drifted them to it, as it had been doing all the way across the Atlantic

And presently a motor-boat put out, and brought them in, and nothing happened to Smith. But he could never forgive Brown, or the small man either.

'I never knew what happened to the small man. I fancy he got safely out of Smith's way and is alive still. But Smith and Brown got to London, two very lean men, who no longer weighed much more than seven stone each, and that was mostly bone. And Brown told me this story. He 'phoned one day to Scotland Yard and said he went in fear of his life. Well, everybody did in those days; it was at the height of the Battle of Britain; and we didn't pay much attention at first. And then I was told to go and see him, and he gave me a rambling story about how Smith looked at him. Of course those looks meant more to him than they did to us. I see that now. You see Brown had been thinking of doing the same thing himself, and with all that on his mind he knew just how men looked when they meant to do that.'

'Do what?' I asked.

'What he meant to do to Brown,' said the old detective.

'And what was that?' I asked.

'We never really knew,' he replied.

'The difficulty of course about any story of crime is that, if you don't ask someone from Scotland Yard what happened, you never get to the actual source. And, if you do, they won't give away what they know; only what has been proved. And there was never very much proved in this case. Brown got lodgings in London and so did Smith. And Smith found out where Brown lodged, and used to hang about near his lodgings and look at him. That was what Brown complained of to the police. Well, there's no law against looking at a man, as I pointed out to him. And then he said a curious thing. He said that Smith looked at him hungrily. Of course I ought to have realized that he knew what he was talking about. I see that now. Brown had been hungry himself, you see, and he knew what hunger looked like. One never really knows another man's job. It's our job to watch other men, and we may get to know something about them. Not much, I expect. But we never get to see the things they see. We never see what an artist sees when he looks at a brick wall, or at anything else. We never see what a geologist sees when he looks at the ground. I don't even know what geology is. We don't even see what a fishmonger sees when he looks at his fish, or what a tailor sees in every man he passes, or a doctor for that matter. And I didn't credit Brown with having seen anything I couldn't see in the revengeful face of Smith. Well, I made my report to the Yard, after my talk with Brown. I made it perfectly impartial, just saying what he had told me, and it was all gone into and my superiors decided that there was nothing in it. They couldn't very well have given a man police protection just on account of how another man looked at him, and in the middle of a great war too. They couldn't. It wasn't their fault. They would do the same again. Anyone would.

'Well, you hear of criminals making mistakes. But sometimes their victims do. There was no mistake in this crime; if crime it was; and, mind you, I know nothing about that. We thought Brown mad at the Yard, and no wonder after a month in a rowing-boat. But he may have been right, and yet mad. For if Smith was all that he said he was, Brown must have been mad to have gone to Smith's house. And it was proved that he did. Smith had a small house in Meanacre Street, where he lived all alone and did his own cooking. And there Brown went one evening. He was seen going in. The theory is, and something Brown said to me about having to help himself if we wouldn't bears it out, the theory is that he was trying to make it up with Smith, as he may have thought that that was his only chance. I don't know what he thought. You can't tell at any time just what a man is thinking, and least of all after he has had an experience like that. But whether he was mad or sane he seems to have been trying to make friends with Smith, for they looked very friendly as they were seen going into Smith's house. Of course nobody saw any hungry look on Smith's face; that was a thing that only Brown could see, having once worn the same look himself. Well, in they went and Brown was never seen again. That much was in the papers. More I can't tell you. It was several days before he was missed, and about a week after that before my superiors at the Yard began to go back on what they had decided. And then one day they began to look for Brown and some of them some while later went all over Smith's house. But it was too late and there was no trace of him.'

And the old detective gazed out to sea, perhaps picturing that scene in the boat, and the furious jealousy of the man that he called Smith when Brown got the small man away from him, perhaps merely looking out there so as to say no more to me.

'I suppose Smith got his revenge,' I said after a while.

'You may suppose whatever you like,' he said. 'But we have to go entirely by what we can prove.'

'And you never found anything,' I said.

'Not a bit of him,' said the detective, and gazed out again to sea.

THE SPEECH

'CRIME,' said the old journalist one night at his club. 'One reads a good deal about violence nowadays; but I never read of a crime that would make a story like the one that there was when I was young and quite new to my job. *That* would have made a story. But it was all hushed up. It was a neat crime, that was. You don't get crimes like that now. I don't know why not. People seem slower somehow. Not so inventive. Oh, well; perhaps it is just as well.' He sighed and was silent. A younger journalist, younger by fifty years, said, 'Would you have a whiskey with me, Mr Gauscold?' That was the old fellow's name. 'Oh, well,' he said, 'I don't mind joining you. Thank you very much.' And the whiskeys and sodas were brought, and five or six others in the room, all journalists except me, sat silent, as though expecting something.

And then the young fellow said, 'I'm not trying to get your story, of course. Because you told me it was hushed up. No doubt for some good reason.'

'Yes,' said old Gauscold, 'they were very careful about the peace of Europe in those days. They used to think a lot of it, and they did all they could for it. I suppose they thought they could preserve it if only they were careful enough; and so they were very careful. The crime itself was mentioned in the Press, but barely mentioned and soon forgotten. Of the reason for it nothing was said at all. They were too careful not to disturb the peace of Europe. And that, you see, was what the crime was about. There was a young man, scarcely remembered now, brilliant although he was. He has had his day. The less said of the incident the better; even yet. But I will tell you his name, it was

160

the Honourable Peter Minch. His old father you would never have heard of. A totally obscure old peer, Lord Inchingthwaite. But people heard of Peter Minch in his time. He was an M.P. and the coming man of the Opposition, one of those coming men that you never hear any more of. It is more often *les enfants terribles* that you hear of afterwards. The energy that makes them such a nuisance when young seems needed later on, to make names that will last. Well, Peter Minch is completely forgotten now, but once he was spoken of as the next Prime Minister but three or four, a promise he never fulfilled. At the time that I tell of, when I was quite new to journalism, he was at the height of his reputation. And he was going to make a speech in the House. Things had been simmering to that point for some time, and now he was going to make a speech, and it was known what he was going to talk about. Well, as I told you, we took a lot of care about the peace of Europe in those days, and what this young fellow was going to say just at that time wasn't going to help it.'

'A firebrand was he?' said someone.

'Well I wouldn't say that,' said old Gauscold. 'A bit of a fire-brand perhaps. But his speech on this occasion was going to be distinctly fiery. There is no doubt of that. What he was going to say would have prodded Austria pretty hard; and, if Germany had supported her in what would have been quite justifiable resentment, Russia would not have liked it, and the fat would have been in the fire. It was like that, and the speech much better not made. But there was no stopping him. The Government couldn't do it, of course. And as for the Opposition, he was their fancy man, and they were probably thinking more of how it would embarrass the Government than how it would annoy the Austrians. None of the rest of them would have done any-thing so tactless as to make such a speech at that time, as young Minch was going to make; but stopping him was another matter. I don't think it even occurred to any of them to try. A party, especially in opposition, never does stop its brilliant young men.

'And then the extraordinary thing happened, the shadow of

the coming event. A man walked into the central office of Minch's party, without giving his name, and said quite clearly that he had sure information that was not exactly a message, but was none the less sure, and must not be taken as a threat but only a warning, that that speech would never be made.

"'What do you mean?" said the Chairman, before whose table he stood.

"'I mean," said the man, "that there is an organization with which I have nothing to do, nothing whatever, who are determined to stop that speech, who know what Mr Minch is going to say, and who are powerful enough to do what they threaten. It is not I that threaten. I only come to warn you."

"'Do you mean," said the Chairman of the Party, "that they are going to use force?"

"'They will use whatever is necessary," said the stranger.

"'Then they are prepared to resort to crime?" the Chairman said.

"'If necessary," said the other. "But I have come to warn you, so that you can stop him by peaceful means."

"'Crime!" said the Chairman. "Are you aware . . ."

'But the stranger hastily said: "I am no accessory. You can give me in charge if you like, and try to prove that my warning is a threat. Then you will have no more warning, and it will happen. Would it not be better to stop him?"

"'Certainly not," said the Chairman. "We will not give way to crime."

"'We," said the unknown man, "that is to say they, consider war to be the greater evil."

"'War?" said the Chairman. "Who says we are making war?"

"'Their information," said the stranger, "is that what Mr Minch is going to say just at this time will bring war nearer. They are well informed, and they have told me they are convinced that their slight violence, even if it causes the death of one man, is preferable to the risk of disturbing the peace of Europe and the loss of thousands of lives."

'Of course they didn't think in millions in those days. Then he went on to tell them that the prohibition only referred to the House of Commons, and to the present time while things were a bit critical in what we used to call the Chancelleries of Europe. He could make the speech outside if he liked. Mob oratory, as he called it, would not affect the situation, but the speech in the House and the debate that would follow were not to take place.

'He was quite right about what Minch might have said outside the House. The Press would have had the sense not to report it, for one thing. But what was said in the House they had to report. And of course the world would read it, whatever was said there. And the world was uneasy just then, and it would not have been good for it.

'Well, as politely as possible, and they used to be very polite in those days, the Chairman told him to go to Hell. And as the man went he turned round in the door and said, "That speech will not be delivered. Under no circumstances will it be delivered in the House."

'There was silence in the central office for a while after that. Then the Chairman said to his secretary. "What do you think we ought to do?"

'"I think we should give him in charge," said the secretary.

'But by then he had gone. What they did do was to tell Scotland Yard. And what *they* did was to take the matter up at once, and to assure the Chairman of the Party that to prevent any interference with any member going to the Houses of Parliament, especially where there was a distinct hint of murder, the entire police force of the metropolis would be available. They took the thing up at once. I think they must have known something about the organization that was making that threat; more than they ever said. They must have known, because they said at once that the man that had called on the Chairman of the Party would have been a man named Hosken. And that's who he turned out to be. The Chairman asked them then if they would arrest him. But the Chief Inspector said Better not. Better leave him at large, and he might give them more information. And he did.

'Police protection on an enormous scale was given to Minch at once. That was on a Monday, and on Tuesday Scotland Yard advised the removal of Minch to a house on the Victoria Embankment, little more than a hundred yards from the Houses of Parliament, and the speech was to be next day. The head office of Minch's Party, having put the whole matter in the hands of the police, got Minch to do as they asked, and he moved to the new house that morning. I don't know what compensation was paid to the owners; but there was no difficulty about that. When he tried soon afterwards to go out for a walk, so many plain-clothes men followed him that he went back to the house; and policemen, both in uniform and plain clothes, waited all round it. While things were like that with Minch the Chairman of the Party was sitting in his office with a burden removed from his mind, for he felt that the police had everything well in hand, when in walked this extraordinary man again. They let him come in, because they wanted to hear what the fellow had to say. They addressed him by his name this time, and I think it gave the Chairman a little childish pleasure to imply by doing so that they knew all about him, especially as knowing all about everybody and what was going on was rather the job of that central office. You can't win elections without that.

'"Well, Mr Hosken," said the Chairman, "is there anything more that you wished to tell us?"

'A faint smile from Hosken greeted the use of his name. And then he said, "Only to say that all those policemen will not enable Mr Minch to make that speech and start a debate in Parliament, while things are as they are just now abroad."

'"If Mr Minch desires to speak in the House, as he has every right to do, he will certainly do so," said the Chairman.

'"I have come to say," said Hosken, "that if he will put it of for a week, so as to give things time to simmer down, the powerful organization with which a friend of mine is in touch will take no action. Or he can make his speech to the crowd outside. But in the House, with things as they are just at present, that organization forbids it."

"'With things as they are at present!" exclaimed the Chairman. "If you mean the state of affairs in Europe, we are not concerned with them. No one in Europe can deny us free speech."

"'It would be an open defiance," said Hosken, "and would lead to war, if that man Minch gets loose in the House with his dangerous hobby. We know what he means to talk about."

"'Under no circumstances whatever," said the Chairman, "can interference with any policy in the House be tolerated from outside."

"'Your policy will not be interfered with," said Hosken. "Anyone else may speak on it. But that young man Minch cannot be allowed to throw his fireworks about just now amongst Europe's gunpowder, and his speech will not be made."

"'Call a policeman," said the Chairman to his secretary.

"'Yes, sir," said the secretary. "Shall I bring him in here?"

'The remark of the secretary was of course meaningless. But it served to remind the Chairman that Scotland Yard had not wanted to arrest Hosken till they were quite ready for him, and that as he was their only source of information about the intentions of the rest of the gang, he might be better at large.

"'Well, not immediately," said the Chairman, and turning to Hosken, "But you must understand that we cannot tolerate any more blackmail."

"'Certainly, sir," said Hosken. "Only there will be no speech in Parliament by Mr Minch for at least a week. And, if you stop him peacefully, there will be no need for violence."

'Then he smiled and walked out.

"'Well, of all the . . ." said the Chairman.

"'They evidently mean business, sir," said the secretary.

I was a guest, I should explain, among all those journalists. And at this point I enquired of old Gauscold if he knew the exact words that were said in that office.

'Well, the Press, you see,' he said, 'has to get information.'

And all the others nodded. And I felt that my query had been rather silly.

'Well, that's how things were,' went on the old journalist; 'tension rather acute in those chancelleries that we used to talk about, and this fiery young man going to start a debate in the House, that would put all the fat in the fire, and perhaps set it overflowing, and scalding all Europe; and a powerful organization of blackmailers, for they were nothing less, determined that that debate should never take place, and that one man's murder was nothing compared to war. As I have told you, we took the peace of Europe very seriously in those days. And against the blackmailing gang was practically the whole of the police-force of the metropolis, warned in good time by what was obviously one of the gang. I needn't go into the precautions taken by the police. They took them all. Minch was constantly under observation by at least two of them: they even watched his kitchen for poison: and they had a man in every one of the few houses between the house in which they had put him and the Houses of Parliament, and every window of the intervening houses was shut and watched. On the opposite side was the river, and there they had a steamboat with police in it. I doubt if anyone was ever more watched in London. You see, murder was only a small part of it: the right of free speech was concerned as well, and the dignity of Parliament, and of course the dignity of the police-force, for they weren't going to have a man they were guarding murdered before their eyes, after due warning by a gang that had impudently proclaimed that it was going to do it. They soon ran Hosken down, but did not arrest him. All they did was to keep him under observation. I fancy they thought that he would be more useful to them that way. Seeing that he was obviously followed, he turned round to a plain-clothes man behind him and actually repeated to him what he had said in the central office, "That speech is not going to be made by Mr Minch in the House." Of course the plain-clothes man pretended that he did not understand.

'That was on Tuesday. On Wednesday morning everything was all ready. Minch was going to speak at 7. The Speaker had been approached, and it was all arranged that his eye should be caught by Minch about 7 o'clock. Minch's whole family were going to be there, his old father in the Peer's Gallery, and all the rest of his family, except one uncle, in the Ladies' Gallery, two aunts and three sisters. They used to sit behind a grille in those days. The uncle, Lord Inchingthwaite's brother, could not attend, because the Strangers' Gallery was to be closed on the advice of the police. And they had some female detectives even in the Ladies' Gallery. The police had a cab for Minch which was entirely bullet-proof, even to windows of plate glass that was over an inch thick. All this may seem absurd, but the police were on their mettle, having been challenged by a gang who repeated their challenge that morning with several anonymous letters, all saying "Mr Minch will not make that speech today."

'Well, the precautions were more than I have told you, more than would have been taken for moving bullion from the Bank of England. They asked Minch to be at the House by 3 o'clock, and he raised no difficulties. And there he moved in the armoured cab with his enormous escort. They could have had soldiers too, but the police would not hear of it. They said they could do the job themselves, and they turned out in force and marched all round Minch's cab, the hundred yards or so to the House of Commons, and there they got him in safety. As they arrived a messenger-boy handed a note to the inspector in charge of the guard. He opened it and saw one more of those anonymous notes, saying, "Mr Minch will not make that speech today." He smiled, because once inside the precincts of the Houses of Parliament murder was quite impossible. Not that a prime minister had not once been murdered in that very house, but there had been no warning then, and now the lobbies were packed with police. Once the Houses of Parliament had nearly been blown up by gunpowder in the cellars, but there were police in the cellars now. Minch walked in, and the inspector breathed easily. He was seen going into the chamber. Even members had been unostentatiously watched, and I believe it had been ascertained, though I don't know how, that none of them had a weapon in his pocket. Of course I heard very little about those precautions, because they amounted to breach of privilege; but they were taken, for all that.

'Minch's family were to arrive at half past 6. At 3 o'clock a dull debate opened. And yet the tension was electric, for everyone present knew the threat of the gang. There may have been secret hopes among a few of the Government's supporters that the threat of the gang would be realized, for it was the Government that had to deal with the trouble that was simmering in Europe and would have to clear up the mess as well as they could if this young fellow Minch should cause it all to boil over. But the dignity of Parliament was at stake, and most of the members, even on the side to which Minch was going to cause so much trouble, put that first. Slowly the tension heightened, as the hands of the clock moved round to 4. And in that heightened tension everyone seemed to know what everyone else was thinking. They knew when any speaker was intending to be funny, and all laughed quickly and nervously, even before the little joke came. The inspector in charge had completed his tour of the lobbies. "Everything all right?" said the sergeant-at-arms to him.

'"All right, sir," said the inspector. "If practically the whole of the police force can't prevent one gentleman from being murdered, when they have had ample warning and taken every precaution, we should all resign, or be sacked."

'The sergeant-at-arms nodded his head.

'"Thank you, Inspector," he said. "I knew it would be all right."

'At 5 minutes past 4 a note for Mr Minch was handed by a policeman to the inspector, who passed it to the sergeant-at-arms, who went into the chamber and gave it to Minch. Minch opened it and turned white.

"'My father is dead," he said to a member sitting beside him. "He's been murdered."

"'I am terribly sorry," said the other man. "What happened?"

'Minch handed the note to him. His father had been shot dead in his house. The murderer had escaped.

"'And your speech," said the other member. "I am afraid—"

"'No," said Minch. "That can't stop me. Nobody could be sorrier than I am. But private grief is one thing, public duty another. They won't stop me making that speech."

"'But look here," said the other member. "I mean you're a peer."

"'I'm a what!" said Minch.

"'You're a peer now," said the other.

"'My God!" Minch answered.

'After a while he muttered something about it not being known yet. Not verified, I think he said.

"'It will be in all the evening papers," the other member told him.

'Well, that was the end of that. The gang had done it. Of course they didn't attack where a thousand policemen were waiting for them. They attacked as any man of sense would always attack, at the weakest point, where nobody was expecting it. And nobody did think of poor old Lord Inchingthwaite. He was quite obscure, and nobody thought of him at any time. But the moment he died Peter Minch became a peer, and could make no more speeches in the House of Commons. And he couldn't even make his speech in the House of Lords, until he had taken his seat, and all that took time. He did make the speech at a meeting that week in what had been his constituency, but Austria took no notice of that.'

'So war was averted,' said one of us.

'Well, yes,' said old Gauscold. 'Not that it made any difference in the end.'

THE LOST SCIENTIST

THE exact address of all laboratories in which atomic fission is studied in England have not been published, and the little village of Thymedale is probably best known beyond its boundary for its fishing, and only minnow-fishing at that, and not at all for what goes on at the Old Rectory. Yet, in what was the rectory of the parish before the clergyman moved into a smaller house, a little group of scientists are at work all the year round on something that Destiny may use one day to decide the fate of a nation. They are quiet amiable men, and when one of them sits on a wall on a summer's evening to watch either boys of the village, or visiting children from London, catching minnows in bottles, you would say that his work was far from the ruin of cities. And so everyone in the village believes. For from the Old Rectory, in its spacious garden among sunflowers and holly-hocks go large numbers of sewing-machines of a new type, which are sold in the neighbourhood at a quite reasonable price, and the work of the quiet men who reside there is believed to be the perfection of these. These five or six men had been working there for some time, when a new one joined them, a certain professor named Matthew Mornen. Not all in the Old Rectory knew what his job was; indeed, only two of them did, the Chief and his second-in-command, Peters and Brown, and they were talking of him in the garden of the Old Rectory one summer's day, just before he was due to arrive.

A rumour had gone round the village that a Cambridge blue was coming to the Old Rectory; but it was a half-blue that he had once had, and a very long time ago. And when further information arrived, and turned out to be accurate, that the half-blue had been earned for chess, there was disappointment; for, judging chess by the pace of its moves, the village felt that the newcomer would be too slow at everything, to contribute at all to its gaiety. And now Peters and Brown were discussing the new arrival, or rather the problem with which he was coming to deal. The problem was a very simple one to explain, and a very hard one to solve. It was this: they had in the Old Rectory a certain Kreisitch, a man who had once worked for Hitler in that close race, that Hitler lost, to discover the atomic bomb. He was a scientist so able that, when his services were to be had, the country could not afford to reject them. But could he be trusted? That was the problem. His work was undoubtedly worth at least half a dozen battleships. For the strength of nations mainly depended once on the number of battleships they possessed, and half a dozen atomic bombs had now quite as much destructive power as the same number of battleships used to have. On this man's work therefore would depend much of the strength of the nation. For there was no doubt of his capacity. On the other hand there was the risk. Nobody had ever sold battleships. But atomic bombs and, worse still, the secrets that made them, might be passed over many counters.

And so from the Old Rectory in Thymedale a letter had been sent to an address that I do not know, asking for help in the solution of this problem. And the answer had been a promise to send Professor Matthew Mornen, who was now coming. Peters and Brown were agreed, as they walked along a path under tall sunflowers, that the new man would obviously be a detective, and their profitless guesses as to what kind of detective he would be covered the whole of detective fiction and some of real life. Naturally those guesses took some time, and they were long in that garden, for they never spoke among walls of anything that mattered. It was long past the time for their tea, and they were at last about to come in, when a maid brought the new arrival through the house, and out to meet Peters and Brown in the Rectory garden. For one moment a thought flashed in the mind of Peters that here was the greatest detective in the world, a man worthy of work so important, and that he was made up with a skill beyond that of any other detective on earth or in fiction. For he looked a dear old man, as mild a figure as that garden had ever known in all the centuries during which rectors of Thymedale had lived there. All three men shook hands, and they talked awhile and walked slowly into the house for their tea. And before they came to the door that opened into the garden, Peters and Brown both saw, not only that the white side-whiskers of the newcomer were real, but that his whole mild manner was real and that no hawk-eyed detective, no tracker of bandits, walked in the garden beside them. They were astounded. Peters and Brown gave one glance at each other, and then walked into the house, showing the mild old gentleman in before them. They had tea there in absolute silence about the one thing that mattered, while other topics were discussed pleasantly. The others had finished their tea, and later the newcomer was introduced to them, including of course Kreisitch. And what went on in that old house that was once a rectory, during the next few weeks, I do not know, because nobody knows except these men who lived there. But I do know that immense progress was made in atomic fission by the work that was done by Kreisitch, and that the power and might of what is left of our empire was very greatly increased by it. The old professor with the white side-whiskers worked hard too. He got down to work as soon as he arrived. But all I can say that I really know of his work is that he supplied lines and fish-hooks to boys that used to fish from the old bridge with glass bottles. And there he used often to sit, watching the catching of minnows. I am sure that this was no cloak to disguise his actual work, but that he sat there on summer evenings whenever he was not working, because he enjoyed seeing boys catching minnows, he who was to catch Kreisitch, if ever Kreisitch should get away with all his secrets to look for a customer for them at a price of about a million pounds, which is what they very easily should have fetched in any good market that dealt in them.

And then one day it was found out that Kreisitch had done that very thing; he had slipped away about tea-time and taken the code-book with him, a book with many blank pages at the end, on which were written the formulæ of all the secrets that Kreisitch knew. Of course nobody could have prevented him walking out of the house, and nobody had prevented him boarding an aeroplane; but information that he had left the country was accurate and exceedingly swift, and was known at Thymedale before he had been gone two hours. But he had slipped away out of the country, and what was to be done now? Everybody was silent in the room in which they all used to have their tea, as soon as the information had been received and announced by Peters. But everybody looked at Mornen with something in their looks that all of them felt must almost crush the old man. Yet he remained entirely composed.

'What has he got?' asked one of the scientists.

'Everything,' said Peters.

Of course they meant Kreisitch. Nobody there was thinking of anyone else. There were a few short sentences then, telling of the safe and the code-book, and the key that had been given to Kreisitch, the only other man to have the key of that safe beside Peters. And then the silence hung heavy again, while they all looked at Matthew Mornen. For all arrangements about the safe, the key and the code-book had been entirely in his hands. It was he who had arranged that Kreisitch should have that key, and that there should be blank pages in the code-book filled with all that Kreisitch knew of atomic research at Thymedale, with all its formulæ written out. That book itself was the goods that Kreisitch would now hand complete over some foreign counter in exchange for a million pounds. If Mornen had not insisted that Kreisitch should have the key, that silence seemed to say, or if he had not arranged that everything Kreisitch knew should have been written out so neatly for him in that book, if all, in fact, that Mornen had done since he came had not all worked to one end, the disaster would not have been so complete. Then the silence was broken by Peters, who said directly to Mornen, 'What do we do now?'

'Now we catch him,' said Mornen.

'But he's over France by now,' said Peters, 'and will soon be crossing Switzerland on his way eastward.'

And then Mornen explained his plans, and all the work that he had been doing upon the code-book. The code-book had been made very compact. There were secrets that Kreisitch did not know. But everything that he did know, and the private code of that research station, were all in the book. And Mornen had had it fitted with heavy pieces of iron inside the back of the binding, so that, if it ever had to be thrown away to prevent any foreign agent from getting hold of it, and if there were water handy, it would always sink. As there was no water near Thymedale except the little Aren, in which boys of the village waded, there had not seemed to the others to be much use in the iron with which Mornen had been having the back of the book fitted. But, as he had been given an absolutely free hand by those who had sent him down to Thymedale, not even Peters had been able to interfere with him.

Glum and silent sat everyone while Mornen made his long explanation; until Peters interrupted him with the words, 'Then they'll have all that in Latvia in two hours from now.'

'Yes,' said Mornen. 'But they'll never use it. Let me explain a little further. You see, that iron arrangement, that you may have thought rather silly, really contains two things: one of them is what we call Atom Z, of which he has all the details written out in the book; but he does not know that he has actually got a sample with him. And of course you all know what Z can do. We are a long way on from those early experiments at Hiroshima and Nagasaki.'

A gasp went round his hearers, and some were about to speak. 'Wait a moment,' said Mornen. 'The other thing in the back of that book is a little wireless-set, which is able to answer to remote control. Now, we don't want it to go up in Switzerland, and I take it we are right in assuming that he is heading for Latvia with that book.'

All nodded their heads.

'Very well then, gentlemen,' Mornen went on, 'we must give him time to get there. And then I have asked the big station at Upwold to broadcast at intervals of five or ten minutes a message for him to pick up; which is, "Uncle Robert offers three times the price. Listen in at 8 p.m. tonight." That will lure him to listen all right. Money is what all men like him are after. And the prospect of three times the amount he is being offered by what I may call the other side is bound to intrigue him, and he will want to hear if he can get it in safety. And then at 8 o'clock Upwold have promised to turn on the number to which the mechanism in the back of the book responds. Small private sets straying on to that number will not affect it. But Upwold, as you know, is one of the most powerful stations in the world.'

I should explain to my reader, what all knew in the Old Rectory, that Uncle Robert was, as it were, the presiding genius of the private code that they used there, and that such phrases as 'Uncle Robert is coming to tea at five' meant something quite different. All these phrases, with their interpretations, were in the book; so that it seemed certain enough that at 8 p.m. Kreisitch would be bending over his stolen code-book to inter- pret the details of the glittering promise of three times what Latvia would offer him.

'Will he get the message from Upwold?' asked Peters.

'I think so,' said Mornen. 'It is known in all prisons that criminals eagerly read all newspapers that they are given. And this man will be especially anxious during his escape and will lap up all the news he can get. That code-book, with all its formulæ, will go up at 8 o'clock in any case. And I think we shall hear no more of Kreisitch. Well, I can do no more now. My work is over. I think I'll go and sit by the river.'

And later, news did filter through, of an accident to a hotel in Latvia; and no more was heard outside the Old Rectory at Thymedale of the formulæ that were known there as Atom Z. As for Kreisitch, I have called this tale The Lost Scientist. He is indeed lost, and in every way. And it is very doubtful if any of the atoms of which he was once composed have any survival in their original state.

THE UNWRITTEN THRILLER

THERE is a club in London which has a cosy room, smaller than any of the rest in the club, in which are no chairs such as one moves about, but only deep soft comfortable ones arranged more or less in a crescent before a large fireplace, in which all through the cold months there is always a fine fire burning, and often one man standing in front of it, not always the same man; and, though he may start the conversation, talk is general, coming up from chair after chair. It is the room that I like best in all the club.

On the evening in which this story begins it was somewhere late in November and things in that room were much as I always remember them, a man before the fireplace, members in most of the chairs, and talk going merrily; until somebody said, 'I hear that Tather is taking up politics.'

It was then that another man leaned forward suddenly from his deep chair, and said with the utmost vehemence, 'If any of you have any influence whatever with Tather, for God's sake keep him from politics.'

Naturally many of us said, 'Why?'

The man sat leaning forward with an intense look in his eyes, a dark-haired man named Indram, with a thin aquiline face, and for some moments he seemed to take no notice of our questions, as though he had said all that it was needful to say.

In silence we watched him, till it appeared to occur to him that he should say something more. 'I can't tell you why,' he said. 'You must take my word for it. But I am not speaking lightly.' Then one of us said, 'I am sure you are not, and we know that you never do. But Tather is going to stand for

Parliament, and if we are to stop him doing that, supposing we can, we must have a pretty grave reason for doing it.'

'There is a grave reason,' said Indram. 'But I can't tell you what it is.'

We were all silent awhile after that. We knew this man Indram; we knew that he meant what he said; but surely it was reasonable to ask for a little more before we backed his judgement, however much we might trust it.

And then the man who was standing in front of the fire summed up the feelings of most of us, when he said, 'We can see that you have some serious reason for what you say, and that you feel you must keep it secret. We are prepared to back your judgement, you know; but you must give us some clue as to what we shall be doing, if we do what you want.'

'Yes,' said Indram, 'yes. Well, then, I can tell you this much. Politics are exciting things and call up a man's utmost energies. If Tather should take part in anything like that, the most serious result would follow. I can't say more.'

'You mean there is some trace of madness in him?' said the man before the fire.

'No,' said Indram.

'Violence, then,' said the other.

'No,' said Indram, 'I wouldn't say that, provided he is not opposed when his utmost energies have been stimulated. There are many activities at which he would be all right. But I can tell you no more.'

When we saw that there was no more to be got out of Indram there was a good deal of talk in low voices, and I don't know what was decided. He had certainly asked a great deal of the two or three who were Tather's principal friends. He had expected them to rely entirely upon his judgement and to act in a high-handed and very unusual way on the strength of it, and I could not make out from what they were saying to each other in low voices what they were going to do. A certain embarrassment seemed to be over all our little party, imposed by the vehemence of his appeal to us, and by the feeling that we were not going to help him. For how could any of us take such action as he demanded, with no more grounds than he gave us on which to act? And we did not like to tell him straight out that we would not help him. So one by one looked at their watches and went out of the room, till no-one was left in those chairs but he and I.

It was not that I meant to help him, where the others were going to fail, or that I felt any less embarrassed than they did at sitting there listening to a preposterous request that in the end one could only refuse. What kept me there was the idea that, if I could talk to Indram alone, I might possibly be able to get from him the strange story that he would not tell in public. For strange I was sure it must be. And talk to him I did, and at first he would tell me no more than the rest. And then somehow I got him to speak. I don't know how. Certainly by no subtle questions of mine. Rather by silences than anything else. He had been sitting silent too. And I let the silence weigh on him. I think that it was to break that silence as much as anything, that he began to speak. But one never knows.

He began like this, 'You know the laws about criminal libel and slander. If you fall foul of any of them, don't come to me for help. I shall say nothing in your favour. If you repeat anything I say, it is your funeral, not mine. Stop Tather if you can, but don't quote me. Stop him: I'll tell you why. I'll go back to the beginning of it. I asked him one day in the club what he was doing, not because I thought he was doing anything. And he told me that he was going to write a novel. I said that I didn't know he wrote, and he admitted he didn't; but he said that the majority of people read detective stories, and that it wasn't so much a question of writing, but that if anybody could invent a perfectly satisfactory way of murdering someone, a murder that would defy detection, there would be at least a million readers waiting for it, and any publisher would pay accordingly. That was his idea.

'He went on to say that he realized that it was not easy, because the whole thing had been exploited for more than a generation, and must be like a mine that was nearly worked out; but that if the murder he mentioned could be invented, then that was the way to make money. And I'm afraid I encouraged him at first. I told him to read several good writers, so as to have some idea of what style was, and to have something ready when his idea came, and I said I felt sure the idea would come to him one day if he worked at it. In fact, I appeared surer of it than he was, because I felt that he wanted encouragement. I'm sorry I gave it now.' He gazed into the fire in silence then, as though his story had been told.

'Why are you sorry?' I asked Indram. And he came back from whatever dream he saw in the fire, and went on with his story. 'One day he told me that he had got the idea, a plot that he had worked out in every detail, the undetectable murder. And he was so sure of it that I believed him. You can always tell when a man has got a good thing. I don't know how. But you can tell. And I felt sure that Tather had done it. So I gave him several bits of advice, so that he should not spoil his good thing. For I believed in him and believed there was money in it. Oh, it was only little things that I told him. I told him not to use nouns as adjectives, and not to mention his stomach because it was not interesting. Too many young writers tell you they felt an uneasy feeling in the pits of their stomachs. And told him something about punctuation. Not how to use it; that was his own affair; but not to let anybody else pepper his story with more commas after he had done: and I told him what hyphens were. All small things. But I wanted him to make the most of the idea that, whatever it was, he had really persuaded me that he possessed. He hadn't decided then whether the hero was to be, as is usual in all detective stories, the detective.

'Being sure that the mystery of this murder of his was insoluble, he felt it would spoil the whole thing to have a detective find it out, and was inclined for that reason to have the murderer for a hero. That would make it a gangster tale I told him, and advised him against it, and he said he would do as I recommended. But people don't really take advice so much as all that. Some days went by, and I saw him again, and I asked him how he was getting on with his detective story, and he said that he had not started yet. I didn't think much of that at the time, seeing no reason why he should hurry, and it was some weeks before I saw him once more; and this time I thought he must be well on his way with his novel, because he had been so keen on it, besides needing the money, as most people do in these hard times, and the Chancellor of the Exchequer most of all; and he gets it. But no, Tather had not started it yet. Why not, I asked? And he was evasive. Again I saw him, a few days after that; and I questioned him then. For I was puzzled. He seemed so like a man with a little gold-mine in his garden, who would not trouble to dig it. Why not, I kept asking Tather? And then he muttered something that is the key to the whole business, if you think it out, as I did. "It's too good to waste," he said.

'I asked him what he meant, and I got all kinds of answers; too many of them; all meaning nothing. In fact, he went on explaining away those words as long as we were together. And the more that he explained that he had meant nothing in particular, the more I saw what he did mean.'

'You don't mean . . .' I began.

'I do,' he said. 'He was going to use it. He was going to put that idea of his into practice. Not at once. I found that out. Not against any particular person, for there was a total absence of any anger in him; but he was not going to waste that idea of his, that idea of an undetectable murder, whatever it was. He was going to keep it. And he was not using it. And I feel sure that one day he will. That is why I say keep him away from politics. There are plenty of things that excite a man nearly as much, but there is not the same rivalry in all of them, not the same temptation. And look at the crimes that are committed in many lands all for the sake of politics. The most and the worst.

So keep him away from that if you possibly can, or I'm sure he'll use that idea of his. Whether it can be detected or not I cannot say, for I don't know what it is, but I am convinced that it is something pretty cunning; and anyway he thinks that it cannot be detected, so he thinks himself safe enough; and, being prepared to do it, he one day will. Do what you can.'

'I will,' I said. 'Have you no idea at all what kind of murder it is, that you think he'll commit?'

'Hardly at all,' said Indram. 'And yet I have one clue. I tried to get it out of him by telling him, what is probably true, that there is no murder that may not possibly be detected, though many are not. I told him that many murderers had thought themselves safe and got hanged, and that his idea might be fallible as the rest. And he said, "A lot can be done with dead caterpillars."

'That is all. It didn't tell me what his idea was; but it seemed to indicate some sort of subtle poison, probably inflicted by some slight wound, perhaps only a scratch. So keep him away from politics if you can possibly do it. I don't know what influence you have over him.'

'Very little,' I said. 'But look here. Couldn't we get a publisher to offer him a really large sum for a novel. That would lure him back to fiction and the proper use of his damned idea. We and a few others might subscribe, and go in and back the publisher, if it is as serious as that.'

'No,' he said. 'When a man has got the idea of doing anything in real life, you will never turn him aside to express it merely in fiction. No, life is the thing. You might as well offer milk to a tiger to keep him away from blood. Do what you can.'

Well, that is the talk that I had with Indram. And I went straight to Tather's flat and found him in. And I asked him to give up politics. Well, you can't do that with any man. It is merely cheek, and no one would listen to you. So I had to back my words with something pretty strong; and when he told me that it was no business of mine, I said, 'Then give up playing with caterpillers.'

That of course was like hitting him hard on the chin. And it had the same sort of effect. He went very silent, and rather white, and he knew that I had been talking to Indram. I don't see how I could have had any effect on him if I hadn't. I had to show there was something behind my words. Had to threaten the man, in fact. I am sorry I did now, and shall be sorry all my life. Tather was going to stand as an Independent against a Liberal in the High Street division. I left him all frozen with fury; against myself, as I thought at the time. And when I saw that it was hopeless to try to divert him, I went down to High Street and saw the Liberal election agent and did all I could to warn him against possible violence, though I could give him little enough reason. But he was an understanding man, and listened to my warning, and said he would take precautions. I cared nothing for Tather's politics or the other man's either, but I was not going to have murder committed if I could prevent it; and after my unpleasant interview with Tather I had no doubt that Indram was right, and that, when feelings ran high and opportunity came, that man would not hesitate to use what he felt sure was an invincible weapon. I wasted a lot of time at High Street. It was not his opponent that he killed. He killed poor Indram. That is my confirmed belief. Nobody will persuade me that it was anything else. Indram was last seen alive on a platform at Charing Cross station. He had come through a crowd at the ticket-barrier, where he had complained of somebody jostling him. He was on the platform for barely five minutes. Then he dropped dead. A doctor said it was failure of the heart's action. But I am not satisfied that there was anything natural about it. Indram was perfectly well when I saw him last.

Now what should I do? But I have decided that already. I have finally decided to be silent. I have not sufficient evidence to prove anything.

IN RAVANCORE

In Ravancore Wilcolt T. Otis, of Hometown, N.Y., was buying an idol. When he had bought it he asked the Indian who sold it to wrap the idol up for him and to tie it with string. The Indian at first appeared not to understand, and Wilcolt T. Otis spoke louder. And then the man said 'No string.'

'But how am I to carry the darned thing, then?' said Otis.

'It will go in your pocket, sahib,' answered the Indian.

'My pocket!' exclaimed Otis. 'A pretty bulge it will make there, and spoil the set of my suit. We don't go about with bulging pockets in Hometown.'

The Indian smiled and spread out his hands, and looked at the crowd that seemed to flow ever so slowly through the bazaar, as though he were saying, 'Here there are no pockets.' And the American realized all at once that he was far from home and that he could not bring all his own customs with him. So he left with that untidy bulge in his pocket, caused by the elephant-god Ganeesh, carved in some sort of gray slate.

That was before he met two of the most charming men with whom he had ever spoken. They slipped like shadows out of the crowd, like shadows softly detaching themselves from their two owners, and came up to Otis with their dark faces smiling. Would he come to a meeting, they asked him, of an old association that had been tyrannically suppressed by the English, and that was to be reinstated now that India was free?

'Why, sure,' said Otis.

The two men were delighted. As they led him towards their house Otis explained to them that he had been the secretary in Hometown, N.Y., of the India-for-the-Indians League, which

was only lately disbanded on India becoming free. And his two
new-found friends smiled more than ever at that. Their effusive
friendliness charmed the American, whose happy contentment
was only occasionally dimmed by one of those passing shadows
that often distress any man who knows and feels that he is not
correctly dressed, and this shadow came from the long thin
bulge of the elephant-god in his pocket. But it would have been
worse to leave that quaint idol behind, a trophy of his travel
that was to adorn his mantelpiece back in Hometown so far
away. And what travel it was! Everything was new to him there;
all the scents, all the songs, and the tunes that suddenly rose
from hidden flutes and as suddenly died away, and the brilliant
colours of the women's dresses, and of the huge flowers and
even of the sky.

Otis was led through queer narrow streets, once wholly
obstructed by a cow lying down; and, just as he was about to
kick the cow to make her get up, his two new friends led him
back and into another street. There Otis noticed for the first
time that someone was following them, an Indian dressed much
as he was himself, but with a rather gayer tie. Once one of his
guides looked round at the same time that Otis did, and the
man behind slouched into listlessness. Once Otis looked round
without the other two seeing, and the Indian who followed
made a quick sign with his hand. But what the man wished to
tell him Otis was unable to guess. As they approached corners,
the man came closer. In the open street he dropped back. What
was it he wished to say? At a turning into an even narrower
street Otis dropped for a moment behind his guides. The streets
were always crowded, and a bunch of men at the corner enabled
Otis to do this. The man behind came up at once. 'Not with
those men, sir,' he said. 'I am an educated man like yourself.
University education. Take my word for it.'

'I like the common man, my friend,' said Otis. 'God made
more of them than of the University boys. And I like to see
them free.'

There was no time for more. Otis's final words were said in a low voice over his shoulder as he hurried to join his two friends, and the man behind may scarcely have heard. 'Common men,' said Otis again to himself. 'That's what God made most of.'

Among cañons of high white walls with small queer doors in them he was led by the two men, till, in a street so narrow that even the air seemed scanty, he was brought to a dome-shaped door that suddenly opened, and he was in a room that was filled with Hindus, who after a few words from the two that had brought him, which Otis did not understand, greeted him with effusion. There were many societies in Hometown and many secretaries, and he had not been a very important figure there. But at last, he felt, his work was most fully recognized, and in the very field for which he had laboured. There were smiling faces all round him. At one end of the room was a dais, to which he was conducted and there given a chair. As soon as he sat down the meeting began, as though all had waited for him, and a man rose from his chair in the centre of the dais and began a speech in English. It was a very crowded room, and though Otis, as secretary of the India-for-the-Indians League, was delighted to be there, he did not like the smell of some wild herb that was almost breathed in his face; and he quietly moved back his chair till it touched the wall behind him. The speaker was asking rhetorical questions. Why had the English, he asked, suppressed their association? Was it for the reasons they gave? No, it was because they were ignorant and jealous of the time-honoured customs of India, and contemptuous of her gods. The speaker paused for breath, the crowded room quietly applauded, and Wilcolt T. Otis leaned forward and asked the speaker, 'Say. What does your Association do?'

'It aids travellers,' said the speaker.

'Well, so we do in New York State,' said Otis. 'But what is there special about your Association?'

'It is our religion,' said the speaker. 'And the English have persecuted it.'

'I don't quite get you,' said the American. 'But I'm sure glad you are free. It was a shame to interfere with your religion.'

The Indian sighed. 'It was a shame,' he said.

And then he went on with his speech to the thrilled and expectant audience. Expectant of what, the American wondered awhile? But as the speech raged on, and the speaker became evidently more inspired, he realized that these people's old religion, that the English had so harshly suppressed, was to be founded again immediately and in that room. And, curiously enough, Otis discovered this though the speaker had long since ceased to speak in English. Very politely, with courtesy and even with charm, one of the Hindus came up to Otis and asked him to move his chair forward a little from the wall, so that all could see more clearly the honoured secretary of the Hometown branch of the India-for-the-Indians League. Otis did not want to be seen more clearly, because of the bulge that Ganeesh was making in his pocket, and he set much store by being neatly dressed among all these people who might never have seen an American citizen before, and who ought to be shown that those citizens dressed decently. Nevertheless he assented, and the Hindu dropped back into the eager crowds, and Otis caught hold of the arms of his chair and was about to move it forward, when between the finger and thumb of his right hand he felt something inserted, and looked and saw that it was an envelope. There were many men standing quite close to him, but he could not see which of them it had been that had put the envelope there. One of them was moving at that moment towards the back of his chair, but Otis did not think that he was the one. In the envelope was a letter and, probably stirred by surprise at that letter's extraordinary delivery, he drew it out and read it before he moved his chair, while the man who had moved closer stood still, as though waiting for him to move it. The shrewd sense of an American business man may not be so acute as the cunning of the East, yet Otis realized that such secrecy in the delivery of the letter deserved a certain concealment, and he read the letter without, so far as he knew, attracting any attention. The speaker spoke on. Something priestly seemed to have come into his manner now, as he intoned his triumph over the bigotry of the English who had suppressed his ancient creed. Otis could see that he was doing that, though he knew no Hindustani, and he could see that the whole dark audience with gleaming eyes was hanging upon every word that he uttered, as if it were inspiration. Yet he interrupted rather abruptly. Waving one hand to silence the speaker, he stood up and addressed the audience himself.

'Say, folks,' he said, 'your boss's speech is bully. And I like to hear it. But I want you to let me do a bit of my stuff too. I want you to put up an anna on that far wall, or any dam coin you like, and see me do my stuff, which is shooting. Don't you fear I will hit any of you when I shoot; for I'll plug that anna, or whatever it is, right in the middle.'

There was authority in Otis's voice, as there had been in the wave of his hand that had silenced the speaker. He had read of the White Man's burden, and scorned imperialism, yet there was something of the stuff of which these things are made in Otis's voice, and it held the audience. 'And don't think,' he said, tapping his pocket now, 'that it's any old six-shooter I carry here; for it's got ten little cartridges in it, and a clip with ten more that slips in in a moment.' The Hindu who was so nearly behind him found the chair still in his way, and Otis was watching him from the corner of his eye and had his hand in his pocket now, holding the head of Ganeesh.

'Well, boys,' he went on, 'you won't put up an anna for me to see me do my stuff. So I'll go away and do my shooting outside. And there's twenty little bullets for anyone who gets between me and the door.' And now he held up his letter with the left hand, while the right hand clutched Ganeesh. 'And I see that my grave is already dug. Well, that's bully, that's O.K.

by me. 'Cause we'll want lots of graves when I pull out my little gun; and I don't want the trouble of digging any myself in this hot climate. Maybe the English were right to stop thuggee after all. Maybe they had more sense than I thought. But I'm not going to interfere with your sport, or any of your damned gods. Only, they are not going to interfere with me. See? Do you see, boys? Or must I draw my little gun? Just as you please. Only, one grave won't be enough for us if I do. And now I'm going away. And I've been charmed to see you. Salaam, or whatever you say. Go on with your speech, boss.'

And Otis walked out with his right hand in his pocket, where the bulge spoiled the hang of his coat, giving quick glances behind him. For it is from behind that the Thugs always work.

But nobody moved.

Some while afterwards Otis met the Indian who had warned him by slipping that letter between his forefinger and thumb, and recognized him as the University man who had followed him in the street. And naturally Otis gave him a fine dinner. And afterwards they had a long talk, the Indian making it very clear to Otis that he and all decent Indians hated thuggee as much as he did, and its gross goddess Dewanee and all the superstitition that went with her abominable worship. So he and Wilcolt T. Otis talked long of these things, quite openly like two enlightened men. And Otis told the story of the bulge in his pocket, and how it had only been Ganeesh. 'Ah,' said the Indian then, 'but you are not the only one that that god has often saved.'

AMONG THE BEAN ROWS

THIS is the story I had from the old retired detective, Ripley by name. There are certain gaps in it and details left out, perhaps because even now there are things in his story that are better not told, but more likely because he was hard at work while he talked to me, planting scarlet runners in his garden at Putney and putting sticks into the ground for his scarlet runners to climb. 'Excitements in my time?' he said. 'Oh, yes, they came my way, as they do to most people one time or another.' And then, having come on a bit of hard ground into which he was trying to shove a stick for his scarlet runners, he said no more for a while, and I was afraid I was going to get no more. And then he said, 'There was one of them that I don't suppose I shall forget. It all began in the reading-room of the British Museum.'

'The British Museum?' I said.

'Oh, yes,' Ripley answered. 'If it should ever be anyone's job to look for our most dangerous enemies, that is the place to look for them. There are not many of them that have not gone there at one time or another, and even spent some considerable time there, reading. That's what they do. They come and read. And they find everything that they want there. That's where it all started: someone overheard two of them talking, which didn't often happen.'

'What were they talking about?' I asked.

'Murder,' he said. 'It was the only thing they were really interested in. Murder on a large scale.'

And as his attention seemed to wander back to his bean rows again, I said, 'Who were they?'

'They all came from Switzerland,' he said. 'But they seemed to be more interested in Russia. Not that they were Swiss, and I don't know whether or not they were Russian either. I don't know where they came from originally, but they came from Switzerland here, and they were picked up in the British Museum, where a little of what was said by two of them was overheard. But they preferred an underground place in East London for their murderous talk, and it was there I was sent to watch them. That of course was not done in a day. In fact, it took nearer a year. I had to get introduced to English sympathizers, and through them I had to get to know the outer circle, as it were, of the men that I was to watch. There were nine of them, men who studied and organized murder as a manufacturer of insecticide studies greenflies and caterpillars. And all the while I was learning bits of the language of the country I pretended to come from, so as to understand what anybody might say in that language; and I was learning to get the accent right. That, you would think, would be the hardest part of the job, and hardly to be done in a year. But it wasn't. Luckily these men talked English, and all I had to do about the accent was to get it absolutely perfect for the two or three phrases that I was going occasionally to throw in. The country I pretended to come from was one of those that used to be included in the term All the Russias. It took me some time to get into the inner circle, and longer still to be initiated with full ceremony.'

'What was the ceremony like?' I asked.

'Oh, it was one of those things,' said Ripley, 'one of those things. . . .' And he got very busy at that moment with a stick that he was shoving down for his scarlet runners to climb. 'It was one of those ceremonies,' he went on. 'And after that I was a full member of their big murder society. We used to meet in a basement in East London. What we used to discuss was massacre mostly; how to fire down streets so as to kill the greatest number of people, and when was the best time of day to do it. Not in England, to start with. They planned to start abroad. It was all a long time ago, when the Czar of Russia was still alive. There was a staircase down from a shop that was owned by a foreigner, to a room with a long table and ten chairs. And there we used to sit and talk about murder. It was very quiet down there, and we always met after closing hours, and nobody could hear any noise we might make, except the man who kept the shop, and he wouldn't mind. I was getting on well, making headway with all of them, talking their kind of talk, and sometimes throwing in the language of the country that I had chosen, and with the accent just right. And of course I was reporting all that I heard. I had all the feeling one has when one is getting on well. The president of the murder society sat at the head of the table, and we were discussing how to make a government respected, and agreeing that you must first make it feared, and that the way to be sure of that was to send men with rifles into the main streets of a big town at the time that women were mostly doing their shopping, and to tell them to fire all day. And I was agreeing with them all and getting on nicely, and everything seemed harmonious when we broke up and arranged to meet next day. So that I was a bit more than surprised when next day came, and we were all there and the president had just sat down, when he got up and just said seven words, "Comrades, there is a spy among us."

'It seemed to me that the thing to do was to look very surprised. But luckily I glanced first at the others, and I noticed the expression of surprise was not very evident. And I just had time to take my cue from that.

'The president was the oldest and was of course in command, but the most forceful man there was one called Brotskoi. He sat next to the president; and he just said, "Search?"

'"Yes," I heard the president say.

'That was all. And Brotskoi turned at once to the man on his right, he himself being on the right of the president, and said, "Pardon me, comrade," and began to take off the man's jacket. The man on the other side joined in, and two more of them lent a hand, and the man he searched made no protest and they searched him very thoroughly, too thoroughly for anything to have been overlooked, as I noticed with a good deal of interest, for I had done a foolish thing. I had been very careful to avoid having anything on me that could give me away, except one thing, and that one thing was the card in my waistcoat pocket that all of us used to carry, just to show that one was a detective. Of course that was as damning as any bundle of documents I could have carried. It was a little card, and I hadn't thought it would ever be seen. But I had never thought of a search. Well, there it was, and they were searching another man now, and the search was coming my way. I could easily have eaten my card. But there were too many eyes watching for that now. It was a bare table and a bare floor; nowhere to hide the card. There was nowhere on me that I could hide it, any better than where it was. Those searchers weren't going to miss anything: I could see that. There was nothing for it but to plant it on someone else, on one of those experts in massacre. So when two men rose up to search the third man I joined in at once. I said, "Pardon me, comrade," and helped to strip him. There were four of us at it. And I found it easy enough to slip the card into one of his pockets. I did not try to find it myself. I left the others to do that. And one of them did. He found the card and handed it to the president in silence, who just nodded his head. Then the man who was being searched broke out. It had been planted on him, he said perfectly truthfully, by one of the comrades who searched him.

'And then the president began to speak. And, do you know, I knew just what he was going to say. I think that in moments like those one sometimes gets acuter perceptions. I don't know how it is. But I knew what he was going to say. And he said it. But before the rest seemed to know what was coming, I wrote a few words on a scrap of paper while they were all watching the president, and I handed it quietly to Brotskoi. Meanwhile what the president said was, "It may be so, as Comrade Dronski says, or perhaps not. But it is demonstrable that either he or one of the four comrades who searched him is the English spy. You all know, comrades, and have all sworn, that the cause comes first. Therefore, although for myself I shall regret it, those five must be liquidated. For one spy endangers the lives of all of us. These five will raise no foolish objections, knowing that it is for the cause."

'And the cause being murder on a very large scale, there was no sound reason why we five should. I mean we couldn't very well raise objections to murder. It would be like joining a chess-club and then saying that one thought chess a waste of time. What I had written on that strip of paper was, "It is our lives or theirs. We must liquidate them. No?" The rest I really did with my eyes, which was not difficult, though to read his was a harder matter. But I gathered that he agreed with me; and, as it turned out, he did. He was obviously more of a driving force than the president, and it cannot be that he had not contemplated succeeding him one day to the position that, whatever we may think of a gang of murderers like that, was to him the highest position on earth. Why should he allow himself to be knifed just to amuse the man that he was looking forward to replace? You couldn't tell much from his face; but I gathered that he agreed. So then with a movement of my head I suggested showing my little note to the others. And this he did, as the president was ending his interesting remarks.

'When Brotskoi passed my bit of paper to the three others I knew definitely that he agreed with me. And not only that, but I knew that those three others would agree with anything Brotskoi said. He was that kind of man.

'And so they did. I began to speak, so as to gain time, while those three were reading my note. They liked listening to talk. "Surely, Comrade President," I said, "the pick of the intelligentsia of the world, and you the most intellectual of them all, cannot be unable to find out the veritable spy, without liquidating us innocent ones." And I went on saying a good deal more, that I have forgotten now. But, though they seemed to be quite interested in what I was saying, it had no effect at all. "But I told you that I regretted it," was all the president said. And he seemed to say it as though he thought his regret would be any good to us.'

'What weapons had you?' I asked.

'Weapons?' said the old detective, turning away from his bean rows. 'We had none, except knives. The president wouldn't allow revolvers. The English police had funny ideas, he said. So he barred revolvers; barred them by oath. But of course they all carried knives. Foreigners usually do. And I carried one myself, merely for the sake of the make-up, so as to be as like as I could to those murderous foreigners. I never thought I should have to use it. But it's lucky I had it, as it turned out. It came in very handy.

'Well, I didn't say much, for I soon saw the other four were ready. And so they should have been; for, after all, it was their only chance. And then I caught Brotskoi's eye, and he went for the president with his knife, and we went for the rest. It was our side of the table against theirs, and we started before they were ready. We ought to have got more of them than we did. We killed two, the president and another, and that left us five to three. The three stepped back, and we came on again. Of course everyone had his knife out by now. There was no more question of any surprise. They were back against the wall, and no one was saying anything. Brotskoi naturally took command over our lot, and with a sign from him we came on again. But at that moment the three of them came for us. They dropped one of our men with a wound under the fork of the ribs, and we killed two of them. That left one. Still no-one said a word, and the one man opposite to us picked up another knife in his left hand and went into a corner and stood there facing us. We were more careful this time, for fear he should get another of us. But we picked up chairs and went for him behind a kind of a shield, and we soon managed to get him.

'There were now only Brotskoi and me and three others, one of whom seemed to be dying. I had to think quickly. I had fewer enemies now, but it was a matter of plain arithmetic that, as one of the five, I was doubly as suspect as I had been when there were ten alive in that room. So I turned to Brotskoi before anyone else could say anything, and said "I am as sure of you, comrade, as of myself. But what of these others?"

'They looked up like angry dumb cattle. But I caught Brotskoi's eye and we acted quickly. Then there were only we two. You may think it's not easy to show so much with one's eye as I had been showing. Unfortunately I showed a great deal more. I let him see that I was afraid of him. When he saw that, he must have had a pretty good idea that I was the spy. But any way he saw that I was afraid of him, and that I had a knife in my hand; two knives by now, for I had picked up a very nice one from one of the others, the longest one in the room. But, though I had this knife, it was nasty being alone in the room with probably one of the most murderous characters who ever studied in the reading-room of the British Museum, who must have known by now that I was a spy, though he said nothing. After that we watched each other for a while.

'And then Brotskoi began to move cautiously towards the switch of the electric light, that had been on all the time. I pulled a match-box out of my pocket then and struck a match, still holding my two knives. What he meant to do when he had turned out the light I don't know, but he wouldn't be able to do that, whatever it was, while I had the lighted match, and I would be able to put out the light when I liked, instead of his being able to do it, provided it didn't burn down to my fingers, which it was fast doing. But when he saw my match he gave up his idea of turning out the light. And we watched each other a bit more in silence. And then I had an idea, and I said, "But we can both prove our innocence, comrade. Here is the spy's signature on his card. Write his name quickly, and I'll do the same. One cannot alter one's signature totally while writing quickly. Sit down and write his name, comrade, and then give the pen to me." My longer knife made it difficult for him to close with me, and perhaps that made him all the more ready to take to my idea. Anyway he took to it. They were good at fighting with knives, those men, but very fond of talk. And he listened to mine. My card was lying on the table and I pointed to it and Brotskoi sat down and pulled out a pen and began writing as I said, with one knife still in his left hand. I don't know what he thought. You can't easily tell with those people. But there he sat, as innocent to look at, but for that one knife that was still in his left hand, as a child at its copybook, writing away with the hand and pen that, had he lived, would very likely have signed the death warrants of thousands of innocent men. And, if he had had a knife in each hand, he might have lived. But with only one of them the odds were on me.'

'And did you kill him?' I asked.

'Well, you see me alive,' said the old detective, 'which hadn't seemed likely at first, when the president first got up. Brotskoi must have forgotten as he died that he had practically found me out; for there was a look of surprise on his face, and he gasped out, "But, comrade, I am a true Leninist-Marxist."

'"Yes," I said. "But I am not."'

'And what did your friends in the police force do about all those bodies?' I asked.

But Ripley was further away down his bean rows now, and more occupied than ever with his straight line of sticks, and evening was coming on and it grew cold, and it hardly looked as if I should get any more out of him. So I left with what I had.

THE DEATH-WATCH BEETLE

'AND what was your biggest case?' I asked the old retired detective one evening in his garden among his hollyhocks.

'Well, we always count murder as the biggest,' he said.

'What was your hardest?' I enquired.

'The one that puzzled us most,' he said, 'the biggest puzzle of all, was a case down in Surrey that looked like never being found out. It was a man named Tipp, a burglar by occupation, and a clever burglar too. He used to watch a house until he knew all about it. He would hang about and often be warned off for his trespassing. Then he would apologize and go. But he always came back again. Often he got to know so well what everyone in the house was doing, that he would walk into it when the owner was in the garden, and take a look round at all the rooms in which he knew that he would not meet a servant. He never stole anything on those occasions; never touched a thing till he knew where everything was and where everyone in the house would be, and then one day or one night he would go in and take everything that he wanted.'

'You get to know every burglar's ways pretty well, don't you?' I said.

'Pretty well,' he replied.

'I read that somewhere,' I said. 'And every burglar has his own different way of working, and you get to know who's done a burglary by the way he has done it, and they never alter their way.'

'That's so,' said the old detective, 'up to a point, and as a general rule. But a general rule won't solve a difficult problem, because a difficult problem always has something special about

198

it, something outside general rules. That's how it was with Tipp. He was a burglar with his distinct way of doing business, which we knew all about. And then he did a very odd thing; he gave it up; not only gave up his way of working, but gave up burglary altogether for something else; in fact for demanding money by threats. It may not seem odd to you; but to us it was like seeing a fishmonger quite suddenly selling boots. Yes, he suddenly changed over to demanding money by threats. What he did was to watch a house, a very old house in Surrey, in his usual way. The owner, a Mr Wetherly, lived there alone with three servants, and he hung about learning their habits. He wasn't often seen, and if he was, he came next time in a different kind of hat, which is usually quite enough to make people think that it is a different person; and sometimes, to make quite sure, he would come back with a pair of spectacles. It was the man's bedroom he meant to rob, and, as the owner of that house used always to slam his bedroom door noisily when he went in, it was quite easy for Tipp to know when he was there. Another thing Tipp got to know was that he habitually left his door open when he went out of his bedroom. You see, it isn't only burglars that have little ways that they keep to. This helped Tipp, because he always liked to avoid the slight noise of opening a door, if it could be done. It makes practically no noise at all, except to a listening ear, but a burglar never quite knows where there may not be some and is nearly always afraid of them, even when there is none there. And he never knows. Well, Tipp was seen several times by one or other of the servants in the grounds of the old house, but not by the same one each time, and it was only by putting everything together afterwards that they knew how often they had seen him, or that it was the same man every time. One of them spoke to him once to ask him what he was doing there, and Tipp said that he didn't know it was private, and walked away and no more was said. That is the day that he must have gone into the house while the owner was in the garden.

'Well, everything was about ready for his burglary, when he suddenly gave up the idea of it and took to demanding money instead. He went up to the hall door and rang the bell and asked if he could see Mr Wetherly. Well, there was no difficulty in seeing him. He was shown in, and when they were alone he simply said that he wanted £200, and that if he didn't get it Mr Wetherly would die within the week. Of course Mr Wetherly threatened him with prosecution; but Tipp replied by threatening him with death, and pointing out that there were no witnesses. He spoke in a low voice, and with an accent as refined as he had been able to get it. Mr Wetherly got up to ring the bell, and Tipp asked for the money again and assured him that it was his last chance and begged him to take it. Of course Mr Wetherly said that he would have nothing to do with the man. And then Tipp did a rather funny thing. He said he had hoped that Mr Wetherly would give him the money, and that if he didn't he would die.

'"And what will you gain by that?" said Mr Wetherly interrupting him.

'"I was coming to that," said Tipp. "If you don't give me money and you have to die," that is the way he put it, "I am going to a gentleman that lives near here and I shall get it from him."

'"Get it from him?" says Mr Wetherly.

'"Certainly," says Tipp. "You may be rash enough not to give it to me. Very likely you don't believe me. And I can't blame you. But this gentleman will believe me, as soon as he hears you are dead. I am going to him now. I am going to tell him what I have told you; that you will very soon die because you didn't give me the money. I am afraid that what I have had to say does not sound very credible. I have tried to make it so for your sake, but you simply won't believe me. So it can't be as credible as I hoped. But the other gentleman will have no difficulty at all in believing me. I would far sooner have the money from you. It's little enough for your life. But I'll get it quick enough from the other gentleman as soon as he hears what has happened to you."

'Well, Mr Wetherly rang the bell and Tipp walked out of the house, and he did exactly what he had said. He went to this other man, a Mr Plink, and was shown in in the same way, and told him that he wanted £200, and that he had asked Mr Wetherly for it and warned him that he would die unless he gave it, and most unfortunately Mr Wetherly had not believed him, so that perhaps Mr Plink would not believe him either, but that he would call again in a few days' time when Mr Wetherly would be dead.

'We think that Mr Plink tried to frighten him by telling him what happened to murderers. Very likely he said a good deal about that short walk that they take after breakfast at 8 o'clock in the morning. But we know very little of what was said in that house, because Mr Plink appears to have got very frightened himself and would not prosecute and would say very little. Mr Wetherly came to us at once and told us everything. He wasn't frightened. But then it was very different for him: he didn't believe in Tipp's threat, and there was nothing to make him believe it. But it was very different for this Mr Plink. Mr Wetherly merely brought a charge of blackmail, which should have been attempting to obtain money by threats, as we explained to him; but unfortunately there had been no one within hearing when Tipp had been talking to him, so that it was only his word against Tipp's. If we could have got Plink's story, it would have corroborated Mr Wetherly. But he wouldn't speak. What we did was to get Mr Wetherly to fix another meeting with Tipp, and we were going to arrange to have his talk overheard. But before that could be done Mr Wetherly died, and we had the most difficult problem that we have ever had. Mr Plink, I should tell you, had paid his £200.'

'What was your difficulty?' I asked.

'Well, to begin with,' the old detective said, 'it had the hall-mark of all the hardest problems; it had a perfectly obvious solution, which was too childishly simple to be the real one. Tipp, you see, had threatened Wetherly with death, and next day he was dead. So what could the solution be but that he had killed him? But then there was the coroner's jury, which brought in unanimously that he had died from natural causes as the result of a simple accident. We tried to get them to consider it again. But they said there was nothing more to consider. Then we went over it all ourselves, and had to come to the same conclusion. It was a mystery all right.'

'What was the accident?' I asked.

'A huge oak beam,' he said, '(it was a very old house), fell on his head.'

'Some kind of booby-trap arranged by Tipp,' I said.

'That is what we all thought,' he went on. 'But the more we went into it, the more certain it became that it was all done by the death-watch beetle. It was a huge beam that went right across the ceiling of his bedroom, and it had been cut through by this beetle at both ends. The house was five hundred years old; so it had had plenty of time to do it. Of course we looked for marks of a saw or a knife, or anything that would have helped to bring the beam down a bit sooner. But there wasn't a trace, and you can't hang a death-watch beetle. That was our problem: why hadn't Tipp murdered Mr Wetherly. The coroner's jury said definitely that he hadn't, and we couldn't prove they were wrong. We couldn't even have him tried for demanding money by threats, when Mr Plink wouldn't prosecute, and Mr Wetherly was so conveniently dead.'

'Conveniently, you mean, from the murderer's point of view,' I put in to call the old fellow's attention back from a tall holly-hock that he was tying to a bamboo at that moment.

'We couldn't call him a murderer,' he said. 'We have to prove things like that, and there wasn't a vestige of proof. There wasn't even enough for a *prima facie* case; except to convict the beetle. There was all the proof you could want for that.'

'Then how did Tipp know that Mr Wetherly was going to have an accident?' I asked.

'That was our problem,' he said. 'And we never solved it. Not for ourselves that is to say. We had to ask.'

'But whom did you ask?' I exclaimed.

'When Tipp had spent his £200,' he said, 'he went back to burglary again, his old business, and he was brought up on a small charge. He never took much at a time. Used to slip into bedrooms, usually by day, and pilfer a few things from a dressing-table. He only got a few months. There's a lot of difference, you see, when they do it by day. And of course Tipp knew that.'

'Why?' I asked.

'Well, that's the law,' he said. 'It's not housebreaking if he just walks in. And it's much better for him if he does it between sunrise and sunset. He got three or four months. We get to know those fellows pretty well. He came into a station where I was. And I got him a cup of tea and began talking to him. And then we talked of old times. He had often been up before. And after a bit I said, "What about Mr Wetherly?" And I got the whole story from him. What he had done was to go into that bedroom to look round in his usual way, so as to see where everything was. He had watched the house already and found out a lot of things about Mr Wetherly's ways, and all he wanted to find out now was where he kept everything, so that he could scoop it all up at once and get away. The longer he took over a job, the more danger there was of being stopped as he slipped out. So whenever he spent more than five minutes in a house, if anyone questioned him as he walked away, his pockets were always empty and he was only a tripper from London, not knowing that it was private. When he burgled he usen't to be in the house for more than a minute. Well, he was looking round Mr Wetherly's bedroom, getting the lie of it. He didn't walk on tiptoe. He did better than that. He slammed the door as Mr Wetherly used to slam it. He had seen Mr Wetherly going into the garden, but the servants did not know that. He calculated that he had plenty of time, and was looking round. And being very wide awake, as he always had to be, and looking in every direction, he thought he saw that old oak beam move as he slammed the door. Of course it had nothing to do with his business, which was to look round and see where Mr Wetherly kept his trinkets and any little things that Tipp wanted; but it puzzled him all the time he was looking round. And at last he thought he would take another look; mere curiosity, he told me. He didn't look at the beam again till just as he was going out, because slamming the door twice might have given him away, Mr Wetherly being, as he had found out, in the habit of always leaving his door open when he left his bedroom. So, if one of the servants was quick, he or she would have known that it wasn't Mr Wetherly, when they heard the door slam twice, but he chanced that; and anyway nothing would be found on him that day, even if he was stopped. So just before he went out he slammed the door again and looked at the beam, which incidentally was straight over his head. And then he realized what a foolish thing he had done. For it was a small room, and the great beam went right across it and the bed was just behind him and in his way, and there was the beam above him and it was trembling. He realized then, all in a moment, that if it came down he was done for. But it did not come down; it dropped a fraction of an inch, as it had done before, and still remained poised, though Tipp doesn't know what could have held it. But he realized clearly enough that very few more slams of that door and down the great beam would come. Even while he had been watching it he had known that there was no time to jump clear. Next time or the time after that, or the time after that and the man underneath it would slam no more doors.

'Tipp went away and nobody stopped him, and on the way down the drive, he said, he began to think that he had a very curious piece of information. He used to like to pick up curious old things that he found in houses, as he found a very ready sale for them in antique shops. Now, he said, he had got a curious piece of knowledge, and the thought came to him, walking down the drive, that there might be some use for it. And then the idea came to him of asking Mr Wetherly for that £200. It wasn't his fault, was the way he put it: the idea just came to him. And then, he said, it seemed a pity to waste it. He never meant Mr Wetherly to be killed. On the contrary, he meant to warn him the moment he paid his two hundred, "my two hundred", as Tipp put it. He seemed to think that the money was actually due to him. And then Mr Wetherly had unfortunately become pigheaded, he said; and what could you do with a man like that? Mr Plink had been an obliging gentleman; but what could he do when Mr Wetherly wouldn't co-operate? It wasn't his fault, he said. He had been as sorry as he could be about Mr Wetherly, and had shed tears about it when he heard he was dead. He really had, he said. And then he began to whine to me, and I didn't talk to him any more. We couldn't prosecute; we had no evidence.'

MURDER BY LIGHTNING

My walks at one time along a lane in Surrey often took me past the garden of John Ripley, the old retired detective. It ran down to the lane from his cottage, and there I used to see him working among his flowers, whenever I went by on a summer's evening. He used to greet me with a wave of his arm if he saw me, and often I used to stop and we would talk for a while. I remember one day in June when I went by and saw him taking down a long strip of canvas and an old blanket, that were fastened at one end to the wooden paling that bounded his garden, and to a row of poles and sticks stuck in the ground. I asked him what he was doing; and he explained that he was taking down a protection against the sun, that he had put up beside a long deep row of Canterbury bells, for it had been a very hot day. 'It's like drink to them, the sun,' he explained. 'It's a great stimulant to them and brings them on grand. But too much of it, and they're finished. Two or three days like this, and they are all brown.' So he had rigged up this odd shelter for them. He had been born in Kent, and either he was a bit jealous of it on behalf of Surrey, or he was home-sick for it. Certainly he set great store by Kent's principal flower. Sometimes he said to me, 'They can't grow flowers like this in Kent. Haven't the soil for it.' At other times he would say, 'You should have seen the wild roses there, the way they used to be when I was young.'

While he tended his Canterbury bells I said to him, just to start conversation, 'What first gave you your start?'

'What gave me my start?' he said. 'Why, I was a village policeman down in Kent, and not likely to get anything better. Not that that wasn't good enough, and I didn't want anything better at the time. And then a murder came our way. And that's what gave me my start.'

'What kind of murder?' I asked.

'A nasty kind,' he said. 'A premeditated murder. Premeditated for years.'

'For years?' I said.

'Yes, years,' he answered me. 'A bad, brooding fellow. A premeditated murder if ever there was one.'

'How many years did he take over it?' I asked.

'At least three, so far as we know,' said old Ripley.

'He had a long time to wait,' I remarked.

'He enjoyed it,' said Ripley. 'He enjoyed waiting. He was one of those malicious types. Malice was what he seemed to live for, as other people live for their different hobbies. I believe he liked to sit and think how one day he would gratify it. I used to see him sitting on a wooden chair in his garden, looking across the valley towards the house of the man he hated.'

'What did he hate him for?' I asked. 'Had he done him a bad turn?'

'There was nothing bad about the other man,' said Ripley. 'And besides that, men don't hate on account of badness; they merely despise it. When a man really hates, it's because of goodness, something good in another man that isn't in them. That's what they hate about, when they do hate. That kind of people don't like it when another man has more money than they have, but that they can sometimes forgive, for they always hope that one day they may get some money too. What they never forgive is any innate goodness; because that is what, whatever they say, they know they can never obtain. That is what that kind hate. Often they get level by inventing tales about good men, which they make up out of their own vices. Such tales are always believed, because they are so full of the right local colour, because the men who invented them know all about the kind of muck they are talking of. That is enough for that kind of person usually. But it wasn't enough for Brix, that was the fellow's name, and nothing would satisfy him short of murder. So murder it was. And he spent three years on it; maybe longer; we don't quite know. I used to see him, as I said, looking across at the other man's house, and something in his face as he watched gave me the idea that helped when the time came; it was somehow so devilish that I knew that he must be the man.'

'The murderer, you mean,' I said.

'Yes, the murderer,' he repeated.

'What was he watching for?' I asked.

'Watching to see that other man struck by lightning,' he answered.

I had been surprised by the old man's simple wisdom till now. Though I should not have been surprised; for life is not observed only by the educated classes in their studies, who put their wisdom in writing, so that we read it and perhaps get the idea from that that they are the only wise men; but far simpler folk have their wisdom too, though they rarely tell it. Old Ripley had been giving me something from the store of his wisdom now, which he had gained from his long and quiet observation of men. But when he suddenly said that he had seen a man watching for another man to be struck by lightning, then I fell back all at once on the old fallacious belief that only the educated classes are capable of observation. I did not even ask him what he meant, because I could not see how a man who made such an odd remark could possibly make any sense of it, if asked to explain. So I merely said, 'Oh, was he?'

'Yes,' the old detective went on, 'that was what he was doing. Whenever there was a thunderstorm he would sit in his garden and watch, looking across the valley. He didn't mind the rain, not even when it was falling in torrents. All he cared about was his spite. I often saw him sitting there. As village policeman it was my job to walk about the village and see that everything was all right. Mind you, I used to look out myself sometimes during a thunderstorm, when it came rolling along our hills from the South, as it so often did; I'd look to see that no house was struck, or to see if any house down by the river had trouble with floods, as they sometimes had; but to watch one particular house like that, which was what he was doing, and to hope that it would be struck, was another matter altogether.'

'How did you know that that was what he was doing?' I asked,

'Well, I didn't, not at the time,' said old Ripley. 'Not enough to say anything about it. And yet I ought to have: there was that devilish look in his face and that concentrated gaze of the wicked eyes, which might have told me what he was up to, and I remembered that look afterwards and put two and two together. At the time I only knew that he was waiting yearningly for something to happen. I didn't know what.'

'The man must have been mad,' I said.

'Not as mad as all that,' said John Ripley.

'But did he do it often?' I asked.

'Whenever there was a thunderstorm,' he said. 'There he used to sit glowering. That, I think, is the word for it. And always gazing the same way. I tell you what it used to make me think of, up there on his side of the valley; he made me think of one of those devils you sometimes see carved in stone on the top of an old cathedral, looking down in envy at the quiet worshippers. Yes, that's what he used to look like when he sat in that chair in his garden. The expression was all in his eyes, and he didn't know it was there.'

'But did he think he was ever going to see what he was looking for?' I asked. 'The odds must have been many millions to one against any one house being struck. Many millions.'

'Not such long odds as that,' said John Ripley.

'Not?' I said.

'No,' he said. 'And one night it *was* struck, and the man whom he hated was killed. And I'd looked in that fellow Brix's eyes as I went by, doing my patrols through the village, and I had seen enough there to set me thinking. And that's what gave me my start.'

'But you said the house was struck by lightning,' I said.

'Yes,' said the old detective.

'Then Brix couldn't have done it,' I said.

'You never know what those brooding devils can do,' he said, 'when they set their minds to it. Malice seems to be a very absorbing occupation, and a man who is addicted to it puts all the energy into it that another will put into love.'

'Still, he couldn't have struck a house by lightning,' I said.

'Couldn't he,' said old Ripley. 'And the man in it too. I will tell you what he did; and I only found out that by knowing that he had done it. If I hadn't seen that man's face and known that he had killed Jassen, that was the other man's name, I could never have found out. But I had the key to the problem to start with, knowing that he had done it, and with that key I was able to solve it. I should never have done it otherwise. And of course I couldn't say a word of my suspicion before I had worked it all out. They would have thought me mad.'

'But you said he was struck by lightning,' I said again.

'I'll tell you what he did,' said Ripley. 'First of all he got into the house. And that's why we said that it must have been over three years since he first premeditated his murder. For he couldn't have had a chance of doing that in the last three years, and working there for some hours, as he did. And the last time Mr Jassen had gone away was three years before his death. Even then there was a servant who looked after the house, but somebody sent her a ticket for a dance: nobody ever knew who, probably Brix. And the dance was five miles away and she didn't get back till the small hours. That would have been his best chance; but we don't quite know.'

'Wait a moment,' I said. 'You did say he was struck by lightning?'

'That's right,' said Ripley. 'Well, this Brix got into the house one night and cut the lightning-conductor high up, and chiselled a hole in the wall of Mr Jassen's bedroom, outside which the copper band of the lightning-conductor ran; and all he had to do then was to bend the band and shove it in through the hole he had chiselled, right up to a leg of the iron bedstead on which Mr Jassen slept, which actually touched the wainscote. Well, it wasn't quite all he had to do, because he had to paint over the hole he had made in the white wainscote and whiten the end of the copper band, not more than a quarter of an inch of it. It was a neat job.'

'But did nobody notice the gap in the lightning-conductor outside?' I asked.

'I am coming to that,' said Ripley. 'He saw to that too. There was a ladder in Mr Jassen's garden, and he must have got hold of that. At least, we suppose that he did. And he brought a strip of lead with him, cut to exactly the width of the lightning-conductor and painted the colour of copper. And it looked like copper, looking at it from below. That was a neat job too; but for one thing.

'Nobody ever noticed anything. And there was the lightning-conductor, running down not to the earth, but to the iron bedstead on which Mr Jassen slept. And it was like that for years. And then one night came the flash that Brix had been waiting for, and it killed Jassen and set the room on fire, which Jassen's housemaid put out with the help of Brix, who hurried up there on his bicycle. And that would have been his opportunity of shoving back the bit of copper, if it was sticking out of the burnt wainscote. But he didn't get any chance to put a step-ladder against the wall, for there were very soon too many people there, to help to put out the fire. But there was nothing much to notice, and nobody did. I had noticed his face: that was all. And I knew he had done it. And that was a great help. So I began looking round to see what connection a man could have with a flash of lightning. And the first thing I thought of was that the idea of a man having anything to do with a flash of lightning wasn't such a crazy idea after all, for men put up lightning-conductors, so that they did control the lightning to a certain extent. And then I saw what Brix had been up to. Saw it in a flash, sitting at home. I still couldn't say a word to my superiors; nothing to go on yet, and not even a motive. Of course his motive was malice; but that was only what went on in his mind. You can't bring a man's spiteful thoughts into court and exhibit them. But then I made my investigation, and found the lightning-conductor had been tampered with. And then I made my report; for that was something to go on. But we were a long way from convicting Brix yet, or even accusing him.

'And then one day I went to a picture-gallery. It's funny how ideas come to one. I noticed that most of the artists signed their pictures. And I wondered if Brix had signed his bit of painting. And sure enough he had: there was his signature deep in the paint on the strip of lead he had painted to look like copper.'

'His signature?' I said.

'Better than that,' said the old detective. 'His thumbmark. You can't forge that. Well, even that didn't help my suspicions. A thumb-mark three years old might have been made by anybody, when the paint was wet. But it helped me. Being certain that Brix had done it, all I had to do was to get a print of his thumb.'

'How did you get that?' I asked.

'Well, we have our ways of getting them,' said the old detective. 'As a matter of fact I got a dozen.

'And we hanged him on that.'

And old Ripley went back to his Canterbury bells, and I went on with my walk.

THE MURDER IN NETHERBY GARDENS

ONE day, walking East to catch a train at Blackfriars with half an hour to spare, as I passed near the Inner Temple, the fancy came to me to look in on Charles Stanter in his chambers there. Nobody who had been at All Angels in his time seemed to remember him very clearly. He had been so quiet; I suppose conserving his powers that were to win him so much fame at the Bar, while others showered their gifts on the air all round them and were remembered, as meteors are, for a brief brilliance, even if they passed on afterwards into obscurity. Looking back now upon those forgotten names I seem to remember a brilliant company. Do not ask me who they were, for the world never heard of them. And yet I feel sure they were brilliant. They had youth, for one thing; and some had other things besides. Well, few of those names are heard of now, and among that once-brilliant company Charles Stanter had appeared dull. Now his career is so brilliant that I cannot recall the failure of a single case he defended. He had difficult cases too, many of them of murder. I should say alleged murder.

Well, the fancy came to me to see him again, and I rang the bell and was shown in by a maid, and there was Charles Stanter sitting in an armchair by his fire; and he rose to give me a kindly welcome.

We talked at first of old days at All Angels, and of the bright glow of many lost ambitions. And then I said, 'I suppose you have scores of interesting cases.'

'Oh, not all of them,' he said. 'Some are extremely dull. But this one is interesting.' And he pointed to a heap of papers lying under a heavy amethyst. 'This has to do with a civic drainage system, and the water by which it is flushed. The source of the water is in dispute and, if it can be traced to the hill from which my clients contend it comes, then we shall be able to obtain an injunction against a firm which we hold is diverting that water for the purpose of obtaining power, that is to say electricity. The whole thing hangs on a right granted by Charles II in a warrant that the other side don't know we possess. There are a great many legal points in it that are of extreme interest.'

'Have you any murder cases?' I asked.

'Yes, we have one coming on soon,' he said.

And at that moment his clerk came into the room.

'Where are the papers of the Plober case, Smurgin?' he said to him.

'Here, sir, I think,' said Smurgin.

And then he handed to Stanter a bundle of manuscript, untidily written, and Stanter handed it on to me.

'You might care to read it,' he said.

'What is it?' I asked.

'It's a clear tale,' he said. 'You'll see, if you read it.'

'Thanks,' I said. 'Murder, you say?'

'Yes,' he said. 'Murder.'

'There's a thrill in murder,' I said. 'I'm sure that your drainage case is very interesting too. But I must say murder attracts me. I suppose it shouldn't. But somehow it seems to. This is nearer to it than I have ever been. I should like to read it, if you don't mind.'

'Yes. Sit down,' said Stanter. 'Make yourself comfortable in that chair.'

And I did. It was a fine armchair and a good fire. Stanter went over to his table and sat down over the heap of papers concerning the drainage system of some city, and soon he was completely immersed in the case. And I turned to the thick bundle of untidily written sheets. This is what I read:

* * *

I went to see Mr Inker, whom I have known for some years. He was not exactly a friend, but I have known him for some time. The object of my visit was purely private, and had nothing to do with what happened. I went to his house at 18 Netherby Gardens and rang the bell, and nobody answered. I rang again and again, but nobody came to the door. Then I wondered if the door in the area was unlocked, and I went down the area steps and sure enough it was. I opened the door and went in, as I wanted to see Mr Inker. There seemed to be nobody in the house; but I knew he would be there. And he was. I went up to the drawing-room, and he wasn't there. But from a little room off it I heard a noise, and I saw him. I saw him before I had opened the door more than a few inches. And he was murdering a man. He was murdering him with a knife. The man was on the floor, and he had stabbed him already, because the knife he was lifting up was covered with blood, and he was just going to put it in again when he saw me. I've read of people saying that scenes like this para-lysed them, whether they meant it or not. It didn't have that effect on me. It set me thinking quicker than ever I thought before. And what I thought was that there was only one thing for Mr Inker to do, now that I had seen what he was at, and that was to kill me too. He wouldn't want me going about, to give evidence against him. I saw that at once. So I went out of that room like the start of a race, and got on to the landing. Anything slower and he'd have had me. I heard him coming after me before I got to the door. He said never a word. Nor did I.

From the landing the stairs went down to the hall and up to the top of the house. The obvious way was downstairs. But would there be time, with the little lead I had, to turn the knob of the latch and open the door and get through? That's what I wondered. And he wouldn't need quite to catch up with me. He could knife me from nearly a yard away. I thought, for one thing, there mightn't be time. And I didn't yet know what his pace was. But one thing I was sure of: downstairs was the obvious way. So I took the other.

He wasn't expecting that, and it gave me a bit more lead. I easily got to a bedroom before he was anywhere near, and locked myself in. Still he had not spoken a word. Neither had I.

You may wonder why I went into a bedroom instead of getting out of the house. But I had to plan: it was no use rushing wildly about. I had not planned anything yet, but I was going to plan quietly in that room. It opened into another room, and I locked that door too. Then I went to look at the window, to see what I could do from there. But there were no means of escaping that way. So I turned back to the room. He was outside the door, and had not even turned the handle. He must have heard me lock it.

And then I saw a telephone at the head of the bed. I couldn't want better than that, and I took the receiver off. Before I had spoken I heard him rushing downstairs. Then I said Hullo. I said it two or three times, and then I got an answer. And I asked for the police. But I got no answer then: the telephone had gone dead.

He must have cut the wire with his knife. What was I to do next? Anyway, he wasn't outside the door any more. It was no good staying in that room any longer; and it was no good being anywhere where he knew that I was. So I unlocked the door and slipped out and went still higher. No good going down. He was between me and the hall door. If I went up, I hoped I might get away over the roof. So I went right up to the attic. And there I found a long uncarpeted empty passage, empty but for one cupboard half-way down, and a turn at the end to some dingy place unlighted by any window. The cupboard was rather an obvious hiding-place, a tall thing with no shelves in it, that would hide me nicely. But I had not been doing obvious things yet, and I thought that he would expect me to go on to the end of the passage and make for the dingy part of it. I don't know why I thought this, but I was thinking very quickly, and knew he would be doing so too. You see, both our lives were at stake. What I thought he would do would be to go to the end and take the cupboard on his way back. It would have been nasty if he had come straight for the cupboard. I had planned to shove both doors violently open, if he did, and then run. But I thought he would go to the end of the passage. And I thought he was doing it that way, at first, when he came. But he walked a few steps past my cupboard, and then I heard him turn back. Then I thought he was going to open the cupboard door. He actually stopped in front of it and listened, and I was just about to burst out on him and make my desperate bid to get away, with nothing to help me but a moment's surprise, when he turned quickly away and went down the stairs. That puzzled me. He must know, I said to myself, that I am not downstairs. He was hurrying too, as though he were after something. But we two were alone in the house, except for the dead man, the man Mr Inker had murdered. It never occurred to me that he knew perfectly well where I was. I heard his footsteps growing fainter and fainter, and listened till the last of them died away, far down at the foot of the stairs. I had no idea what he was up to. You see, I had been trying to surprise him all the time: now he was trying to surprise me, and I wondered what the surprise was. It was very still in the house and I had plenty of time to wonder, and nothing to disturb my wondering. I thought of lots of things that he might be doing, but never thought of the right one. I do assure you I never guessed what he would do. I hadn't the faintest idea of it. It never entered my mind. It was a shock when I found out, as great a shock as I ever received.

There's nothing more to tell. You know he came back with a policeman, and I was arrested for the murder that Mr Inker committed. They found me hiding in the cupboard, with the knife on the floor outside. He had thrown it down there. I've asked the inspector about finger-prints more than once; but he says that there are none. I point out that Mr Inker could have cleaned the knife just as well as I could. But they won't listen to me when I say that.

I looked up from this dark story into the light of the room, and felt as though I had left dim caverns for daylight, with a moment of relief that it would have taken Dante to picture. Stanter was bending still over his other case, and brooding upon its intricacies as though he had forgotten that I was there, as I had forgotten Blackfriars and the train I had meant to catch.

'What do you make of it?' I asked.

Stanter looked up with a start. And then he said, 'It's a perfectly clear story. That is the case for my client. What you have read, of course in confidence, is my instructions for the conduct of the case. Our whole defence will be based on it.'

'But what really happened?' I asked.

'Oh, that,' he said, 'will be for a jury to say.'

THE SHIELD OF ATHENE

WHEN Richard Laksby went down from All Angels he decided, to the pained astonishment of his father, to choose an occupation to suit himself. He came of a family whose sons had always been sent into something by their fathers, so that to Richard's father his idea was entirely new. By the will of another relative he had enough money to live on, so that the thing was possible once he was able to pull away from the almost overpowering force of the idea that he must be sent into something by his father; and when he did pull away he naturally chose a profession that was outside the few that his family had ever considered possible. 'It all comes of wasting his time reading trashy detective stories,' his father said. For the young man's extraordinary ambition was to be a great detective.

'How are you going to set about it?' his father asked, hoping that the logic of that question would put an end to the boy's scheme. But young Laksby was not going to be checked by knowing nothing of how he was to set about it: all he wanted to do was to start. And start he did, in spite of anything that his father could say; and he took a flat in London and read every unsolved criminal case that was reported in the Press. As soon as one was solved and a man brought to trial, he dropped it and looked for another. Of course he didn't get very far. All this, I may say, was some years before the war, when there was no question of the State doing what his father could not do, and putting him into something.

I went round to see him one day, for I had known him well for some years, and found him in his flat, reading evening papers. He offered me a cigarette, and I asked him, without meaning in any way to embarrass him, how he was getting on at his new profession. I forget what he said, but, whatever it was, it became perfectly clear that he had done nothing at all, and that his idea of going to Scotland Yard after solving a crime that had puzzled all the police and asking for employment upon the strength of that, was no more than a childish dream. And this somehow became so very clear, that I could not help feeling that I was as welcome in his flat as a friend with a pin would be to a child who was blowing a beautiful soap-bubble. So I left, and we did not see each other for some time. And then one day he rang me up on the telephone, and I was very glad to hear his voice, for, all unintentional as it was, I felt that a coldness between us had been my fault.

'You were asking me how I was getting on,' he said

'I didn't mean to trouble you,' I told him. 'All I meant to do was just to ask. That was all.'

'It was no trouble at all,' he said.

'I am afraid it was just idle curiosity,' I replied.

'Not at all,' he said. 'But, if you would like to come round. I will tell you.'

What pleased me about all this was that his voice was particularly cheery, and he evidently bore me no grudge for having clumsily dragged the futility of his absurd ambition into the light of day from its proper place among vague dreams. 'Come round to tea,' he said.

What I thought was that he felt he had been a bit unwelcoming, as I felt I had been rather tactless, and that he wanted to put it right. That he could have had any progress to show me I never imagined.

It was by then half past three, and by a quarter past four I was there. He was in the same armchair in which I had seen him last, with a small light table in front of him, on which had been several newspapers. But now he had an album on the table. We shook hands and he said, 'Look here,' and he opened his album. It was full of cuttings from newspapers gummed in 'Read that,' he said.

It is always tedious to be set to read things when you come to have a talk; but I was anxious to atone for my gaucherie, and I read every line. What he and his album were driving at I hadn't the slightest idea. It began like this, a critique of some work of a sculptor: 'An unbalanced piece of work with unnatural pose, making a fetish of realism, and yet with hands that seem smaller than life, and a stride that is going in no particular direction, all trousers rather than legs. It is doubtful if in real life the body would be supported at all.'

The next critique in the album also criticized the legs of this statue, and then went on in these words, 'All Mr Ardon's figures show the same horror in their faces. The expressions vary, but the horror is always the same. One can use no milder word for it. This is unnatural and can only emanate from a decadent mood in the sculptor. If this be thought to be libellous, let anyone look at a thousand faces and see if he can find in a single one the look of astonished horror that is clearly observable in every one of Mr Ardon's works of art, if such a description may be applied to them?'

I plodded on with my reading through that album, sitting in Laksby's chair, while he stood watching me. I must have read a dozen critiques, saying all the same thing. And then I suddenly came on a totally different cutting. It said, 'Miss Jane Ingley has been missing from her home since Tuesday afternoon. The police of the Yorkshire area have made careful search, and no trace of her has been discovered as yet.' The cutting continued with an appeal to the public to telephone to the local police any knowledge that might come to them of the girl's whereabouts. I turned the page and there were more cuttings about this girl, and no more critiques of sculpture, so far as I saw. But when he saw me turn the page, Laksby interrupted and, somewhat to my relief, said, 'You needn't read any more for the present.'

I looked up.

'That girl has been recognized by her brother,' he said.

'Recognized,' I said. 'Then she's alive.'

'No,' said Laksby.

'What happened to her?' I asked.

'You know what my ambition always was,' he said.

'You wanted to be a detective,' I answered.

'No,' he said. 'I wanted to be a great detective. You can be humdrum in any profession. I didn't want merely that. Any profession may throw up one or two great followers of it in a generation. I wanted to be one of them. Pick the wrong profession, make a steeple-jack of a man born to be a pearl-diver, and you only get mediocrity. I felt that my profession was the one I have chosen. I felt that in that profession my opportunity waited. Well, it has come.'

I thought he was merely trying to excuse himself for his rather unusual choice, and I was just tacitly agreeing with all he said; and then came those last four words that astonished me. Could he mean he had done something useful? What could he have done? There was nothing in that album to explain it. I could only ask.

'Your opportunity has come?' I repeated.

'It has come,' he said.

'And what was it?' I asked.

'Well, that's the difficulty,' he said. 'Nothing that I can prove as yet. Nothing that a jury would believe. Nothing that you would believe. I don't know how to tell you.'

'Oh, I'll believe you all right,' I said.

'I ought to explain,' he went on, 'that it's nothing that has ever happened before, anyway not since the Norman conquest, and long before that.'

'But what is it?' I asked.

'It is something that I suspect,' he said, 'and have got to prove. But I take it you would expect a brother to be able to recognize his own sister.'

'Oh, yes,' I said.

'Well,' said Laksby, 'if you admit that, I ask nothing more. If you admit that, you can believe the rest.'

'Of course I admit it,' I said.

'Well, that is the evidence on which I base the whole case,' he went on.

'On a brother being able to recognize his sister? That will not strain my credulity,' I said.

'No,' he said. 'But there's more in it than that. I had better tell you the whole story.'

'Do,' I said.

He sat down opposite me and began.

'James Ardon,' said Laksby, 'is a young sculptor. At least, so he says. I have made the most careful enquiries, complete enquiries, and nowhere can I find that he studied anywhere. He says he learned sculpture by seeing statues in Greece.'

'Has he travelled in Greece?' I asked.

'Yes,' said Laksby.

'What is he doing now?' I asked.

'He has hired a studio in York,' Laksby explained.

'Where the girl disappeared,' I said.

'Exactly,' said Laksby.

'And made the figures that are criticized here,' I said, patting the album.

'Yes,' said Laksby. 'And no one knows where he got his marble. The marble of his figures is all the same, identical with that of the earliest statues in Greece, statues before Praxiteles. But I have not been able to trace how he got it to Yorkshire.'

'How do you think he got it there?' I asked.

'Well, that, you see,' said Laksby, 'is the essence of the whole thing. That is what you won't believe.'

'If it's anything to do with a brother recognizing his sister,' I said, 'I ought to be able to believe it.'

'That,' he said, 'is the evidence on which the whole thing must rest.'

'I interrupted you,' I said. 'Please go on.'

And he went on. 'He sent his statues to Bond Street, and hundreds of people saw them. Many said they were true to life.

Some said they *were* life, as no sculpture had been before. But the critics didn't like them. There was a good deal of talk about them for a while. And the talk died down. And then one day this young fellow from Yorkshire, who had come to London to see a football match, walked into the exhibition; no one knows why; it was just one of those incalculable chances. And in one of the statues he recognized his sister, the girl who had disappeared.'

'I see,' I said. 'His model. And you think he has murdered her. Well, I congratulate you on finding it out before the police. I can believe it all right, every word you have told me. But I don't quite see why you said it has never happened before, or not since the Norman conquest. I think I remember reading about a case—'

'Wait a moment,' said Laksby. 'The brother recognized his sister. But he also says that she never gave any sittings to any sculptor. He can't say that she never knew him, but he does say definitely that the long sittings that must have been needed for such a likeness never existed.'

'As a witness,' I said, 'the brother seems rather to contradict himself.'

'I don't think so,' said Laksby.

And then his telephone-bell rang, and he asked me to excuse him, as he expected some details that he had asked for to assist his investigation. And that is what it turned out to be, and somebody seemed to be telling him something about Ardon's studio. I left Laksby then, quietly waving my hand to him as I passed him at his telephone, and he looked over his shoulder and just said, 'Think over what I have told you.'

And I did think it over till late that night, and could make nothing of it. For one moment a dark and fantastic suspicion threw its shadow upon my mind, a suspicion that left my thoughts as soon as it came. But I should not have let it go, for it was the right one.

Laksby rang up next day, saying nothing of that strange case; but he did ask me to come to tea again, and I knew he meant to go further with our interrupted talk. I went, and the first words he said after he had made me comfortable and poured out a cup of tea for me were, 'Others have disappeared too.'

'In Yorkshire?' I asked.

'Yes, in Yorkshire,' he said. 'But we can't find out where they have gone. Some of them may have gone to London, or elsewhere, to look for a job. But one should bear in mind that they have disappeared.'

And then we got down to the point at which we had left off when his telephone rang. 'You say that the girl never gave any sittings to Ardon,' I said.

'Yes,' said Laksby. 'Her brother is sure of it.'

'And the likeness is perfect?' I asked.

'Well, her brother recognizes her,' he said, 'and is prepared to identify the statue as being that of his sister, on oath, in any court to which he may ever be summoned.'

'And he never studied sculpture?' I went on.

'I have made the most exhaustive enquiries,' he said, 'and no-one has taught him.'

'And then he has imported no marble,' I continued.

'That is so,' said Laksby.

'And bought none from any English firm?' I enquired.

'I have tried every one of them,' he said, 'and none of them ever supplied him.'

'And he has travelled in Greece,' I said, 'but never brought any marble back with him.'

'That is so,' said Laksby.

'And of course he could never find any in Yorkshire,' I said.

'Of course not,' he answered.

'Then how did he make that marble statue of Jane Ingley?' I asked.

'There's only one answer,' he said.

Laksby has often surprised me. He is rather an odd fellow. And he surprised me then. 'I don't like to be disbelieved,' he said. 'And I don't like to strain your politeness. *You* shall tell *me* what has happened. I've told you most of the facts. And I'll tell you any more as I find them out. You shall tell me. You shall test the facts and give me the answer. Remember he has travelled in Greece.'

'Ancient or modern?' I asked; one of those questions that one regrets the moment one utters them, because they are so foolish. How could he have travelled in ancient Greece? Some ominous fancy at the back of my mind that had taken no form must have prompted it. I knew at once I had said something foolish. And yet those words gave me the clue.

'Ancient,' said Laksby at once, before I could withdraw or explain away my question. And then I was thinking no more of geography or imports of marble, but my thoughts ran back past history and away among legend; and among old legends, a horror amidst the darkness of time, they saw Medusa's head and the shield of Pallas Athene.

'The head!' I gasped.

And he nodded.

'But how could we prove a thing like that?' I said.

'He's found the shield,' said Laksby, 'and we must get it.'

'How on earth did he come on it?' I asked.

'That we can't say,' said Laksby. 'But Greece is full of wonders. Look at the Parthenon. Look at the Venus of Milo. Compare it with modern sculpture. There is a miracle for you. Begin by explaining that. They got the human soul looking out of a face. Why not the other thing? They are all beyond us.'

'But wait a moment,' I said. 'Medusa's face was flesh. Pallas Athene put it in her shield. But would it have kept?'

'Yes,' said Laksby. 'Those immortal things must have had something in their blood that we haven't, and evidently gorgons don't decay.'

'You believe in them then,' I said.

'I must,' he answered. 'What other answer is there? A man who has never studied sculpture, never learned anything whatever about it, makes statues that, whatever the critics may say, are life, as life has never been shown in marble before, barring the Greeks. You might as well go straight out of this room now and build a battleship without any study whatever. And I have made the most careful enquiries. I haven't been idle.'

'But you are asking me to believe the incredible,' I said.

'Isn't the alternative incredible?' he asked.

'I suppose it is,' I replied.

'And besides,' said Laksby, 'I am not asking you to believe anything. You must believe the most likely. I cannot control your belief. Nor, I suppose, can you.'

'He might have found a marble statue in York,' I said. 'It was the old camp of Eboricum.'

'Certainly,' said Laksby. 'But not a statue of a modern girl in modern dress, recognized by her brother, and all her little trinkets and ornaments recognized too.'

'It could do that?' I asked. 'Could turn the dress and the trinkets to marble?'

'If you mean Medusa's head, it could,' said Laksby. 'Her, and anything that was touching her at the time. All those statues of his were completely clothed, in dresses and jackets of marble.'

'I see,' I muttered.

'Or you may prefer to believe,' he went on, 'that he picks up marble whenever he wants it on Yorkshire moors, where there is none, and knocks off these perfect statues without any training.'

'No,' I said. 'It must have been as you say. He must have found that shield of Athene. Saw a rim of it, perhaps, sticking up through the anemones, and dug it up. But how did he escape being turned to stone when he saw it? All the legends say it could do that. And we've got to believe them if we can see no other way of his having made those statues.'

'What other way could there be?' said Laksby.

'Then how did he escape being turned to stone when he found it?' I asked again.

'It must have been face downward,' he said. 'And then, when

he had picked it up by the handle, perhaps a goat saw it, or anything, and was turned to stone, and he saw what he had got. Then he must have been pretty careful with it, or he wouldn't be here.'

'It's odd,' I said.

'So is the alternative,' Laksby insisted. 'A sculptor without any training, and without marble, for the matter of that.'

'No, I can't believe that,' I said.

'Well, I am glad you can't,' said Laksby. 'We can get to business now. What's to be done?'

'I'll go and look at his studio if you like,' I said. 'I'll get in somehow, and give you an independent point of view, and evidence to back you in any court, if you like.'

'No, you don't,' he said. 'There's nothing to see there but one thing. And if you see that . . .'

And for some seconds neither of us said any more.

And then Laksby said, 'I don't think you would make a very good statue.'

'But I'll keep my eyes shut,' I said.

'Then you won't see anything,' said Laksby.

And that was obvious enough. But I would not give up the idea.

And then I said, 'Didn't Perseus use a mirror?'

'Look here,' said Laksby. 'That man has got his neck to protect, and if he sees you walking in with a looking-glass he'll know what you are after at once, and you'll have a nasty reception and a quick exit, if you are lucky. And I'll tell you another thing: those mirrors they had three thousand years ago, when Perseus got the gorgon's head, weren't made of glass like ours. They were only polished metal, and Perseus wouldn't have seen so much. With a modern looking-glass the ricochet would probably get you. I'd be very glad of a witness, but I am not going to send you to that.'

Well, we argued up and down, and the more we talked the keener I got. 'I could take a revolver,' I said.

'For goodness sake don't think of doing that,' said Laksby. 'I have no evidence whatever that would protect you if you did. It is illegal to carry revolvers, and you'd go to prison for having a firearm with intent to endanger life. That is how it goes. Don't have anything to do with it.'

'He must be a nasty fellow to approach unarmed,' I said.

'That's as it may be,' said Laksby, 'but the Law doesn't know that.'

'Why does he do it?' I asked.

'Some people will do anything for art,' said Laksby. 'And that I can understand. But this man would do anything to be thought an artist, though he knows nothing of art whatever. His is a cheap and flashy method. Pressing the button of a camera is as artistic, and certainly far more moral.'

'I'll go and see him,' I said.

I had made up my mind and I got the man's address out of Laksby, a studio overlooking the main street in York.

'I hate the risk you are taking,' said Laksby. 'But between the two of us we may save lots of lives. I could do nothing alone. They would merely say I was mad and lock me up.'

'Well, I will go,' I said.

'It is sporting of you,' said Laksby. 'And, look here, that shield he has found will of course be hidden. The moment he moves towards a cupboard or curtain, shut your eyes and clear out, and you will be all right.'

And that is what I did when it came to it. The man had done at least half a dozen statues already, and it was time he was stopped. Laksby and I sat smoking and making plans, but they were not particularly useful. It all depended on what I found when I got there.

Well, I left Laksby and took the train to York. I went quite unarmed except for a walking-stick, and foolishly enough I brought a stick of the lightest and brittlest wood, quite useless for any defence. And yet I think it was that stick that saved me. I walked from the station up the street and knocked at the man's door, which he opened himself. I told him that I had seen his exhibition, greatly admired his faithfulness to life, and would like to ask him to do a life-sized statue of me. All this in the passage between the door and the dingy staircase. As we came to the staircase I could see he did not think much of the reason that I had given for having entered his house. I don't know how I saw it in that dim light. I must have felt it, rather.

At the top of the stairs we came to a door, and into the light of his studio. It was I that had been leading us upstairs, for he showed no readiness to let me in. When we got into the studio he turned round and looked at me, and I saw that he was not a man to be trifled with. Which was of course what I was doing. The room was tidy; there were no chips on the floor, and no mallets or chisels that I could see. I thought he might at least have bought some chisels. But I suppose he was too sure of himself to have bothered about that. One marble statue stood in the room, the statue of an ordinary young man in ordinary modern clothes, and on his marble face an extraordinary look of horror, the look that all the work of Ardon had. It made me feel cold, apart from the fact that I felt that at any moment I might myself be a block of marble with that terrible look on its face.

I looked round for cupboards or curtains, and saw a cupboard quite close.

'What did you say you want?' said Ardon.

And he said it in a tone of a man who requires an answer at once. But my eyes were fixed on that terrible marble face, and I found no words for an answer. And Ardon was looking at my expression, as I looked on the face of his statue. And the horror in the face must have been partly reflected in mine, and Ardon saw that reflection and must have known I suspected him. He turned at once, not waiting for any answer from me, and went to the cupboard. Outside the motors hummed by continually, going to the station and some coming away from it. Inside Ardon opened the cupboard door. Three thousand years seemed to lie between it and the street. I turned round at once and took one glance at the door, and then I shut my eyes, and I did not open them again until I was far from that house. I put both hands to the wall, though my stick was in one of them, and groped my way to the door, and was soon there and slipped out. That one glance I had had of it helped, but outside it was more difficult. Several times I was tempted to take just one glance with half-opened eyes, which would have given me a view of the whole staircase, but could equally have given me a view of the Gorgon's head. For Ardon was close behind me, and I knew that he had the shield. I had heard it bump against the cupboard door as he took it out. And of course he could move twenty times faster than I, on strange stairs with my eyes shut.

The mistake he made was in not hitting me over the head. He could have done it with the edge of the shield, or with anything. I didn't like to put up a hand to protect my head, for fear of giving him the idea. I was expecting a blow every moment, as I groped my way down those stairs and could even feel the warmth of Ardon's breath on my neck. He never spoke a word and I got to the door, and still he was close behind me. And then I felt a cold and awful chill in my face, and I knew he had slipped the shield forward over my left shoulder and had turned its face towards me. Of course I knew he must have averted his own head when he did that. And that gave me time to open the door to the street, which he might easily have prevented me doing by gripping my wrist. But he left the job to Medusa and she couldn't do it, because my eyes were tight shut.

They say that every criminal sticks to his own way of doing things. A man, for instance, murders a woman in her bath, and women will be safe with him except in a bathroom. I think that is the peculiarity that saved me, when he might have hit me over the head. I opened the door and the fresh air blew in my face, cold, but not with the deadly chill I had felt on my cheeks from Medusa. I was not safe yet. A statue on a sculptor's doorstep would not have been out of place. He could have done it yet, and nobody might have noticed. What would he do next? What could I do, blind there in the street? And then it suddenly came to me: if I must be blind, and I must, I would go the way of the blind, and rely on the help and mercy the blind receive. I walked straight into the traffic, tapping the road before me with my stick in the way that the blind do. I daren't open an eye for a single moment to see if a motor was near, for I should have seen Medusa instead. I knew that chilly shield was still hovering about my face, but I listened, and could hear that no car was at any rate within ten yards of me, and then I went straight on, tapping my stick. And it worked.

There was a scream of one or two brakes, and then the stream of the traffic lulled and I walked safe to the middle of the road and heard the opposite stream lulling already, and I got to the other side. The traffic went on at once; too quick, I hoped, for Ardon. But that I could not tell. I turned to my left and went tapping down the pavement towards the station, still with my eyes tight shut. And presently an arm took mine to lead me over a crossing. Of course I could not be sure that it was not Ardon. But I thanked the kind fellow and, when he spoke to me, it was the voice of an honest Yorkshireman. I asked him if he would mind guiding me a little further, and he did all the way to the station. I did not think Ardon would dare to get up to his tricks there, but I did not take any chances and never opened my eyes till we left York. A porter led me into a carriage.

You want to hear the end of it. I went back to Laksby and told him everything, and he told the police, and I went with him, so that each could back what the other told of this strange story. The police were doubtful at first and very standoffish, and took our addresses and asked us to call again. And we went next day, and while we were there their manner suddenly altered: they had news from one of their men in York by telephone. Then they were all politeness. What happened was that

Ardon knew well enough after my visit that someone had found him out and, however sceptical Laksby and I had found the police, they had 'phoned to York to investigate, and a policeman called on Ardon. And the moment Ardon saw him he lost his head. He added one more statue to that extraordinary collection of realism and horror, neither of which have been equalled by any living sculptor, if by any sculptor at all, a statue of a policeman. Then he knew it was all up, and he lifted the shield of Athene and turned it inwards and looked full at the face of Medusa; and he, and it, turned to stone. The statue has been exhibited more than once: the marble shield is perfectly harmless now. Some may remember seeing that strange white figure. In the catalogue it was entitled Young Man Trying a Shield.

THE END

LORD DUNSANY

BORN in 1878 to the second oldest title in the Irish peerage, Edward Plunkett, 18th Baron of Dunsany, was a writer and dramatist, mostly of fantasy. He published more than 80 books as Lord Dunsany, including hundreds of short stories, as well as successful plays, novels and essays. Educated at Cheam, Eton College and the Royal Military College, Sandhurst, he served in the Boer War and both World Wars, moving in the 1930s from County Meath to Shoreham in Kent. Dunsany worked with W.B. Yeats, and was a significant influence on such writers as H.P. Lovecraft, J.R.R. Tolkien, Arthur C. Clarke and Isaac Asimov.

In addition to his writing, Lord Dunsany was an influential campaigner for the scouting movement, the British Legion, and for animal rights. He set chess puzzles for *The Times*, was a pioneering writer of radio drama and appeared in early television programmes including the BBC's *The Brains Trust*. A Fellow of the Royal Society of Literature and of the Royal Geographical Society, Dunsany received an honorary doctorate from Trinity College, Dublin, and was nominated for the Nobel Prize for literature. He died in 1957 of appendicitis, aged 79.